THE LAST SPEAKER OF SKALWEGIAN

ALSO BY DAVID GARDNER

The Journalist: A Paranormal Thriller

THE LAST SPEAKER OF SKALWEGIAN

DAVID GARDNER

Encircle Publications
Farmington, Maine, U.S.A.

The Last Speaker of Skalwegian © 2021 David Gardner

Paperback ISBN 13: 978-1-64599-239-4
Hardcover ISBN 13: 978-1-64599-240-0
E-book ISBN 13: 978-1-64599-241-7
Kindle ISBN 13: 978-1-64599-242-4

Editor, Encircle Publications: Cynthia Brackett-Vincent
Book design and cover design by Deirdre Wait
Cover images © Getty Images

Published by:

Encircle Publications
PO Box 187
Farmington, ME 04938

info@encirclepub.com
http://encirclepub.com

ACKNOWLEDGMENTS

So many people have contributed to my writing over the years that I don't know where to begin. Their feedback, patience and encouragement has been invaluable, and I owe much of my success to them. I want to thank Bill Regan, Jane Roy Brown, Richard Bolt, Vicki Sanders, Peggy McFarland, the late Steve Gordon, Alyson Miller, Erica Harth, Arlene Kay, Kevin Symmons, Elizabeth Lyon, Judy Giger, David Gallant, Ray Anderson and especially my wife, Nancy, also a writer, who understands my need to write and understands me (as much as I'm understandable).

I would also like to thank Cynthia Brackett-Vincent and Eddie Vincent for bringing me into the family of Encircle Publications and Deirdre Wait for her clever cover designs.

DEDICATION

To the memory of SP/4 William McNeil

"Why document the Skalwegian language?" Charlie Fox asked. "The answer to your question should be obvious: I want to save the language of my Scandinavian ancestors and preserve their culture for future generations. I'm no longer young, and if I don't act soon, Skalwegian will disappear forever. And give Professor Lenny Thorson a lot of the credit. He's a linguist—I sure couldn't do the job without him."

—regarding the last speaker of Skalwegian, *Newsweek*

CHAPTER 1

Weegan

*A word in the Skalwegian language loosely
translated as butthead (impolite usage)*

Lenny Thorson watched the red pickup roar into the parking lot, a statue propped up in back. It was the Ghurkin College mascot, an eight-foot-tall gerbil.

Charlie nudged Lenny. "You sure you want tenure at a college with a rat for a mascot?"

"It's a gerbil. And yes, I do. Jobs are scarce."

Gerry Gerbil stood on his hind legs and stared into the distance, a football clutched in his right front paw, his rat-like tail draped over his left. He looked hot and humiliated.

Lenny too felt hot and humiliated, and he guessed that Gerry hated parades as much as he did. Lenny tugged his sweaty shirt away from his chest. It was a sunny September afternoon, with heat waves shimmering off the blacktop in front of the building where he lived. He badly wanted the day to be over.

The pickup swung around with a screech of tires and backed up to Lenny's beat-up Chevy. Two college students in matching black muscle shirts stepped out. Brothers, Lenny guessed. They were a wide-shouldered pair with mussy brown hair and long ears.

Lenny reached out his hand. "I'm Lenny Thorson and this is Charlie Fox."

"Yeah, I know," the taller one said, glanced at Lenny's outstretched hand, then climbed onto the back of the pickup and untied the statue.

Lenny and Charlie dragged the wood-and-papier-mâché gerbil from the bed of the pickup, boosted it atop Lenny's car and stood it upright.

One brother thumbed his phone while the other fed ropes through the open doors and around the mascot's ankles.

The boy was careless as well as rude, Lenny told himself, and he was tempted to order him to untie the ropes and start over, but Lenny hated confrontation. Once he was around the corner and out of sight, he would stop and retie the knots. He didn't want anything bad to happen to Gerry Gerbil.

On second thought, did he really give a damn?

Charlie threw his right leg over his motorcycle, gripped the handlebars and bounced once in the saddle. He wore jeans and a T-shirt that read 'So Are You!' He nodded toward Gerry. "He looks like a *weegan*, and so will you when you parade him through the center of town."

Lenny hadn't yet learned that word in Skalwegian. "*Weegan?*"

"'Butthead.'"

Lenny nodded. He was a *weegan*.

Charlie looked particularly worn and shrunken today, Lenny thought, especially astraddle his beefy black Harley. His hair was gray, his skin leathery, his chin neatly dimpled from Iraqi shrapnel. He was fifty-one—seventeen years older than Lenny—and eight inches shorter.

At six feet four, Lenny was always embarrassed by his size. He wished he could go through life unnoticed. He wondered if Gerry Gerbil ever felt the same.

The shorter brother slapped the mascot's foot. "Have fun at the parade, professor."

Both brothers laughed.

Lenny didn't expect to have fun. His gut told him that the day would go badly.

*   *   *

Bob One wasn't happy about whacking a professor. He specialized in crooked bookies, wise guys who'd flipped, and casino managers caught skimming. But never a civilian. Bob One believed in upholding the ethics of his profession.

He parted the tall tan grass at the side of the road, pinched a mosquito off the tip of his nose and peered westward. No cars yet, but the guy who'd hired him had said his target always took this route on his way into town and would have to slow to a crawl here at the switchback. Bob One figured he'd have plenty of time to pop up, rush forward, blast the guy at close range, then get the hell back to Chicago where he belonged.

*   *   *

Lenny eyed the brothers, now slouched against his car's front fender, both lost in their phones. He couldn't remember ever seeing them on the Ghurkin College campus, the fourth-rate institution an hour west of Boston where he taught French and linguistics. "I didn't catch your names."

The taller one glanced up. "You don't know who we are?"

Lenny shook his head.

The boys exchanged puzzled looks. The taller one said, "I'm Tom Sprocket, and that's my brother Titus."

The names sounded familiar, but Lenny didn't know where he'd heard them. He could memorize entire pages of the dictionary in one sitting, but he was terrible with names.

Tom pocketed his phone and looked Lenny up and down. "Did you play football in college?"

"No," Lenny said.

Tom snickered. "Afraid of getting hurt?"

"I was afraid of hurting someone else."

Tom snorted. "Man, that's all the fun."

No, it's wasn't, Lenny told himself. Hurting someone wasn't fun at all. Twenty-one years ago, while fighting underage with a fake name, he'd killed an opponent in the boxing ring. Guilt still clung to Lenny, ate into his soul.

Tom gestured with a thick thumb over his shoulder toward the office building behind the parking lot. "You live on top of that thing?"

Lenny nodded.

"You're weird, man."

Lenny stiffened. He did feel weird for living in an abandoned rotating restaurant atop a ten-story insurance building, but didn't particularly enjoy being told so.

But in spite of Tom's rudeness, Lenny wouldn't let himself get angry with the boy or even with Dean Sheepslappe who, for some reason, insisted he participate in the Gerry Gerbil Alumni Day Parade, even threatening to block his tenure if he refused. Lenny had grown up angry, had fought with rage in the ring, but after that last fight, he'd promised himself he would never again lose his temper. Some people found this strange, Lenny knew, some sweet. Others used his good nature as a way to take advantage of him. Lenny knew that too.

Titus Sprocket smirked and said, "I heard the place starts up running sometimes all on its own."

The Moon View Revolving Restaurant had failed financially in just six months, when its motor took to speeding up at random moments, knocking staff off their feet and sending diners sliding sideways off their booths and onto the floor. Lenny moved in shortly afterwards. He was paying minimal rent in the abandoned restaurant in return for serving as its live-in caretaker. He found it oddly comforting to be the world's only linguist who inhabited a rotating restaurant.

"Sometimes it makes a couple of turns in the middle of the night," Lenny said, "then shuts down. It's no problem."

It was in fact a problem. When the deranged motors and gears got it into their head to noctambulate, they did so with a terrific bellow and jolt that made Lenny sit up wide awake, and which frightened Elspeth so badly that she'd stopped staying overnight.

But Lenny wasn't bothered by the smirking Sprockets. In fact, he felt sorry for the boys, regarding them as underprivileged lads from some sunbaked state where children ran barefoot across red clay all summer and ate corn pone for breakfast.

Lenny wondered what corn pone tasted like and—more importantly—what was the origin of the word *pone*? A Native American term? Spanish? Skalwegian even?

He turned to Charlie, astride his motorcycle and fiddling with one of its dials. "Is *pone* a word in Skalwegian?"

"It sure is," Charlie said without looking up. "It means 'He who makes a big *weegan* of himself by driving an eight-foot rat through the center of town.'"

"You're no help."

"I've heard that before."

Lenny drifted off to ruminate on *pone*. The campus newspaper had labeled him the most distracted member of the faculty—misplacing his briefcase, forgetting to show up for class, walking into trees. But he'd also been one of the most popular until he'd flunked a pair of star football players. The school newspaper excoriated him, and fans called him a traitor. A few students considered him a hero, however. Lenny wanted to be neither.

Charlie tightened his helmet and slipped the key into the ignition. "I got to get back to the farm because Sally must have lunch ready by now. Besides, I don't want to stick around and watch my good buddy make a big *weegan* of himself."

"Can you come over tomorrow? We got only halfway through the G verbs this morning."

"Tomorrow I got to work on the barn roof. Maybe the day after.

Or the day after that."

Charlie started the engine, leaned into the handlebars and roared away in a blast of blue smoke.

Lenny watched him go. There were times when Lenny felt like quitting the project. Charlie used him as a resource—"What's a gerund? Where do hyphens go? What in hell is a predicate complement?"—but had given him no real role in documenting the language itself. Although this was frustrating and puzzling, it was never quite enough to force Lenny to drop out. He took great pride in helping save a language, not to mention that it was a hot topic in linguistic circles and would go a long way toward saving his teaching job.

Tom and Titus simultaneously tucked their muscle shirts into their waistbands. Titus said, "We was football players."

"Oh?" Lenny said. He paid no attention to team sports but closely attended to subject/verb conflicts.

"Yeah, that's right," Titus said. "But we got cheated and ain't never going to get our whack at the NFL."

Distracted, Lenny tugged on Gerry's ropes. Yes, they'd definitely need retying. It pleased him to hear someone say *ain't* so naturally and not merely to make an ironic point. He said over his shoulder, "NFL—that would be the National Federation of... uh...?"

"Holy shit on a shingle!" Titus said. "I'm talking about the National Football League—big money, fame and all the poontang a guy could ever want."

Lenny had read somewhere that *poontang* descended from New Orleans Creole, from *putain*, the French word for *prostitute*, but he wasn't absolutely sure. He would look into this later, along with *pone*. He turned to the brothers. "Something went wrong?"

The Sprockets looked at each other in wonder. "Yeah, you could say that," Titus said. "We got screwed."

"Yeah, screwed," Tom repeated.

Lenny said, "That's a shame."

"Yeah, well, we're gonna get payback," Titus said and patted Gerry's foot.

Lenny climbed into his car and eased out of the parking lot. Ropes squeaked against the door frames, the statue's base creaked on the Chevy's roof, and Lenny was sure he heard Gerry groan in anticipation of the dreadful day ahead.

In his rearview mirror, Lenny watched the diminishing Sprocket brothers waving and laughing. What an odd pair, he thought.

Lenny decided to take his usual route through the arboretum on his way downtown. The beauty and isolation of the place soothed him. He hoped it would today.

*   *   *

Bob One spotted a car approaching and got to his feet. It was an old black Chevy with a maroon right front fender. Don't all professors drive Priuses?

But it had to be the guy on account of the statue on top like he'd been told to look for. What was that thing? A squirrel? A rat? Look at how the damn thing wobbles! About ready to tip over.

Bob One slipped closer to the road, crouched behind a bush, pulled his pistol from his belt and slapped a mosquito off his forehead. He examined the bloody splotch on his palm. Shit, stick around much longer, and the damn insects would suck him dead.

*   *   *

Lenny was scared.

In two days, he had to go on live television with Charlie and discuss their Skalwegian project—not easy for someone wanting to go through life invisible. Would he make a fool of himself? Say dumb things he'd later regret?

Probably.

Lenny's thoughts turned back to the Sprocket brothers. Strange last name. Scholars could trace *sprocket* back as far as the mid-sixteenth century as a carpenter's term but hadn't yet located an ancestor.

Tom and Titus Sprocket!

Of course!

He'd flunked them in first-year French because they never showed up for class, which cost them their eligibility to play football. The dean had been furious with him but not with the errant guard and tackle. Jocks normally took Spanish with Juan Jorgenson—the other candidate for the language department's one tenured slot. Juan automatically gave A's to athletes just for registering.

Lenny reached over and cranked up the radio for the boisterous ending of Beethoven's Fifth Symphony, then glanced up to see he was driving much too fast into Jackknife Corner.

Panicked, he jammed on the brakes and twisted the steering wheel hard left.

He felt the car tilt to the right and heard a loud *Thunk!* just as Beethoven's Fifth swelled to a crescendo. Puzzled, Lenny drove on, with the Chevy pulling to the right. Probably something to do with tire pressure, Lenny guessed. He'd have that checked later.

*   *   *

Bob One lay on the side of road. Blood flowed out his left ear and down his cheek. His head buzzed, and his eyes slipped in and out of focus. He pulled himself to his feet, wobbled, then toppled into the ditch. He crawled into the marsh, still gripping his unfired handgun. Puddles soaked his knees and elbows. A possum trotted past. An airplane roared low overhead. Or was that inside his skull?

Bob One's left temple hurt like a son-of-a-bitch. That damn rat had toppled over and whacked him on the side of the head. Or was it a guinea pig?

Bob One curled up beside a bog. Half-conscious, he watched a fat snapping turtle waddle toward him, stop two feet from his nose, look him up and down, then open its jaw. Shit, Bob One said to himself, the thing's got a mouth the size of a catcher's mitt. Bob One didn't like animals or much of anything else in nature. He tried to crawl away, but things started going dark—warm and dark—not such a bad feeling, actually.

Bob One awoke to see the turtle biting his right forefinger off at the second joint. Bob One felt no pain and noticed that one of his shoes was missing. As Bob One slipped comfortably into his final darkness, he wondered if a missing trigger finger would hinder him professionally.

*   *   *

Lenny reached the parade route late and swung in behind the school bandsmen in their sky-blue uniforms with "Skammer's Fine Meats" embroidered in bright yellow across the back.

Spectators to Lenny's right shouted and pointed. Some ducked, some knelt, some even dropped to their stomachs. Lenny shook his head in disbelief. Had students and townspeople taken to prostrating themselves before the college mascot? Did he really want tenure at a batty place like this?

At the end of the block, a policeman holding a Dunkin' Donuts cup stepped into the street, raised his palm, and forced Lenny to brake.

As Lenny stepped from his car, he realized that he'd forgotten to retie the ropes.

Gerry Gerbil lay sideways across the car's roof, projecting five feet to the right, the ankles tied precariously in place. Someone took a photo. Someone fingered the slack ropes and spoke of slip knots. Lenny touched a patch of something red and damp on the mascot's forehead. Lenny rubbed thumb against forefinger. The stuff looked like blood.

Since when did gerbil statues bleed?

CHAPTER 2

Ceme nak ool ank espaska

"You have shit for brains."
Common Skalwegian saying (vulgar usage).

Lenny sat in the WDRK studio, his mouth dry and sweat running down his back. A television camera zeroed in on him from just a few feet away.

"Good afternoon, viewers, this is Bradley Noyze, and today we have a special treat for you out there in television land. With us are the two leading world authorities on the Scalpwiggin language and…"

"*Skalwegian*," Lenny quietly offered. "Broad 'a' with the accent on the second syllable."

Bradley didn't miss a beat: "Which can also be pronounced as 'Skalwegian.' So I'd like to start things out by asking a question of Mr. Charlie Fox, who *Newsweek* referred to in a recent article as 'the last speaker of Skalwegian.' Why did they say that about you, Charlie?"

Charlie leaned forward and rested his forearms on the shiny round table. He wore a neat blue suit with a striped blue tie. "Perhaps because I *am* the last speaker of Skalwegian."

"How interesting," Bradley said, and turned to the woman seated to his left. Like him, she wore a maroon blazer with *WDRK* over the left breast pocket. "Now, all of you know Daniela, my junior assistant co-anchor on News at Noon and who just happens to be the niece of Mr. Fox. And finally, I'd like to introduce the gentleman seated across from me, Professor Lenny Thorson, who teaches at Ghurkin College. Doctor Thorson, could you tell me why you've chosen to assist Mr. Fox in documenting the Skalwegian language?"

Lenny had hoped no one would ask him a question, had hoped he could get through the next half hour unnoticed, hoped in fact to go through all of life pretty much unnoticed. He cleared his throat, started to speak, produced a baritone gurgle, cleared his throat again. "Of the roughly six thousand languages in the world, a third have fewer than a thousand users. Every week or two, somewhere on the Earth the last fluent speaker of a language dies. When a language expires, a people lose their past, and the world is a poorer place. Language and culture are—"

"But is that so bad, Doctor Thorson?" Bradley said, lifting a forefinger in coordination with his left eyebrow. "I mean, fifty years from now, everyone will be speaking English anyway, and that'll lead to a better understanding between the peoples of the world. We'll have fewer wars and will no longer have to put up with annoying subtitles."

Lenny caught Daniela rolling her eyes. Tall, slender and in her early thirties, she had large dark eyes, a wide forehead, straight black hair parted in the middle and the face of a goddess. An absolute dream.

She smiled at Lenny, which he recognized as an attempt to get him to relax, but her efforts had the opposite effect. Beautiful women frightened him.

Lenny turned his attention back to Bradley Noyze—dark hair, six feet tall, and chiseled chin—who was now explaining to his viewers that people in foreign countries often spoke foreign languages. Lenny tuned out. He rarely watched WDRK, which supplied the town of New Skalvik and the surrounding region with antique reruns of

"Hogan's Heroes" and "The Andy Griffith Show" and on occasion an uplifting interview in the loose hope that a member of the licensing commission had tuned in.

The camera rolled closer to Lenny and hovered a few feet from his face. Now what was he supposed to do? Smile? Wave? Make a funny face?

Lenny caught sight of himself in the monitor, and his stomach seized. Was that how he looked to the world? He dwarfed Charlie and Daniela and was even several sizes larger than the sleek Bradley. His head was too big, his hair untamable. Lenny reached up as casually as he could and flattened it on top, but it popped back up. He should have gotten a haircut before the show. Sometimes he went a couple months without noticing he needed one.

It always puzzled him why women seemed to find him attractive.

From somewhere Lenny heard Bradley say, "Mr. Fox, what is your opinion on the subject of dying languages?"

Charlie looked at his hands. "There's a Skalwegian saying appropriate for this occasion: '*Ceme nak ool ank espaska.*'"

Bradley wore an expression of fake interest. "That's certainly an interesting-sounding language. It reminds me of Hungarian or Dutch, although I don't speak either of those tongues. Could you translate what you said for us?"

Lenny broke in before Charlie could open his mouth. "It means 'To lose a language is to lose a treasure.'"

Bradley turned toward Lenny and said, "How interesting," in a voice betraying little interest.

Charlie turned to Lenny and chuckled.

Lenny congratulated himself for his fast thinking. What Charlie had really said was, "You have shit for brains."

But Lenny was surprised that Charlie had said *neke* ('four') when he should have said *ank* ('for'). How could he have made such a basic mistake? Maybe he was rattled by the cameras. But that's not like Charlie—a decorated army veteran.

Bradley turned to Daniela. "Do you speak Skalwegian?"

She wrinkled her nose. "None. No one taught me any. In fact, when I was a child, I never heard my father or Uncle Charlie utter a single word of the language."

She gave Charlie a suspicious look, Lenny a soft one, which frightened him even more.

Lenny had seen her on television a few times, and from an interview that he'd read in the *Boston Globe*, he'd learned that she'd taken a job at WDRK after getting her master's degree in sociology from Harvard. Lenny guessed she was working as an info-babe for the money and the attention. Lenny didn't trust women this meltingly beautiful.

Bradley continued. "But from just a purely cultural point of view, Daniela, wouldn't it give you some sense of duty to continue the language of your ancestors?"

"I'm one-quarter German, one-quarter Hungarian and half Skalwegian," Daniela said. "I haven't learned German or Hungarian, and I'm much too busy to learn a near-dead language."

"But Daniela," Bradley said, wrinkling his forehead and lifting his chin, "recall what Mr. Fox said. Uh... would you please repeat that lovely saying for me and our viewing audience?"

Again Charlie told Bradley Noyze that he had shit for brains. Charlie was having fun.

Lenny was not having fun. His only pleasure was in glancing from time to time across the table at the gorgeous Daniela. Lenny considered her everything that a woman should be, unlike his disheveled and self-absorbed Elspeth.

The director—a tiny man with long ears and an aquiline nose—tapped his watch and waved a clipboard.

Aquiline, Lenny knew, came from the Latin *aquilinus*, as in *eagle*. The word always made him think of the constellation Aquila (the Eagle), which in turn led him to reflect on the glorious names of other constellations such as Orion (the Hunter), Leo (the Lion) and...

And Bradley cleared his throat. "I said, Doctor Thorson, how did you and Mr. Fox arrive at your collaboration?"

Lenny noticed that everyone around the table was staring at him. A camera hovered a few feet from his nose, which he always thought much too large.

The elfin director frenetically flapped the clipboard.

"Uh… I was his wife's student in high school," Lenny said. "Sally and I kept in touch over the years. After she started working at Ghurkin College, she told me about the opening for my current job in the language and linguistics department. A couple years after I was hired, Charlie contacted me through her and asked if I'd help him document the Skalwegian language."

"I see. And how long have you and Mr. Fox been working together?"

"About three months."

"And how much longer do you expect your work to take?" Bradley asked, his chin vibrating as he smothered a yawn.

"We're scheduled to turn the manuscript over to our publisher in late December. It's a small house, subsidized by a group of New England colleges and universities. The book won't be a money-maker, I'm afraid."

"Speaking of money-makers," Bradley said, straightening up, "we must take a quick break for our sponsors. But don't go away folks. We'll be right back."

A tiny, aproned woman rushed over, comb and makeup brush in hand. She straightened Bradley's tie, then stepped behind him, brushed down his silky black cowlick, gave it a shot of spray and made a funny face that drew a snicker from the little man with the clipboard.

Daniela kicked off her right shoe and massaged her toes.

Lenny leaned over and whispered to Charlie. "You seem to be taking this in stride."

"I sure am. What about you?"

"I'm scared."

"Don't be. No one's shooting at you. When they start shooting, that's the time to get scared." Charlie yawned, then stared off in the distance. "You take it too seriously, you know."

"The TV show?" Lenny asked.

"No. Life."

"Oh."

"That's right," Charlie said, still not looking at Lenny. "Nothing we say or do here today makes one damn bit of difference."

"Then why are we doing this?"

"For the money, of course."

Lenny had heard this before and always found it puzzling. There was no way that the project would be profitable. Too bad, Lenny thought, because Charlie had debts all over town. His military retirement was pocket change because he'd been busted down to private four months before his discharge. It was Sally's college paycheck that kept them solvent. It amazed Lenny that Charlie could always be so optimistic, could always think so positively, could always believe that, with the next throw of the dice, he'd roll snake eyes.

Or was rolling snakes eyes something bad? Lenny had never gambled. As soon as he got home, he'd research the expression. Maybe it had something to do with how the single dot on each die looked like the eyes of a snake.

"'Pip' was the technical term for the dot, Lenny recalled. Same for dominoes. Also the small hard seeds that birds eat and... and then Lenny noticed that all eyes were on him, and once more he'd gotten lost in thought.

They'd gone live. The director flapped his arm like a one-winged bird.

Bradley smiled at Lenny. "To repeat myself—and this is not the topic of today's discussion, I'll admit, but it should be of interest to our many viewers. Is it true that you were the driver of the car carrying the statue of the guinea pig named Cherry that tipped over and forced spectators to throw themselves to the sidewalk?"

"It's a gerbil," Lenny said. "Named Gerry. And sabotaged knots were to blame for the... uh... incident."

Lenny thought back to the mysterious blood on Gerry's forehead.

"Is it true you're getting threats, Doctor Thorson?"

"A few from overwrought fans. They'll calm down."

"I see," Bradley said. "And is the gerbil safe? There are reports that it's been damaged."

Idiot, Lenny thought. He's bringing all this up to humiliate me because he saw how much attention I was getting from Daniela. Lenny leaned closer to Bradley. "Gerbils are tough little critters and can withstand all sorts of abuse. In fact, they're rowdy by nature and are killers in the wild. Other animals run from them. In packs, they can bring down a full-grown man."

Daniela smiled ever so slightly.

"Yes, well… thank you," Bradley said, doubt in his voice. "Thank you for enlightening our viewing audience. Now, just before the break, you asserted that your research will result in little or no monetary gain. So why undertake the project, Doctor Thorson?"

Lenny never referred to himself as *doctor* and wished this Bradley person wouldn't either. But Lenny warmed up to the subject. "Three reasons: I'll be helping to save a dying language; the project could advance my career; and perhaps most of all, because I love the work. Putting down on paper a language that has never before been written… well, it makes me feel like an explorer. I know that sounds strange, but it's true. I feel like I'm venturing into wild and uncharted territory where—"

"Yes, I understand," Bradley said, stifling a yawn and turning to Charlie. I believe you have a Purple Heart, Mr. Fox. How did you earn that award?"

"I was standing too close to the spot where a rocket-propelled grenade hit."

"Ah yes. And you were in the Marine Corps for how long?"

Charlie's eyes lost focus. "Army, I was in the Army for thirty-one years."

Bradley turned to the excitable director, then back to the camera. "Right now, we have to take another short break for a commercial message. Don't go away, folks."

Bradley signaled to the makeup women and pointed with irritation at his cowlick.

Daniela gave Bradley a withering look, then turned to Charlie. "What are you up to, you old scoundrel?"

Charlie's expression didn't change.

Daniela turned to Lenny. "What's he up to?"

Lenny shrugged.

Daniela said, "Be careful."

"I can take care of myself," Lenny said, knowing full well he almost never could.

Daniela's expression softened. "I don't suppose you remember me, but we met a long time ago when Charlie was an Army recruiter in Boston. He took me to the school where Aunt Sally taught, and I spent the day with her. You were a senior in her English class. I was just a sophomore and thought you were really cool."

Lenny couldn't remember anyone ever referring to him as 'cool,' and certainly never 'really cool,' but now he did recall Daniela. He remembered her as the prettiest girl he'd ever seen, and the nicest. Now he thought that she was the prettiest woman he'd ever seen and he hoped she was still just as nice. He wanted to get all this across to her somehow, to say something witty and memorable, something really cool. He said, "Uh huh."

"My aunt said that you were her brightest student," Daniela added.

"I'm certain others were a lot smarter," Lenny said and shifted in his chair, which creaked underneath his 205 pounds. "I was going through a bad time and ready to quit high school, but Sally talked me out of it and convinced me to go to college. I owe her a lot."

"That's interesting," Daniela said, and sounded as if she really meant it. "Do you live in town?"

"Not far from the campus," Lenny said. He hoped she didn't ask for specifics.

Daniela shifted in her seat. "Uh... where do you hang out when you're off work? Do you ever go to the coffee shops in Harvard Square?"

Rarely. Whenever Lenny drove into Cambridge, it was to do

etymological research at Harvard's Widener Library, which wouldn't impress a dreamy goddess like this. "I... uh... usually go to The Monsoon Mist."

He'd been there once and had tipped a pot of chamomile tea onto his date's lap.

"No kidding?" Daniela said. "I go there a lot. Funny we haven't run into each other by now."

"Funny," Lenny said.

"Ten seconds," the director said, and banged his clipboard on top of his head.

Bradley straightened up to show off his broad shoulders, then turned to Charlie. "As I understand it, before you brought Dr. Thorson onto the project, you worked with Harvey Hanssen."

"Right. But just for the couple months before he died."

"I've heard he was a fanatic about the Skalwegian language and all things related to the culture, and that he—."

"Harvey wasn't a fanatic," Charlie said. "More like someone deeply involved in a favorite hobby."

"A hobby? He bought the entire Skalvik island and planned on repopulating it with—"

"He was a kind and charitable man," Charlie said, leaning in. "He did a lot for this community."

"Uh, yes," Bradley said, leaning back. "One final question on the matter, Mr. Fox. With Mr. Hanssen out of the picture, why have you continued documenting the language?"

"I promised him on his deathbed that I would finish the project. It's payback for something he did for me when was a teenager."

"And would you like to tell our viewers what that was?"

"Not a chance."

Bradley paused, then turned to the camera. "With just a couple minutes left, I think we should end with Mr. Fox sharing a favorite saying in Skalwegian, perhaps something romantic. Would you be so kind, Mr. Fox?"

Mr. Fox nodded. He would be so kind.

The camera wheeled in closer. Charlie turned toward Daniela. "*Mekut nat di weegan!*

Lenny hurried to translate: "The eyes of… umm… a pretty woman are like the sun in the sky."

Bradley looked disappointed.

Lenny admitted his fabrication lacked originality, but so did, "That man is a butthead."

Relieved, Lenny watched the camera's red light go out, the director's shoulders slump, and Bradley—like the butthead he was—jump up and hurry away without a word to anyone, slapping his cowlick flat with both hands as he went.

Lenny was puzzled by Charlie's insistence that they'd ever make money documenting the Skalwegian language, but even more baffled that he'd used *neke* when he should have said *ank.*

CHAPTER 3

Krakont leefonta

"Badger rats"

Daniela stood at her office window and watched Lenny and her uncle climb into a beat-up car with a dented roof. Charlie was small and thin, Lenny tall and muscular. Charlie took short quick steps, Lenny long strides. He's that rare, good-looking guy who doesn't seem to know it, Daniela mused. Strong jaw, wide shoulders and not an ounce of fat. Huggable.

And she'd liked him for his honesty, his shyness, even his mussy brown hair. He hadn't looked at her the way most men did, didn't give her the up-and-down. His expression was soft, scared, even vulnerable—someone others took advantage of.

Her uncle, for example. She hoped the old goat hadn't drawn Lenny into one of his schemes. She wasn't convinced he was continuing the project because of a death-bed promise to Harvey Hanssen. That didn't sound like the Charlie she knew.

Charlie and Harvey Hanssen were an unlikely pair to have teamed up on a language project in the first place, Daniela mused. She'd interviewed Harvey the day he turned ninety. He'd given her a tour

of his Skalvik museum, pointing out this and that with his cane. A
self-effacing man, lonely and sweet. Later, Bradley would refuse to
air the interview because she'd wouldn't go on a date with him.

Daniela watched Lenny and Charlie drive away, then she slumped
in her desk chair. Her phone's red light was blinking. Bradley's direct
line. He no doubt had something stupid to say. It embarrassed her to
work with the creep. During the show, Lenny had given her a look
of pity. Did he also see her as a sellout, someone on TV just for the
money? Probably. Which she was.

Just one more year, two at the most, and by then she'd have saved
enough to start a nonprofit. Something she'd kept secret from WDRK.

Daniela pressed PLAY.

Bradley said, "You seem to have forgotten that during interviews I
ask the important questions and you—"

Daniela stabbed the delete button.

What an idiot, she thought. And a groper. The next time he lay his
hand on her knee, she was going to break his thumb right there on
air.

Her desk phone rang. Bradley again. Don't answer.

Her thoughts drifted back to Lenny and how uneasy he was on
television. Most people lack self-confidence to some extent but learn
to hide it. Not Lenny. Part of his honesty, Daniela guessed. Some days
she herself was nervous about going on the air, afraid she'd make a
fool of herself. But then she told herself she was just playing a role:
I'm the newsperson, and you're the audience—my job and your job.

People assumed by her cool demeanor that she had her act
together, but she still felt like the outsider, the scholarship kid at the
fancy private girls' school. Her classmates hadn't treated her badly.
In fact, they'd gone out of their way to be polite and pretended not
to notice when her father picked her up after school in his battered
blue pickup. But no one invited her to their home, or to go skiing, or
to take in a movie. They became a bit less friendly after she made top
of the class.

The phone rang. Bradley again. Daniela ignored the call.

Aunt Sally had told her that Lenny lived in an abandoned restaurant, but Daniela figured she must have misheard. Sally probably said he owned a restaurant.

She'd also told Daniela that Lenny had a girlfriend on the faculty, Elspeth Something-or-Other. No doubt some brainy beauty, Daniela imagined, someone who drives a Prius, summers in Italy, can't stop discussing wine, and makes fun of TV anchorwomen.

Daniela took a deep breath and opened an email from her station manager. He was sending her to a county fair seventy-five miles away to judge an apple pie bake-off.

Daniela groaned. Two more years of this, max.

*   *   *

Charlie glanced up at the den's wallpaper and its duplicating Dutch boys with their handlebar mustaches. He smiled to himself, then turned back to his desk. Where had he left off the day before? Right, it was verbs, middle of the *G*s.

Gouge. Charlie didn't think that was on the list he'd given Lenny. Let's see... uh... *Looigtu,* yeah, that sounded just right for *gouge.* He licked his pencil tip and added *looigtu* to his list of Skalwegian verbs.

Grate, as in, to grate a... a what? What gets grated? Carrots, he guessed, but not potatoes. Or do they? He wished he could ask Sally, but that was out of the question. He didn't think his Skalwegian ancestors used graters anyway, so just shorten the English verb and add the *tu* to turn it into an infinitive: *grattu.*

Charlie moved his finger down the page of his English dictionary. *Greet.* What does *greet* sound like? Try *feegtu.* Yeah, *feegtu.* Fun word. Sometimes this was fun.

But mostly it was a hell of a lot of work.

He'd never been a reader and certainly not a scholar, but he prided himself on his steel-trap memory. For thirty-one years, the Army had wasted his smarts. On the battlefield he'd earned two Silver Stars and a Purple Heart. During peacetime he earned a demotion and a discharge as a lowly private with a crappy little pension.

What he'd have become if he'd finished high school, he didn't know. But he'd had no choice. Get drunk, joyride someone's car, then wreck it, and you're lucky the court let you enlist instead of sending you to jail. He'd promised himself he'd be out after three years, but he ended up liking the Army. Most of the time, anyway. They'd at first stuck him in an intelligence unit on the basis of his entrance-exam scores, but he'd insisted on a transfer to the infantry because he wanted to be a real soldier. Through all those years of service, he'd stayed in close touch with his parents and his younger brother Oscar, but rarely returned to New Skalvik.

Charlie glanced out the window. The barn needed repairs. So did the house, the fences and the plumbing. He had debts up to his neck and he was going bug-fuck shut in like this much of the day, messing with conjunctions, interjections and predicate nominatives, stuff he'd never heard of until he'd asked Lenny for help.

Did Lenny catch his slip up on TV? Probably, but he didn't say anything. Lenny's a good kid, Charlie told himself. Bright as all get out. A bit naïve, but that's okay except when people took advantage of him. Daniela liked him, that was pretty obvious. She's a good kid too. Still pissed at me, though, for supporting her father when he enlisted, but who'd have guessed the army would take a thirty-five-year-old and stick him in the infantry? But they did, and they sent him to Afghanistan, where a rocket-propelled grenade blew up his Humvee and scrambled his brains. After he got home, he mostly worked as a dishwasher. Before enlisting, he'd been a supervisor in a tire factory.

Daniela's smart like Oscar had been before his wound—Wellesley College on a scholarship, then Harvard for a year of grad school. Maybe a bit spoiled by her good looks, but still a good kid. It was too bad a train killed Oscar before he got to see his daughter on TV.

Charlie turned back to his dictionary. *Grout*, the verb. Pretty obscure. Hold off on that one. He didn't think his Skalwegian ancestors ever grouted anything anyway, never had bathtubs. Charlie glanced out the window toward the barn. Where did a person take a bath on the island? Did they even take baths? Probably not, because the place was eighty miles north of Norway and always damn cold. He and Harvey had visited a month before the old man died. The place looked like a frozen version of hell—flat, windswept and overrun with cranky rats the size of badgers. No wonder everyone had packed up and left. Mid-1700s, Harvey had said, and that must be right because the guy knew more about the history of Skalvik than anyone else did, and way more than anyone else wanted to know. Harvey said their ancestors had left town after it burned down during a lightning storm. The last straw, he said. Fishing had already gone bad, and the soil was over-farmed.

Charlie figured that everyone also must have been damn sick of going three months in winter without seeing much of the sun, but he hadn't said anything. Charlie's feelings got hurt too easy.

Grumble. Charlie leaned back in his chair. Had he given that one to Lenny already? He thought so. He'd have to check his notes. One of these days he'd hand Lenny the same word with two different meanings.

What a clusterfuck.

Retirement had turned into a full-time job.

After thirty-one years as a grunt, all he'd wanted was to get the hell out and find peace and quiet back here on the family farm. Live out the rest of his life. Get away from military regulations, from uniforms, from fuzzy-faced lieutenants ordering him around, from cranky Third-Worlders firing Kalashnikovs at his head.

Now here he was, cooped up in his study every day, struggling to get the project done before the end of the year. Luckily he had Lenny pushing him to finish. Lenny's better organized than me, Charlie admitted, probably something learned in the family junkyard. He wants a bigger role and deserves one, but that's out of the question. Lenny should get angry over how I'm treating him but he doesn't. I'd like to see the guy blow his top once in a while. Do him good.

But this whole goat rodeo would be worth it if he could make enough money for Sally to quit that damn job she hates so much. Also, he'd be helping out a lot of folks who deserved a better life and at the same time prevent a mobster and his wife from getting richer. Finally, he was saving the Skalwegian language. Well, sort of.

CHAPTER 4

Ena nan soku

"Hog butt"

Sally stepped into the den and stood there for a moment watching Charlie. He didn't look up. She slipped her suit jacket off and lay it across a chair. She owned five business suits, one for each day of the week, working as an administrative assistant for Dean Sheepslappe, a hellish job for an asshole boss. She noticed that Charlie had on that damn 'So Are You!' T-shirt with the stained armpits. She'd thrown it out the evening before, but he'd found it again. Next time, she'd rip it to shreds. It no longer fit him anyway.

He'd put on ten pounds sitting around documenting a language no one gave a rat's ass about, while at the same time she'd dropped ten pounds and weighed about what she did when she'd been a dancer back in Atlantic City. Her legs looked great again, she knew, but otherwise she wasn't happy with her appearance. She hated her face—round with fading freckles—and she hated her frizzy red hair, now with a touch of gray. To annoy her, Charlie liked to call her Carrot Top. At least he'd have to stop that after she'd gone all gray.

Why had she left for work so angry with him that morning? She couldn't remember. She was often mad at him, largely because she hated her job and resented the fact that he had none, at least none that paid. Whenever she griped about her work, he'd just say, "Lady, just be happy you're not in the infantry."

Which made her angrier.

Sally settled into a brocaded armchair with a loose leg, folded her hands across her lap and said nothing. Charlie liked his quiet when working. Interrupt him and he'd grumble. Sally took a deep breath, kicked off her shoes, and looked around.

They'd named the first-floor den the Dutch Windmill Room for its yellowed wallpaper with the faded blue windmills and the grinning boys in their wooden shoes. For a similar reason, they'd named the second-floor bedrooms the Daffodil Room, the American Flag Room and the Drummer-Boy Room. The house had been wallpapered to death when they'd moved back to the farm that had been in Charlie's family forever. During their absence, the last renter had turned the place into one of those cutesy bed and breakfasts that New Englanders couldn't seem to get enough of.

Every room was filled with the faux Colonial cuteness that the previous occupants had abandoned when they'd skipped town without paying their final month's rent: framed embroidery ("A House is Not a Home without Love"), a pair of stuffed squirrels on the mantelpiece, and a dozen cockamamie spinning wheels to trip over every time Sally turned around.

Charlie grunted, then said to himself, "*Oopack? Oopink?...* no, *oopank. Oopank* it is." He nodded, licked the tip of his pencil, and scribbled into his notebook.

Sally thought it was time to finally get rid of all the kitsch. From time to time, she and Charlie would stomp a spinning wheel into kindling and feed it to the fireplace, or they'd draw Sharpie mustaches on the bewildered Dutch boys, or go out behind the house and shoot holes in one of the embroidered pillows ("Every Time You Have a Mean Thought, You Make an Angel Cry").

Through the west window, Sally caught sight of The Widow

Bahr in the corral next to the barn, atop a nag that was inscribing insane circles in the powdery dirt. Hers was the only horse they still boarded. After the others fell sick, their owners had trucked them away in a huff. The Widow Bahr's horse—Angel Warrior—never got sick. He was also a nut case that was just as likely to walk backwards as forward.

It wasn't out of loyalty that The Widow Bahr boarded her deranged horse at the farm, Sally knew, but the fact that no one else would let her ride naked, which she was doing right this minute.

To spare herself the sight of The Widow Bahr and her jouncing bare bosom, Sally stood up and moved to an east-facing window. The late afternoon sun shimmered off a pond crowded with frogs that kept her awake half the night. On the slope beyond lay the buried remains of her brother-in-law, Oscar.

Sally shuddered. If she died tomorrow, would Charlie and his buddy bury her next to Oscar? She hoped not. Then again, would it really matter?

Charlie mumbled, "*Konktu?* Uh... *Konkentu?* No, stick with *konktu.*"

Sally turned and watched him bend close to his notebook, write a few words, then lean back and chew his pencil eraser. Noticing her now, he smiled faintly in her direction and went back to work.

He looked much older than when he'd retired just four years back. Newer wrinkles had formed over older wrinkles, and his hair had turned gray. It was crazy to work so hard all these months on that damn language. Make Lenny do more of the work, she thought. It's his profession, after all. She'd told Charlie this a hundred times, but he'd never listened. Then she remembered this was what they'd been arguing about before she'd gone to work, how he never listened.

Sally wanted to bring the subject up again because she was in a bad mood, but from Charlie's look, she could tell that he was in an even worse one, and he probably wanted nothing more than to be left alone. But she wasn't going to be driven away. This was her place too, damn it. She turned her back to Charlie, looked out the window and started humming, which always drove him crazy.

He harrumphed a few times, then said, "Hey, Carrot Top, in a few minutes I'm walking up the hill to visit Oscar. Want to come along?"

Sally shook her head. Every day, summer or winter, blistering sun or knee-deep snow, Charlie visited the grave of his brother, Daniela's father.

It was almost two years ago to the day that the train had crushed Oscar's Buick. It was a restored steam engine pulling five open-sided red cars, and it ran only in summers to take tourists through the countryside. She and Charlie were on their way home from a horse show in New York State, driving a mile behind Oscar. They turned the corner and there it was: Oscar's flattened Buick and the cherubic engineer standing beside the wreck, wringing his billed blue cap with both hands and bawling like a baby. A grotesque circle of observers surrounded him: one tall Superwoman and one short Superwoman, a Batman with a beer belly, an aged Spiderman in a sweat-stained hat and sunglasses, all snapping photos. It had been an outing for Amway dealers, dressed as superheroes.

A lump grew in Sally's throat. As clear as yesterday, Sally could picture Charlie standing there while the rescue team extracted Oscar's wrecked body from the twisted vehicle. Charlie remained dry-eyed, expressionless, jaw set, stiff and at attention. The good soldier. The sad soldier. The lonely soldier.

Oscar had two graves, the real one up the hill and the official one in the town cemetery a couple miles to the west. The day after Oscar's death, one of Charlie's army buddies drove out to the farm with a bottle. Andy Deezel worked as a clerk in the Massachusetts State House and was a member of the National Guard. Charlie had mentioned that he'd have liked to have Oscar buried at the farm so he could visit the grave every day. It was just an offhand remark, but Andy, half-drunk by then, took it to heart.

So Andy stole Oscar from the funeral home, resealed the coffin, then tucked the body into the wooden crate that he'd spirited from the National Guard armory and which at one time had held 150 pounds of canned ham. Andy drove Oscar to the farm on the back of his pickup. Charlie was overwhelmed by gratitude. Also drunk. He rarely drank, but he did that day. A lot.

Sally had watched Charlie and Andy shovel late into the night, drink bourbon, and take turns bawling. A full moon lit the meadow and reflected off the pond. Frogs croaked, crickets chirped, ducks splashed about, and the shovels went *thunk, thunk, thunk* into the hard ground. Finally, the two men lowered Oscar's makeshift coffin into the ground and covered it with dirt. Charlie sank to his knees and wailed.

And there Oscar would lie forever, Sally told herself, turning away from the window, with his knees scrunched up inside a crate that once housed 150 pounds of Gallahad Canned Ham.

Oscar had never much cared for ham.

CHAPTER 5

Gurblok

"Bodyguard to the Exalted One"
(specious Skalwegian for "gerbil")

As soon as Lenny stepped through the door, Dean Sheepslappe said, "I'm on your side," but didn't elaborate. Still not looking up, he gestured for Lenny to sit, then continued to fuss with the papers on his desk.

Lenny's stomach churned whenever he was summoned to his dean's office, especially when greeted with "I'm on your side."

The dean's broad, mahogany desk overflowed with football paraphernalia from the man's merry days on the gridiron: lace-up cleats, a scuffed purple helmet, an autographed ball from a bowl game that Lenny had never heard of, and three color photos of the dean as a tight end in grade school, high school, then college, with him increasing in girth from left to right as his numbers increased neatly by twos: 83, 85, 87.

Lenny said, "Why did you want to see me?"

The dean stapled two sheets of paper together, slipped them into a manila folder, dropped them into a desk drawer and continued to ignore Lenny. He often ignored Lenny.

The dean's head hadn't kept up with his expanding body since the days the man sported number 87. To Lenny, the head resembled a small and alien orb balanced atop a mound of corpulent pin stripes. Buttons strained, seams screamed. The dean's black eyebrows formed an inverted V when their owner was puzzled (rarely), suspicious (often) or scheming (quite often). Well over six feet tall, he had surprisingly delicate hands and dapper little feet that he always enclosed in pointy black shoes. The dean gave Lenny the impression of having been constructed from mismatched parts, as if a careless toymaker had snatched components from random bins.

Because the dean lacked a teaching background and an advanced degree, everyone on campus puzzled why Lawrence Ghurkin, the addled founder of the college, had appointed him to his current position.

Dean Sheepslappe raised his eyebrows into an inverted V—which Lenny interpreted as a bad sign—and said, "Have you rectified the Sprocket brothers' grades from the spring semester, per my request?"

"They never came to class."

"Still, they are good boys. And they do great work on the playing field."

"And they don't know a single word of French."

The dean snorted, stood up, turned his back to Lenny and linked his little hands behind his back. He rose on tiny toe tips, then settled down. "Exactly how would the world benefit if the Sprocket boys ever *were* to learn a single word of French? And if they did, would it remain in their skulls beyond the first hard helmet blow from an opposing lineman— providing, of course, that you cooperate and let them play? And why *should* they learn French? In your wildest dreams do you ever picture those two seated at a sunny sidewalk café on the Champs-Elysées, ordering croissants and café-au-lait in the local lingo?"

Lenny wished the dean had stumbled over 'Champs-Elysées,' but he'd nailed it. Knowing the answer before he posed the question, Lenny could nevertheless not stop himself from saying, "Who gives passing grades to jocks who never come to class?"

Dean Sheepslappe raised on his toes, settled, re-raised, re-settled, then turned to face Lenny. "Juan does."

Lenny groaned inwardly.

Juan Jorgenson had been born to Norwegian immigrants who'd had him christened as 'Bjorn.' But while in graduate school pursuing a PhD, he'd changed his name to *Juan*, claiming it meant *Bjorn* in Spanish.

Juan had dated Elspeth before Lenny showed up on campus. Juan tried in every way to humiliate, undercut and harm Lenny out of jealously over her and especially because he and Lenny were competing for the single remaining tenure-track position in the language department. The loser would be out on the street.

"I won't change the Sprockets' grades on principle," Lenny said. "And besides, it wouldn't be fair to the students who do come to class."

The dean lifted the purple helmet from his desk, held it in both hands and appeared for a moment ready to pull it down over his shiny dome and rush in from the sidelines to replace spunky number 84, his ankle shattered in the previous play. But he set the headgear down and said, "Refresh my memory—which courses *do* you teach?"

"I have five—and as you well know, no one else in the department teaches more than four, with some just three. I teach two first-year French courses, two second-year French courses, and a class in linguistics at the junior/senior level. In addition, I spend many hours a week doing academic research."

The dean seized the inscribed football with his right hand and bounced it up and down as if ready to send Lenny out for a pass ('Fake short, then go long.'). "Research?" the dean said, eyebrows raised. "I wouldn't exactly call what you're doing *research*. Research is what that white-coated bunch does down in their labs, analyzing pond water or measuring the distance to stars, stuff like that. As for your teaching load, I'm not sure that you're carrying your weight. Perhaps I should find more for you to do here."

"Like driving Gerry Gerbil through the center of town?"

"Well, yes, that's a start. And by the way, that's another reason I asked you to see me. You caused quite an uproar, you know. I'm getting angry calls from alumni about how you tried to destroy the school's mascot. Some are threatening to withhold donations, and you know how that could hurt us financially."

"Maybe we need a new mascot that can carry *its* weight," Lenny said. "A cute green gecko, for example, like the one in the insurance ads on TV. We could bill the company every time the colorful little fellow appears at a football game or rides in a parade atop some poor jerk's Chevy."

The dean paused, lifted his left eyebrow, then his right. He could never tell when Lenny was joking.

Lenny made a mental note to check the derivation of *gecko*. Some sources claimed it had a Malay origin, with the name supposedly imitative of the cry of the frisky little lizard.

Eyebrows back to neutral, the dean said, "In fact, I've been considering a new mascot ever since I started here. Lawrence Ghurkin chose the current one when he founded the school. Just between you and me, I think the deranged old duffer has an unhealthy preoccupation with gerbils. Filthy little creatures, I've always felt. Juan Jorgenson recently came up with a good suggestion for a new mascot: The Banshee Raiders. That would put fear into our gridiron opponents. I could have an ad agency create a big yellow cat with long claws. Terrifying."

"In spite of what many people think," Lenny said," banshees aren't cats. They're mythical creatures from Celtic folklore, females who wail outside a home to warn the family inside that a death is imminent."

The dean's beefy shoulders drooped. "Are you sure?"

"It's my business to be sure about such matters." Lenny said, turning his attention to the photo of the dean as #85, when even then his head appeared underdeveloped. "Take my advice, stick with the gerbil. Few people are aware of this but—ounce for ounce—the gerbil is one of the toughest creatures in the world. In the wild, a cornered gerbil can kill a bobcat. Three working in concert can bring down a grizzly. In fact, the Skalwegian word for 'gerbil' is *gurblok*, which means 'Bodyguard to the Exalted One.'"

Lenny had learned storytelling from his father, a man with a quick temper, hermit tendencies and an unbridled sense of humor. People often sold junk Fords to Jake Thorson or bought junk Fords from Jake Thorson just to hear his jokes and tall tales.

Lenny's mother, a cultured woman who never once visited the family salvage yard, remained unresponsive to her husband's stories and sharp observations on day-to-day life. Rarely leaving the house, she read romance novels from morning to night and tended her sickly houseplants until she died the day before Lenny's ninth birthday.

The dean gave Lenny a puzzled look, then turned his back and gazed down at his beloved new stadium eight stories below. Back up on his toes, he said, "The check for your government grant arrived this morning."

Lenny leaned forward in his chair. "Great. With the $200,000, I can hire student assistants and pay Charlie a salary. This will greatly speed up our research."

"The school has to take its cut, you know. Administrative costs and that sort of thing. I warned you about that when you first put in your application."

"Right, I remember. But there'll be plenty left over. And as I told you, I'm not taking anything for myself."

The dean turned around, settled into his swivel chair with a wheeze, twice rotated back and forth, slid the helmet closer to the two silver trophies, shifted the photos (but retaining their increasing numerical order) to the spot recently vacated by the helmet, and carefully aligned the cleats—which Lenny now noticed were bronzed—parallel with the edge of the desk. Dean Sheepslappe didn't look up. "I've asked the finance department to cut you a check for $3,000."

"Three thousand dollars?" Lenny asked. "Three thousand? That's what, one-and-a-half percent?"

"Uh… yes."

"And you're keeping $197,000?"

The dean still didn't look at Lenny. "The stadium needs repairs."

"It was completed just three months ago."

"Nevertheless, it needs a touch of work here and there."

"Who built the damn thing, the Sprocket brothers?"

The dean swiveled his chair sideways and began sorting through papers in the desk's filing drawer. "You'll get by fine. Maybe you can find volunteers to help you on this little project of yours. Yes, that's it, find volunteers. They always do the best work anyway."

Lenny watched the dean move the same piece of paper around from file to file. Lenny said, "You won't get away with this."

But he knew the dean would.

"I'm not *getting away* with anything. You signed a paper agreeing to reimburse the school for overhead. It's all legal. Now I have to rush off to a meeting with the college president. Rules are rules. But you'll get by just fine. And remember this—I'm on your side."

Lenny stood up. He knew he would get the money if he changed the Sprocket brothers' grades, or at least get a bigger chunk of it, but he wouldn't give in. He paused at the door and looked back at the dean, still fussing with his filing, still not looking up. For a time he'd been adamant that Lenny abandon the Skalwegian project, but now for some reason he no longer was. Did it have something to do with the $197,000? Lenny didn't know. But one thing he knew for certain: The dean sure as hell wasn't on his side.

CHAPTER 6

Bleefuma

"Crooks, cheats, liars"

The dean watched the school's linguist close the door behind him. Lenny was surprisingly light on his feet for someone so tall and muscular. Moved like a boxer but didn't act like one. Anyone else, the dean told himself, and I'd have had a fight on my hands. It looked for a while like the guy was getting really angry, then—just like that—he cooled down. Some people can take care of themselves, and some people can't. Assistant Professor Lenny Thorson obviously can't. Too bad in a way—in spite of everything, the dean kind of liked the fellow.

Without Sally's nagging, he nevertheless wouldn't have hired Lenny three years earlier. She'd informed Lenny of the opening, and he'd shown up to interview, a head taller than all the other candidates and—from what the dean could determine—one of the few who hadn't padded their résumés. Now the dean wished he hadn't listened to her. But Sally was Sally. It was hard to deny her anything. It had always been that way.

She hadn't put out as he'd hoped back when he'd hired her, or even later when he'd done her a favor by hiring Lenny. But in spite of her sass, she was efficient and hardworking, and she now and then dropped valuable tidbits about how Lenny and Charlie were progressing with the Skalwegian language.

The dean picked up the football and gave it a squeeze. A bit low on air. He'd get one of the Sprocket brothers to pump it up.

Was Lenny serious about gerbils being that tough in the wild? Probably. Lenny's the no-nonsense type, the dean said to himself, not a person to make up some cock-and-bull story.

Yup, the dean thought, he kind of liked the guy.

Too bad he had to go.

Too bad it wasn't Juan instead. The dean hated how Juan had made a fool of him with his brainless suggestions for a new mascot. He should have known better than to listen to an idiot who'd changed his name from Bjorn to Juan. He worked with idiots.

The dean stood up, went to his window and gazed down at his flawed stadium. Four workmen had just lifted Gerry Gerbil onto his platform halfway up the north side of the inside of the stadium, and now they were standing around smoking. The dean opened his window and shouted down for them to get back to work, but they either didn't hear or pretended not to.

The dean loved the stadium, and he expected the school to name it after him when he left in a year or two.

He'd taken flak for building a stadium with a capacity of 22,000 for a school of 3,400. Some snotty Boston architect had even gone online and labeled it 'ugly and grandiose,' but the dean prized the structure and had in fact made the initial sketches. He saw it as a blending of Harvard Stadium and the Coliseum in Rome, which he'd once visited with Penelope. Or was it Angelina? One of his ex-wives, anyway. Sheepslappe Stadium—he liked to think of it by that name—was shaped like a horseshoe, open at one end, with arches running around the first two exterior levels and topped by Corinthian columns. A massive glassy luxury box hung high up the north side of the stadium—that snooty Boston architect had great fun with that—but the dean knew how to keep wealthy donors content and how to make money for the college. And for himself.

A woman in white coveralls was getting ready to spray gray paint on a column next to the entrance. The dean grabbed the binoculars off his desk and squinted through them. The graffiti read, "Dean Sheepslappe Eats Shit!" Same as yesterday, same as the day before. Why can't the campus police catch the culprits? Slackers.

Two construction workers drove a pickup into the stadium, climbed out and grabbed their toolboxes from the back. The Stadium wasn't built with the best of materials, the dean had to admit. Every other concrete-clad steel support beam was in fact pure concrete, a money-saving modification that slipped past the building inspectors. Architects always designed structural redundancy into their buildings, the dean knew, or guessed he knew. The place didn't have to stand for two thousand years. It wasn't the Coliseum, for god's sake.

Current repairs came in at $125,000. The dean thought he could whittle that down to $115,000. Subtract that number from the $197,000 left over from Lenny's grant, and that's what the dean would pocket: $82,000. Not bad, the dean told himself, especially when the place would be named after him.

Had he squeezed the concrete contractor as hard as he should have? Or had he been just too nice? The dean feared that he could sometimes be just too nice. Had the electricians also cheated him? Maybe they had. The dean hated cheaters.

The first construction company had done solid work on the stadium's south side, but then the owner went fishing, fell off the boat and drowned. An accident, Police Chief Bart Skammer concluded, even though the widow said she'd never known her husband to fish. Several companies put in bids to finish the project. The dean convinced the college to give the contract to a construction company owned by Luther Skammer, brother of the police chief and a man the dean had known from way back. His bid was the lowest, his kickback the highest—three million dollars in fact, as yet to be handed over because Luther's various businesses were in a slump. This worried the dean. Still, he'd get his payoff if this inheritance thing with Luther's wife came through. If not? The dean didn't want to think about that. He was afraid to put pressure on Luther. The man had underworld contacts, like that specialist he'd brought in from Chicago.

And where had the jerk gone? Had he pocketed the down payment and skipped town? Probably. The dean shook his head. Ethics in our day and age. No one could be trusted, no one followed up on commitments. Maybe the next hitman would be honest.

The dean stepped into his bathroom to straighten his tie. Today he lunched with the college president and would have to explain the additional stadium repairs to the daffy old geezer and later to the compliant and bribable trustees. He wouldn't mention Lenny's grant money.

While the dean was retying the knot, a cloud of doubt slid over him: Had he perhaps stepped over some ethical boundary when he'd engaged a hitman to kill one of his own faculty members?

Dean Sheepslappe tugged the tie into place, studied his reflection in the mirror, patted his bald spot, then smoothed down his remaining hair. Was this the face of someone who'd done something wrong? No it wasn't. No, not at all. Anyone else in his position would do the very same thing.

CHAPTER 7

Klanktu

"To desecrate, discredit"

Lenny sat grading papers at his desk before his 10:00 o'clock class. He shared an office with Henri LeBeau, who taught upper-level French courses and was Lenny's best friend on the faculty. Thirty-eight and Parisian-born, Henri enjoyed telling everyone that he was dating a pair of nineteen-year-old underwear models. Only Lenny knew that the twins were in fact thirty-one and working toward their master's degree in computer science at MIT.

At 9:15, Henri burst into the office, snatched up the teaching notes for his 9:00 class, gave Lenny a bright smile and said, "Guess I'm late, partner."

"Hard to believe."

Newly citizenized and fascinated by all things American, Henri called everyone *partner*, owned a bloated Ford SUV, wore cowboy boots, and sometimes taught in a Red Sox cap turned backwards. His students loved him, especially the coeds. Henri was a tall, slim-hipped man with a strong jaw and dark eyes. Once when Lenny was crossing the campus with Henri, he saw him smile at two girls and heard them squeal. Lenny didn't know that sort of thing happened in real life.

Henri was a smiler. He once told Lenny that the French didn't smile enough. Lenny sometimes looked up from his papers to see Henri at his desk, working over his class notes—or more likely his private genealogical studies—and practicing his smile.

"I'm late because I drove Joan to the airport," Henri said breathlessly, shoving a paper into a textbook entitiled *Fun with French II*.

Lenny nodded.

"At least I think it was Joan," Henri said over his shoulder as he scampered out the door.

Henri couldn't always tell Joan from Jane.

He was back after five minutes. "I gave the little buggers an essay to write in French," he said, plopping down behind his desk. "That should hold them for a few minutes while I catch my breath. The twins tire me out, partner."

"I'll be glad to take one of them off your hands," Lenny said, looking up from a test paper covered with red marks.

"Things not going so well with… her?"

Henri disliked Elspeth so much that he refused to say her name.

Lenny shrugged. "About the same as usual. And you're not supposed to know about her and me."

Henri snorted. "*Mon ami,* everyone in the department knows you're bedding our shapely chairperson."

"Just as long as the dean doesn't find out."

Henri frowned, put on his Red Sox cap, rotated it backwards, then took it off and dropped it back on his desk. "You Americans can…" He started over, "We Americans can be pretty old-fashioned when it comes to matters of the flesh." Henri got up and walked over to Lenny's desk. "Still grading quizzes?"

"Still grading quizzes."

Henri slapped Lenny on the back. Henri considered backslapping to be very American. "That's a waste of your valuable time, you know. The dean should turn your classes over to someone else—not me, of course—and let you devote all your time to your Skalwegian research."

"The dean doesn't call it research."

"He's an idiot," Henri said.

The English word *idiot* descended through middle English from the Old French word *idiote*, Lenny knew, meaning an ignorant and common person, and then the word reached back through Latin to Greek.

Lenny dropped the paper he was grading, reached for Chambers *Dictionary of Etymology* and joyfully spread it open on his desk.

Henri lay a two-month-old copy of *Newsweek* across the dictionary. "Autograph this for me, partner."

Lenny looked up. "I didn't write the article, you know."

"I know," Henri said, and gave the magazine a tap.

Lenny signed the article. "It's mostly about Charlie. My name appears only once, and *Newsweek* spelled *Thorson* with two S's."

Henri took the magazine back and frowned. "You should have written bigger."

"It's not in my nature."

"Well, it should be. You should be proud of what you're doing. Me, I'm just here teaching a bunch of doofuses—is that a reasonably acceptable pluralization?"

"It's good enough."

"Anyway, I'm teaching French from a moronic text to morons, while you're saving a language from extinction. That must make you proud."

It did in fact make Lenny proud. Also very uneasy, especially these past few days. But he didn't share his growing doubts with Henri. Instead, he said, "I find great satisfaction in my work. I'm not curing some horrible disease or ending poverty, but I'm glad to do the little I can to save a dying language and culture."

Henri nodded. "That's exactly why I volunteered to help Harvey trace immigrant families that settled in New Skalvik. He's gone now, but he got me so interested that I'm still working. I haven't gotten very far, though. What are you up to now, partner?"

"I'm trying to fit Skalwegian into the proper family of languages, but I'm stumped. I can trace a few common words to Norwegian— *dog, run, house*—but most are like nothing I've seen before. It's almost as if…"

Lenny stopped talking when Juan appeared at the door. Or at least Lenny assumed it was Juan. All Lenny could see were scuffed brown shoes, brown-and-gold argyle socks and brown baggy pants. The face and upper body were hidden behind a copy of the school newspaper, the *Gerbil Bugle*. Its entire front page was taken up by a photograph of a toppled mascot atop a dilapidated 2001 black Chevy. The headline shouted in bright red, "Desecration!"

Lenny groaned. Henri burst out laughing.

Juan lowered the paper to reveal himself to be a long-bodied individual with dull brown hair combed straight back and a nose like a pickle. "It's a terrible shame," he said, his favorite expression.

"It was an accident," Lenny said.

Juan screwed up his mouth. "Psychology teaches us that there are no accidents."

Lenny knew that Juan had supervised the newspaper's coverage of the gerbil incident. In his dogged quest for tenure, Juan had volunteered for everything in sight: faculty adviser to the school newspaper, representative on the Town/Gown Relationship Committee, cafeteria consultant—to name just a few.

Lenny also knew that in normal usage the word *desecration* applied to sacred objects. Was Gerry Gerbil a sacred object? Had he ascended to that level?

Before Lenny could put forth this observation, Henri bellowed, "Get out of here, you halfwit, before I throw you out!"

Juan backed into the hallway and scampered away.

Henri turned to Lenny. "You were getting ready to debate that evil elf on some linguistic point, weren't you?"

"Maybe."

"*Maybe.* Lenny, *mon ami*, my partner, my office companion and fellow sufferer at this soul-sucking institution, you've got to learn to talk when it's time to talk, and to kick butt when it's time to kick butt."

Henri was constantly attempting to toughen Lenny up, to get him to lose his temper, to punch out an office window, to kick butt.

Lenny had told Henri nothing of his brutal year in the ring as a teenage heavyweight fighting with a fake name and bogus papers, nothing of the opponent dying at his feet, nothing of the guilt, the regrets, the ongoing nightmares.

Elspeth stepped into the office.

Henri grimaced. "*Bonjour, ma princesse!*"

Elspeth glared. She had once told Lenny that, were Henri not the sole native-speaker in her department, she'd have fired him long ago for sass and insubordination.

Elspeth had a round face, plump cheeks, untamed brown hair and a stunning figure. She ate all the right foods, exercised daily, and pressed Lenny to follow her example. She said, "Happy birthday."

Lenny had forgotten he'd turned thirty-five during the night. "Oh, right. Thanks."

"Let me buy you a birthday lunch at the faculty café."

Henri snorted.

Elspeth was a famous tightwad.

"Great, I'd like that a lot," Lenny said, adding a lilt of enthusiasm to keep Henri from saying something snarky. "See you at noon."

Lenny often found himself protecting Elspeth, whether she deserved it or not.

After she left, Henri said, "I have a special birthday present for you, but it's not ready yet."

Lenny groaned. Last year it had been a hot-air balloon ride, which had caused him to throw up onto a cornfield 300 feet below. The birthday before that, a 200-lb woman showed up in his office with an ancient boombox and lumberingly disrobed to *Greensleeves*.

"No balloon rides," Lenny said. "No portly strippers."

Henri shook his head. "This year I'm getting you something a bit more *ordinaire*. It won't make you disgorge your breakfast, and it won't swivel its ample derrière to the execrable *Greensleeves*."

"Good," Lenny said. "I'm relieved."

But he wasn't.

CHAPTER 8

Muntudo opanut vevlaktu kuk opanut

"Expect a fox to behave like a fox."
(Skalwegian folk saying)

Lenny found a corner table in the faculty cafeteria, a windowless puce basement room that had once served as overflow for the library's aging periodicals. There lingered in the air a moldy whiff of *The New York Review of Books* and rumors of mice families. Lenny studied the chalk-board menu above the counter in hopes of finding something new. He didn't. Today's special was tuna melt, same as the day before and the day before that.

Until this year, professors had eaten lunch in the student cafeteria, but Dean Sheepslappe contended that—like officers and their enlisted underlings—faculty members shouldn't mix in casual settings with their students. The dean often turned to military doctrine, even though his only experience in that area was when he posed as General George Washington during the ludicrous Revolutionary War reenactment that took place each year on the soccer field.

In previous years, Lenny had devised excuses for not participating but—with his tenure hearing approaching—he knew escape was impossible this time around. An historian friend on the faculty maintained that the incident had been more of a scuffle than a battle, that a handful of turkey hunters ran into a few Hessians under the command of a British lieutenant, exchanged wayward shots, then got drunk together. The only casualty was the British officer, who stumbled down a dry well and broke both ankles.

The faculty cafeteria had in fact nothing to do with the harmful mixing of ranks but everything to do with economics: For the same bland fare, prices in the faculty café were double those in the student cafeteria.

Lenny reread the all-too-familiar menu and wondered how he and Elspeth had ever become a couple. Well, he did know. Three years before, she'd asked him to walk her home after the meeting for new faculty—of which he was one—then displayed her stunning bare breasts, seduced him on the kitchen floor and declared them a couple.

Elspeth spoke with an on-again/off-again British accent, even though she'd been born forty-one years earlier in Dayton, Ohio. This annoyed Lenny, second only to her bossiness. But to his happy surprise, Elspeth was vigorously experimental in bed, which often caused him to fondly think back to his summer of love between undergraduate and graduate school when, at the end of his second week hitchhiking through France, he'd hooked up with a moody, wide-hipped Albanian bareback rider, and for two months they traveled together, communicating in French and copulating in hostels, vineyards and dusty deep roadside grasses, her powerful equestrian thighs clamping him to her in exquisite pain.

Elspeth wrote poems that Lenny found incomprehensible, even though he read a lot of poetry. He wondered sometimes if he weren't being deliberately dense. In any case, she'd published dozens of her works, with several in *The New Yorker*, and had a growing reputation in poetry circles, so Lenny guessed she must be talented.

He told himself he should just end things and wait for someone better to come along. But would someone better ever come along?

Maybe, maybe not. Besides, there were moments when Lenny told himself that Elspeth wasn't so bad. After all, she didn't smoke, use drugs or snore.

Lenny realized these weren't good traits so much as the absence of bad ones.

Would he ever have the courage to break up with her? Lenny wasn't sure. It would hurt her terribly, and he didn't want that. After the fatal boxing match, he vowed he would never hurt anyone ever again.

Lenny was horrified that he'd ever stepped into the ring.

Boxing had been his father's idea, a way to offset the losses at the salvage yard. Lenny had liked learning a new skill, the training, watching his muscles grow. But he didn't much like hitting other people and he was gentle in the ring. Until the final fight, he never knocked out an opponent and rarely knocked them down. He developed a reputation as a softy, but didn't care. He won every match.

"I saw your car in the faculty parking lot."

Lenny looked up. Elspeth had just entered the cafeteria. He stood up and pulled a chair out for her.

She sat down. "How did your roof get so dented?"

"I was attacked by a gerbil," Lenny said and sat back down. "Which, as you are no doubt aware, happens to be one of the fiercest creatures in all of nature. I was lucky to escape with my life."

Elspeth rotated in her seat and studied the chalkboard menu. "Lenny, you've never been in mortal danger in your life, especially from a domesticated rodent. You've led a life singularly free of significant events. And I simply cannot understand why a well-educated and eminently sensible individual such as yourself should always be making things up."

"It's my way of coping with stress."

"Well stop it," Elspeth said. "Just stop it. Your propensity to make up silly little stories like that nonsense about gerbils does nothing to make you a better person."

Elspeth constantly strove to make Lenny a better person.

She added, "What are you getting?"

"Fish and chips."

"No. You should avoid fried foods, and you've got to watch out for mercury. You should get the spinach salad with tofu and bean sprouts."

They went through the cafeteria line. Elspeth got the spinach salad with tofu and bean sprouts, and Lenny got fish and chips.

The girl at the cash register smiled at Lenny. She was one of his best students, a sweet girl from Sri Lanka with a hint of mustache and a tinkling giggle. Lenny was helping her transfer to a better college, which would be one more black mark against him were the dean to find out.

Lenny and Elspeth carried their trays back to the table. She said, "You and... and that *man* that you share an office with can be brutal with Juan."

"Juan deserves what he gets."

"Juan is a misunderstood individual. Few of his colleagues realize that he possesses a sweet soul and a fine mind."

"He's a horse's ass," Lenny said.

"He is not," Elspeth said, sitting down. "He is a fine man with a heart of gold."

"Maybe you should go back to him," Lenny suggested, half in jest, half in hope.

Elspeth sniffed. "Maybe I will. Maybe I just will. There are times when I don't feel appreciated by you."

She picked up her napkin and scowled. It read, 'Skammer's Harley Heaven.'

The dean had convinced Grace Skammer—Luther's fierce wife and manager of their motorcycle dealership—that the college faculty presented an untapped market for their throaty-motored products.

Charlie had bought a motorcycle he couldn't afford at Harley Heaven. Sally didn't speak to him for two weeks.

Elspeth sipped her water, then said, "I heard you met with the dean."

Nothing occurred on campus without Elspeth's finding out.

"That's right," Lenny said.

"Did he mention tenure?"

"He did."

"And...?"

"And what he said wasn't encouraging."

Elspeth puckered. "I'm tebbly sorry, Lenny, just tebbly sorry."

She always pronounced *terribly* as *tebbly*, an iffy Briticism that drove Lenny nuts.

She added, "I just wish there were something I could do for you, but I simply cannot. I know this sounds tebbly implausible coming from your department chairperson, but it's the truth. My hands are tied."

Lenny knew this was true. The dean made all the hiring and firing decisions.

Elspeth speared a chunk of tofu. "How is your research going?"

"It's going."

"That's good news," Elspeth said, not picking up the tension in Lenny's voice. "Someone told me you looked ill-at-ease on that news show. I'd have tuned in but, as you very well know, I never watch television."

"Even when it's someone you know as well as me?"

"No, not even then. One cannot makes exceptions."

Lenny wanted to tip his water glass onto her lap, the way he'd once accidentally dumped chamomile tea on her in a coffee shop in Cambridge. Or had he done that on purpose? Maybe Juan was right—maybe there are no accidents?

Elspeth ate quickly, describing her latest poem between bites while Lenny let his mind wander to the friendly Sri Lankan behind the counter, whom he hoped to help get into Brown University in the fall term but whose hirsute smile he would miss at lunchtime, then his mind drifted to the Albanian with the thunderously powerful buttock muscles—where was she now? Lenny's mind glided to the origin of the word *buttock*. The word derived from the Middle

English *buttok*, which in turn descended from the Old English *buttuk*, which meant—sweet surprise!—'small piece of land.'

Lenny's thoughts turned to Elspeth's shapely small piece of land.

From somewhere a voice drifted into his zone of consciousness: "which I feel pleasantly unites theme and form, color and cadence, tone and tune. Don't you agree?" Elspeth asked.

Lenny nodded. He agreed.

Elspeth reached out to pat his hand, then quickly withdrew after apparently recalling that their relationship was that of chairperson and underperson. She stood up. "Well, I'm off to the gym."

Lenny watched her go. She spent two hours a day in the gym, firming up her small piece of land. After showering, she would douse herself in perfume, of which Lenny's futon reeked. Lately the problem had lessened because Elspeth refused to stay overnight anymore in his randomly rotating restaurant.

Lenny chewed slowly and reread his plate: "Harley: The Man's Motorcycle."

He was worried.

Charlie had made a mistake on Daniela's news show, and Charlie's latest list of verbs contained *looigtu* "to gouge," but just three days earlier he'd told Lenny that *looigtu* meant "to plant corn."

And why won't Charlie simply sit down and speak into a recorder? That would be by far the most efficient way to proceed. That's how other researchers captured a dying language. Instead, at irregular intervals, Charlie handed him a line or two of syntax or a couple of hand-written pages of words and their meanings. Just why, Lenny asked himself, would Charlie insist on working in such a clumsy and inefficient fashion? Why parcel out the language in such small pieces, such tiny *buttuks*? What was Charlie up to?

It was almost as if he were making the language up as he went along.

Lenny held that thought but dropped his sandwich. Tartar sauce splashed onto his tie.

It was almost as if he were making the language up as he went along!

Lenny jumped to his feet. *"Fuck! Fuck! Fuck!"*

Diners turned. The girl from Sri Lanka let a tuna melt slide off a plate and onto the floor. A pot-bellied sociologist said, "Language, professor! Language!"

Lenny grabbed his fish sandwich and hurled it against the wall. *"That bastard!"*

CHAPTER 9

Estome di nervu ank opanut di uknervu ank tokluk.

"What is right for the fox is wrong for the hen."
(Skalwegian folk saying)

Lenny lay awake most of the night, furious with Charlie, but even more so with himself. He had a PhD in linguists, for god's sake, but still hadn't caught on that Charlie's language was counterfeit. When this leaked out, his reputation would be ruined. Others in his field wouldn't meet his eye at conferences, would snicker behind his back. The Skalwegian language would become an enduring joke in linguistic circles.

The restaurant jerked into motion six times during the night, twice the average. Even the Moon View Revolving Restaurant has lost all respect for me, Lenny concluded.

The next morning, he dragged himself to the college, taught four courses in a fog, then headed to the farm, talking out loud as he drove, practicing how he would rip into Charlie.

Lenny found him in his barn, forking hay to the one horse he still boarded. Charlie glanced up. "You look beat."

Lenny nodded. "We have to talk, goddamn it!"

"You sound pissed."

"I am."

"Good. You need to get angry once in a while."

"I drove out here to tell you that—"

"Sally's still at work, so I made sandwiches for both of us," Charlie said, and leaned the pitchfork against the stall. "The weather's nice. Let's head up the hill."

Charlie grabbed the bag of sandwiches and two cans of beer and took off.

"We have to talk!" Lenny shouted after him.

Charlie kept walking.

Lenny followed.

They climbed the knoll overlooking the farm pond. Barn swallows carved figure eights overhead, and the early evening moon hung pale and fat over the horse barn off to the right. Charlie sat on the damp evening grass and held a sandwich up to Lenny.

Lenny shook his head. "You've made me look like an idiot. In fact—"

"You don't like ham?" Charlie said.

"Huh?"

"I asked if you didn't like ham."

"I thought it was turkey."

"It is," Charlie said. "But I'm asking about ham."

"Not especially. And listen, you have to—"

"Oscar hated ham," Charlie said. "Especially the canned stuff, and I've always felt guilty about it."

Lenny sat down. "Uh… about what?"

Charlie bit a big corner from his sandwich, sipped his beer, burped quietly and then patted the ground. "I've never told you this, but he's right here."

"Who?" Lenny asked.

"My brother Oscar. I buried him here."

"No, you didn't. I went to his funeral. He's interred in the town cemetery. I saw his coffin."

"Did you look inside?"

"Of course not—it was sealed."

"He's right here beneath us," Charlie said, again patting the grass. "He always said he wanted to be buried on the family farm. Listen, I want you to make me a promise: When I bite the bullet, I want you to bury me beside him."

"Uh… is that legal?"

Charlie snorted. "Does it matter?"

"Does Sally know about Oscar?"

"She watched me and Andy bury him."

"What about Daniela?"

"She'd rip my head off."

Lenny took a deep breath. "Listen, I have to know if the Skalwegian language is—"

"Are you going to eat your sandwich?"

Lenny shook his head. "Ever since we went on TV, I've been—"

"That pounding is The Widow Bahr's demented horse trying to kick down his stall door," Charlie said, biting into Lenny's sandwich. "He does that every night. I don't know why I board that horse," Charlie said. "I guess it's because—"

Lenny jumped to his feet. "Fuck! I don't want to hear about some goddamn horse! Or ham! Or nocturnal burials! You know exactly why I'm here, don't you? That's why you're stalling!"

Charlie took another bite of the sandwich.

Lenny put his hands on his hips. "Is one goddamn bit of it real?"

"What are you talking about?"

"You know damn well. On TV you misused *neke,* and you gave me two meanings for *looigtu.*"

Charlie broke off a corner or his sandwich and tossed it to a duck.

"Well?" Lenny said.

"Are you going to finish your beer?"

Lenny handed him the can. "I'm waiting."

Charlie took a sip, set the can down and peered off in the distance. "Some. The words I learned as a kid from my father and grandfather:

horse, dog, fox and a few verbs like *jump, run, throw.* The sort of thing a boy would want to know."

"Not very much!"

Charlie drank more beer. "One, maybe two percent."

"As a kid," Lenny said, drawing out his words, "I never threw a rock through a neighbor's window or shoplifted a candy bar. As an adult, I've never padded an expense report or fudged on my taxes. And now look at me: Not only am I a fake, but I'll have to pay $200,000 back to the government, which I don't have, and I'll go to jail for lying on the grant papers."

Charlie grunted. "You won't go to jail because no one will know."

"I have to tell the truth."

"Okay, tell the truth if you feel you have to. But give yourself a couple of days to think about it first. There's an old Skalwegian saying that goes, 'What's right for the fox...'"

"No, you don't! I don't want to hear another one of your goddamn bogus sayings!"

"Okay, but just promise me you'll think things over, then make your decision."

"I've already made my decision," Lenny said. "I'm telling the truth!"

"That's your right. But ask yourself how much you have to lose by telling the truth, and how much you have to gain by keeping quiet? Besides, are we hurting anyone?"

Were they hurting anyone? Not really, Lenny had to admit. He sat down and looked off in the distance.

If he quit the project, he'd never get tenure and would lose his job at the end of the school year. Maybe earlier. The college sucked, but seventy-seven other candidates had applied for the position he'd been hired for three years earlier. If he went looking for work, there'd be another seventy-seven fresh PhDs to compete with, and this time there would be no Sally to help. Worst of all, his name would be forever associated with the ludicrous Skalwegian language.

The moon settled behind a cloud, the dog stopped barking, and The Widow Bahr's steed drifted into goofy dreamland.

Charlie took a sip of beer. "Want to hear how this all got started?"

"No."

"Well, you're going to anyway because it's a funny story, and I can see how much you need cheering up right now. A while back, I popped into Harvey's museum to get out of the rain. I was standing in front of a cheesy diorama of a Skalwegian family sitting around a campfire when this pretty woman asked if I was from around here and if I knew Skalwegian. I told her I did and then made up a few words that I translated as: 'Your beauty brings sunshine to a rainy day.' She was impressed. So was Harvey, who'd overheard me and assumed I was fluent. He'd already hired researchers to find written versions of the language, but they'd had no luck. That's when he asked for my help. I said no at first but finally gave in."

"Why?"

"It goes way back. I was a wild kid in high school—I drank, caroused, stole stuff. One night I downed a six pack, boosted a car, lost control and drove it through the front window of a taxidermy shop. I destroyed a stuffed grizzly, a family of porcupines and a new Cadillac—Harvey's, I later found out. I already had a police record and this time was heading to jail for sure, but Harvey talked a judge into letting me enlist in the army instead. Harvey didn't even make me pay for the Caddy. That's why I agreed to help him. Also, he was old and lonely, and I felt sorry for him."

"But you're faking the language."

"Yeah, mostly. Like I said, I remembered a few common words that my dad had taught me, and some others I more-or-less remembered, so I added them to the vocabulary list. When they ran out, I started making up new words."

"Didn't you feel guilty?"

"I was making a nice old man happy in his dying days. What's wrong with that?"

Lenny didn't answer.

"Well?" Charlie asked.

"Didn't Harvey get suspicious?"

"Nope."

"Because his mind was slipping?"

Charlie shook his head. "Harvey was as sharp as he'd ever been. That is, he was as sharp as anyone is who builds a museum that no one visits, buys a desolate island off the coast of Norway, and expects people to move there and learn Skalwegian."

"Since that's not going to happen, why are you still working on the language?"

"Like I said on TV, I'd promised Harvey to finish the job."

"But you're making it up."

Charlie shrugged. "What difference does that make?"

Lenny didn't know quite how to answer. "Why in hell did you get me mixed up in this?"

"I needed an expert. I realized I was getting things wrong— duplicating words, getting confused about parts of speech, that sort of thing."

"That doesn't make sense because you brought me in after Harvey died. Why would your mistakes matter now?"

"Uh… because I would know."

"That's the only reason?"

"Of course? What else could there be?"

Lenny couldn't come up with an answer. What he did know was that he'd been a fool. Wait until his fellow linguists found out about this. Their laughter will resonate for miles. They'll shame him out of his profession, and he'll be forced to move several states away, change his name and go to work in a salvage yard.

His father had warned him against going to college.

Lenny watched a crow wheel overhead. "Until we went on television, you had me completely fooled."

"Thanks," Charlie said. "Thanks. That means a lot coming from a professional like you. Sally always said you were the brightest student she'd ever taught."

"Don't try to make me feel better."

In spite of himself, Lenny had to admire Charlie. The syntax was solid, and—except for those recent lapses—so was the vocabulary. He was impressed that Charlie could rattle off Skalwegian as if it were real. "How can you keep so much detail in your head?"

"I could barely read before I started taking night classes in the army, which means that until then I'd had to memorize everything. Believe me, that'll give you one hell of a memory. I thought it would breeze me right through the project, but it turned out to be a hell of a lot harder than I'd expected. But it'll all be worth it."

"You keep saying that. How?"

Charlie set his beer can aside. "Lenny, here's something that should appeal to you as a language professional. Consider this: Besides me, you're the only person in the entire universe to learn the new Skalwegian language."

CHAPTER 10

Cutkoske

"Lobster" (literally, "ugly sea dweller")

Lenny sat at booth number four of the rotating restaurant and stared at the inch-thick stack of ungraded second-year French quizzes that lay on the table before him. A *click-click-click* warned him that The Moon View Revolving Restaurant was warming up for a merry evening twirl. Exactly twenty-two seconds later, the room jolted into motion, sliding the darkening landscape from left to right, and soon the view of the dean's stadium was replaced by the more pleasing vista of the fading purple sky over the college arboretum where Lenny and Elspeth had on several occasions gotten joyfully naked.

Lenny selected a different booth each night from which to grade papers and to watch the world glide by. There were eighteen booths, but only seventeen were free because number two supported a four-by-eight-foot sheet of plywood topped by a futon redolent of Elspeth's perfume. On those nights that the restaurant chose to gyrate—which was most—Lenny awoke at dawn to a fresh panorama: sometimes the leafy campus, sometimes the white church steeples of the town, sometimes the meadow where one misty morning he'd spotted a nervously nibbling doe. Lenny liked to think that he was the only person in the world to wake up in quite this fashion.

Eat first or grade papers? He couldn't decide. He guessed he'd have frozen lobster tails and boysenberries for dinner, even though he'd had the same meal the night before and the night before that. Also the two previous breakfasts.

For a nominal $300 a month, the owner had turned the defunct restaurant over to Lenny as its tenant and guardian, visibly impressed by his bulk and air of responsibility. Anything left in the freezers was his to eat, the owner said. Also, he could help himself to the wine. Lenny asked why the remaining food and drink hadn't been sold to another restaurant, but the man looked sideways and muttered something about taxes and burdensome paperwork. Lenny didn't press.

The Skammer Construction Company had been given the contract to build the shoddy restaurant atop an existing ten-story insurance building. Grace Skammer—Luther's wife—had overseen the construction. The eatery's owner had complained bitterly to Lenny that Grace had bought the central motor secondhand from a bankrupt pipe manufacturer. Three times the size needed for the job, the motor sometimes went three times too fast, completing a circuit in two minutes and in less than one when particularly cranky. Dishes slid off tables, waitpersons tripped, and clients complained of motion sickness, never to return. Restaurant reviewers had a field day. Aware of Grace's temper and Luther's reputation for violence, the owner had decided not to sue, choosing instead to close down.

Lenny chewed the end of his red pen and watched New Skalvik's downtown slip into view, first the white spike of a church tower with its rose window, then the red-brick fire station and neo-Renaissance library, and finally the Museum of Skalvik and Skalwegian Culture, located in a former wig factory.

Elspeth had dragged Lenny there a couple years earlier. Harvey Hanssen himself had done the tour, pointing his cane at glass displays of farm tools, spears, stew pots and an unconvincing diorama of a stiff Skalwegian family singing around an open fire, the father a dead ringer for Harvey, a tall thin man with a bushy gray mustache. The fireside version of Harvey had a family, but the real Harvey lived alone.

Harvey answered Elspeth's questions plus many not asked. They lingered a half hour over the table-top model of the future Skalvik— tiny cottages, tiny fishing boats, tiny people and dogs. Harvey had bought the island ten years earlier. For a song, he'd reported, pride in his voice.

Lenny decided to grade the French exams first and eat later. Best to build up his appetite. He was tiring of lobster tails and had never much cared for boysenberries.

He'd recently calculated that he'd eaten a hundred pounds and ten pounds of lobster during the past months, which left him approximately three hundred pounds to go. He guessed he'd also consumed about fifty pounds of boysenberries in that time. Several hundred bags remained in the freezer.

Lenny had never counted the wine bottles. He drank little. His only contact with heavy drinking was during his summer with the bareback rider, whose myriad problems included alcohol abuse. Lenny fondly recalled how, during their frequent sessions of frisky and utterly delicious love-making, she would blow her tippler's breath at him as she leg-clamped him in place.

Had he enjoyed wine, Lenny knew, he'd have been disappointed, at least according to Henri. The one time Lenny had invited him over for lobster and boysenberries, Henri had spit the red wine back into his glass and declared that the restaurateur's abandoned wine had been "Pumped directly from a *pissoir.*"

Lenny didn't consider himself a wine expert and took Henri at his word. People growing up in salvage yards rarely became oenophiles.

Lenny wondered about the derivation of *oenophile*. He would look it up, but only after he'd finished his grading. Otherwise, he knew he would wander down a dusty side trail leading to words related to *oenophile* and over the next vined hill and onto other forking paths, and it would be midnight before he hoofed it back to where his French quizzes lay ungraded at booth number four.

Three clicks and twenty-two seconds later, the restaurant started to turn again, but shut down after rotating barely ninety degrees.

Lenny wondered why it was called a revolving restaurant rather than a rotating restaurant. In many instances the words were interchangeable, but *rotating* means "to turn about a central axis," whereas *revolve*, while sharing *rotating's* meaning, can also refer to one object circling another, as is the case of the moon circling the Earth. Lenny supposed that the shifty-eyed and somewhat smelly restaurant owner had simply preferred the sound of *revolving* over *rotating*.

He guessed that the man didn't share his own obsession with words.

He also guessed that he was letting his mind wander because he didn't want to confront what was bothering him, namely, the ethical swamp Charlie had led him into. And he worried about Charlie. Why was he working so hard to make up a language? Why the obsession? Had a screw come loose?

Lenny experienced a whirling mixture of guilt, puzzlement, sadness, disappointment, shame and—and this was hard for him to admit—a tingle of a thrill. He now stood unambiguously on the wrong side of the line that divided right from wrong, good from bad, the white hats from the black hats. He felt unshackled, liberated, lighter-than-air, and for a moment pictured his rotating abode breaking free of its bolts and brackets and spiraling into the limitless heavens like a flying saucer.

As for Charlie's obsession with Skalwegian, had the man's behavior changed recently? Had his mind deteriorated? Who knew him well? Should he ask Sally? No, that would just upset her. What about Daniela? After all, she's known Charlie all her life.

Lenny took out his phone, then stopped. A woman like Daniela wouldn't believe he was calling from out of the blue just to quiz her on the mental state of an uncle. She'd probably heard every lame excuse from guys trying to hit on her.

Was he trying to hit on her?

Of course not.

Lenny lay the phone aside, then picked it up again. Of course he was trying to hit on her.

She answered on the second ring. Her voice—bright, pleasant—dissolved some of Lenny's fears. "I'm worried about your uncle Charlie," Lenny said. "Could you spare me a minute or two?"

"I can spare you more than that, but I'm not sure you want to get me talking about the shifty old goat. Anyway, what do you want to know?"

"As I said, I'm worried about him."

"And I'm worried about you," Daniela said.

"Me? Why me?"

"Because my uncle's apparently gotten you mixed up in something."

After a pause, Lenny said, "I can take care of myself."

"Let's hope so. Anyway, what do you want to know?"

"Well, have you noticed any changes in Charlie's recent behavior? Also, are there any instances of… uh… mental… uh… instabilities in your family?"

"To the first question, I'd say 'No, I haven't seen a change.' To the second—except for my remaining at my job at WDRK, which is insane—I don't think my family is any more unhinged than most. But maybe we shouldn't discuss this over the phone. I was going to get a quick bite and then go rollerblading. Do you want to get together?"

Lenny was stunned. He wanted very much to get together. He said, "We could… uh… meet in some nice restaurant. You choose."

Lenny wanted her to choose because he knew of no nice restaurants. Frugal Elspeth insisted they eat either at the faculty café or at her place, where she overcooked lumpy, English-style meals. And on his own, Lenny Thorson—the junkman's son—felt out place in upscale eateries.

"Um, maybe not," Daniela said. "I don't go out to eat very often because people recognize me from television and keep coming over to talk. They're always nice enough about it, but it gets tiresome."

"You should consider retraining as a linguist," Lenny said. "That's a faceless profession. Sometimes even the dog doesn't recognize you when you come through the front door."

Daniela giggled. It was a pretty giggle, like the Sri Lankan girl's in the cafeteria, only fuller and lower. Lenny had never heard Elspeth giggle. "What do you have in mind?"

"Well, I could bring some take-out. I'd invite you here, but my apartment smells of fresh paint. What about your place?"

"Uh… I'm not sure you'd be comfortable here."

"Why not?"

"Well, it's sort of like… well, it's a bit unusual, and it's up high… and… um…"

"It sounds like a tree house," Daniela said.

"It sort of is. But I allow girls in."

"I'm glad to hear that—times are a-changing. Now where exactly do you live?"

Lenny paused. "Uh… do you remember that revolving—better, rotating—restaurant that you can see from the stadium, the one that went out of business so quickly? Well, I'm sort of the guardian of the place. It's rather unusual digs."

Long pause. "You're a rather unusual person."

"You don't know me well enough to say that."

"I'm sorry," Daniela said. "I meant it in a nice way."

"I know you did. I was jerking your chain. However, when you do get to know me better—uh… if you ever did get to know me better, I mean—then feel free to refer to me as an unusual person. I am, and I guess I like it that way."

Another giggle. "What about 7:00?"

"That's fine. I own a pair of rollerblades, so bring yours. I'll make you dinner. I hope you like lobster and boysenberries."

CHAPTER 11

Flekont Chootora

"Boysenberries" (literally, "blue lips")

"Maybe you shouldn't microwave them," Daniela said, spearing a chunk of lobster tail with her fork and holding it up. They were seated at booth number 14. She wore jeans and a baggy blue long-sleeved shirt, as did Lenny. He considered that a good sign.

"They are a bit chewy," Lenny admitted, "but the only way I know how to cook them is in the microwave."

"Next time you might consider sautéing them in butter."

Lenny wondered if *next time* meant the next time he cooked lobster or the next time he had her over for dinner. He hoped it was the latter. "You put that nicely."

"What do you mean?"

"I mean that you didn't just come out and tell me I'm a lousy cook."

Daniela shrugged. "Some guys know their way around the kitchen, some don't. I guess your mother didn't teach you."

"My mother died when I was nine."

"Oh, I'm sorry."

"She was a superb cook, however. She was from Quebec—that's

how I learned French. She'd been taught cooking from her own mother—who by the way abandoned her family and ran off to California, but that's another story."

"That must have been painful for your mother."

Lenny nodded. "After Mom died, Dad and I lived on take-out or ate from cans."

"And you probably sat in front of the television set."

"Dad hated television, so we'd eat at the table in the trailer's kitchenette and tell stories. He mostly told them, I mostly listened. He was a natural storyteller."

"So that's where you acquired the skill."

"It seems so."

Lenny watched Daniela rearrange the boysenberries on her plate. "You don't like them?"

Daniela shrugged. "Not a lot. My dad always called them *poison berries*, and that prejudiced me against them."

"They're named after a horticulturist named *Boysen*. He crossed the raspberry, the blackberry and—I believe—the loganberry."

Daniela giggled, bit her lower lip, giggled again.

"What's so funny?" Lenny asked, smiling with her.

"You. But in a nice way. How do you know so much about words?"

"When I was ten, someone towed a Mercury into our salvage yard with its engine shoved into the front seat. I found a stack of porn magazines and a dictionary in the trunk. Dad took the porn and handed me the Webster's. That summer I had a lot of down time alone in the salvage yard office between customers, so I read the dictionary straight through. Twice."

Daniela set her fork down and placed her hands on each side of her plate, palms down. "I don't know where to start: Do I first ask if you've actually read the dictionary all the way through, or do I ask if you really worked in a junkyard?"

"I not only worked in a salvage yard—that's the preferred term—but I also lived there in a mobile home from the age of nine on. And, yes, I've read the dictionary all the way through and still do now and then. I went through it probably a dozen times during the years between high school and college, when I ran the family business and took care of my ailing father in his last years."

"That was a kind of you."

"He was my father."

Lenny wanted to change the subject because he didn't want to think about his dad's lingering illness. Also, he guessed that women probably weren't all that attracted to men who grew up in salvage yards. "You don't like the wine?"

"It's fine," Daniela said. She held her glass up to the light. "Where did you get it?"

Lenny pointed his fork at the storeroom at the immobile center of the restaurant. "From there. I have a couple hundred more bottles if you'd like some to take home."

"Are you serious?"

"I'm always serious. Linguists are a serious bunch."

"I've only met one," Daniela said. "And he certainly was a sober, down-to-earth guy who lived in an abandoned revolving restaurant, drove around town with a gerbil statue tied to the top of his car and kept boxing gloves hanging over his futon. What's the story behind them?"

"Uh... they were here when I moved in."

"Why are they in shreds? And why do you still keep them?"

Atonement, Lenny told himself. He nipped the end off of a lobster tail. "Who can account for the weird behavior of the male members of our species?"

Daniela eyed him for a moment, then ate a single boysenberry.

Lenny drifted back twenty-one years. The phone had rung while he and his dad were jacking up a corner of the trailer where a cement block had split. It was Lenny's trainer. Your opponent didn't come out his coma."

Lenny's dad had hugged him, patted his back, spoke in a soothing voice.

Lenny broke free, rushed into the trailer, grabbed a razor blade and made slashes in his boxing gloves. He never put then on again.

No matter where he lived from then on, the gloves always hung over his bed like a bad dream.

Lenny thoughts drifted to the word *coma*. It had arrived in English through modern Latin and from the Greek *kôma*, meaning "deep sleep." Appropriate, Lenny thought. He liked to tell himself that his opponent had only fallen into a deep sleep, soon woke up, got married, had kids, and that he…

"You're lost in thought," Daniela said, staring.

Lenny nodded. He wanted to tell her everything, but he didn't, and he guessed he never would. Only Sally knew—through tears, he'd confided in her back in high school. Only Sally would ever know.

Put on a happy face, Lenny told himself. "I'm an academic. I'm supposed to go through life lost in thought."

Daniela pointed her fork at his stack of ungraded quizzes. "Speaking of the academic life, that looks like hours of merriment."

"Probably not quite the expression I'd use," Lenny said and lay his fork down. "Now, about Charlie. I… uh… hesitate to bring this up, but has he ever done anything dishonest?"

Daniela turned her eyes toward the ceiling. "Not exactly dishonest," she said, dragging her words out, "but he's come close a few times."

Lenny finished his boysenberries. *Rudolph*—that was Boysen's first name. He considered revealing this interesting fact to Daniela, but decided against it. "If you had to decide between doing what's ethical and doing what's not ethical but would save someone close to you from getting into trouble—even if they don't completely deserve your concern—which would you choose?"

"Does this involve Charlie?"

"Uh…"

"Want to tell me what's going on?"

Lenny shook his head.

"I thought not. Listen, Lenny, I think you're a good person, and I'm sure you'll make the right decision if you haven't already. I can't be your moral advisor, and I doubt very much that you need one."

Daniela glanced around the restaurant. "You need a decorator and a nutritionist, not a moral advisor."

Lenny nodded. It was his dilemma, not hers. Besides, he'd already pretty much decided to stay on the project. He nodded toward the paper bag next to Daniela. "What's in there?"

Daniela set the bag on the table. "You said you lived in a tree house, so I stopped on the way and got the stuff we need. Did you have a tree house when you were a kid?"

"In fact I did. I made it from four car doors—two blue and two red—and for a roof I used the hood from an old Hudson Hornet. No doubt your tree house looked pretty much the same."

Daniela giggled. "I never had one, but I always wished I did. I'd have spent all day in it dressed up as a pirate."

She pulled a black eye patch from the bag and snapped it in place, then put on a three-cornered green hat with a purple feather. She shoved the bag toward Lenny. "Arrrh, matey."

Lenny put on his hat and eye patch. "Arrrh. Put on your rollerblades."

"Shouldn't we wait until we get down to the parking lot?"

Lenny adjusted the patch. The elastic dug painfully into his skin, but he said nothing because he didn't want to draw attention to his big head. "Do you prefer left-hand circles or right-hand circles?"

"Uh... I don't know."

"Then we'll try both directions."

After their first turn around the restaurant floor—counter-clockwise—Lenny was so pleased to find out that he was the better skater that he did a showy 360-degree spin.

"I'm impressed," Daniela said. "You're remarkably light on your feet."

Like a boxer, Lenny said to himself and thought about how his final opponent was rotting in his grave while he was goofing around with this long-legged goddess.

Daniela tugged his sleeve. "Teach me how to make that turn."

Lenny lifted his eye patch and gave Daniela a severe look. "Can't.

Only boys get to learn to do that turn. My tree house, my rules."

"But you let in girls."

"Yup. Times are a-changing."

"I know that I'm not the first girl you let into your treehouse," Daniela said between puffs, "because I found a mascara wand in the bathroom. Do you have a little friend who comes to visit?"

"I used to."

"Did the two of you break up?"

"No, but we should. Do you have a little friend—or a big one?"

"Sort of."

"Is it your strong-chinned and weak-brained co-anchor? I saw how he drooled over you."

"He's been trying to get me into bed ever since I started at the station, but no, it's someone else."

No doubt someone rich and handsome, Lenny thought, with a normal-sized head and a normal abode. Daniela was beautiful, successful, a solid money-maker and considerably far out of reach. Stick with Elspeth for now, he told himself. Or maybe forever. He was a fake, he drove a beat-up Chevy, and he'd loaned all his savings to Charlie. He'd never get his hands on a woman like Daniela.

He grabbed Daniela by the waist and held her tightly.

She swatted at his hands. "Hey, what's this all about, mister?"

"Just be quiet and listen."

The Moon View Revolving Restaurant was coming awake.

"Hear that ticking sound?" Lenny said.

"Yes. But let go of me."

"Hang on."

The restaurant stirred. Daniela hesitated, then hugged Lenny around the waist. "Don't tell me this is happening."

"It's happening."

"How often?"

"A couple times a day—or night. But this is the first time it's provided me with the opportunity to grapple with a famous info-babe."

"I'm not famous, and I'm not sure that I want to be called an *info-babe.*"

"Fair enough," Lenny said.

He and Daniela clung to each other, wobbled and shook.

The restaurant made several turns, then slowed. For once, Lenny wanted it to go on longer, forever maybe. Releasing Daniela, he said, "Try this then: Never before has my rotating residence provided me with an excuse to grapple with a fetching lady pirate."

Daniela giggled.

The restaurant stopped, Daniela took Lenny's hand, and the two started skating again.

"You sure know how to show a girl a good time, Doctor Thorson."

"I know," Lenny said. "And a unique one. Think of this: At right this minute, in the whole wide world with all its billions of inhabitants, we have to be the only two people dressed up as pirates while rollerblading ten stories up in a cranky, rotating ex-restaurant."

A half hour later, they removed their skates but not their pirate hats and eye patches, and they drank a glass of wine before Lenny escorted Daniela down the elevator and out to her car, a dented, eight-year-old red Miata, its top down. She leaned against it and said, "Thanks for the dinner, for finally giving in and teaching me how to make that fancy turn, and for all the funny stories. But thanks especially for the rest."

"The rest?"

"You know."

"No, I don't know," Lenny said.

"I mean, thanks for not trying to lure me into the sack. That was really decent of you."

"Oh," Lenny said. "That would have been rather… um… impolite."

Daniela cocked her head. "So it didn't cross your mind?"

"No," Lenny said. "Not at all."

Daniela twisted her mouth.

Lenny added, "Well, I guess it did."

Daniela stepped forward, went up on her toes, pulled Lenny's head down and gave him a peck on the cheek. "I'd feel insulted if it hadn't."

Then she kissed him lightly on the lips. Lenny could smell her hair, taste her lipstick, feel the light pressure of her breasts.

There was much he wanted to say, to tell her how much fun she was and how he wanted to see her again, how he would learn to sauté lobster tails and find a suitable substitute for boysenberries.

Instead he pulled his pirate's hat farther down his forehead and said, "Arrrh."

Daniela laughed, climbed into her car, blew him a kiss and drove away.

With his unpatched eye, Lenny watched the convertible's brake lights blaze red as Daniela paused at the street, then turned left and disappeared.

*   *   *

And Bob Two watched from a car parked in the shadows across the street. He let out a low whistle. Look at the shoulders on that dude! But size don't matter. He'd whacked big guys before.

CHAPTER 12

Eskunowo di oska nan rako oola.

"Life is a bag of horse droppings."

Charlie shoveled horse droppings into a green, ten-gallon plastic bag, while The Widow Bahr's riderless white steed, Angel Warrior, walked backwards in the corral—his favored direction—and enthusiastically passed gas into the morning mist. The Widow Bahr had driven out to Charlie's farm two hours earlier to ride Angel Warrior, and now stood watching Charlie clean the horse's stall. Finally, she said, "Just what *are* you doing?"

"I'm shoveling horse doots into a green, ten-gallon plastic bag."

"I can see that," The Widow Bahr said, her voice rising in pitch. "What I am really asking is: Why?"

"Because a five-gallon bag is too small."

The Widow Bahr placed her hands on her hips, her favorite gesture of impatience. In her early 60s, narrow-shouldered and wide in the rump, she wore tan riding breeches, a white blouse and a brown riding helmet from which dangled a long gray ponytail.

Charlie wore black rubber boots, Army fatigue pants and a stained T-shirt that read, "So Are You!" His favorite. Sally kept throwing it out.

The Widow Bahr said, "You know what I mean."

Charlie tied the bag closed, set it next to the barn door and started forking fresh straw across Angel Warrior's stall. Some days The Widow Bahr was good company, but at other times her advice in that screechy high voice of hers irritated the hell out him, even though he admitted she was smart as a whip and her ideas were usually worth listening to. "A rich guy down the road pays me $50 a bag for the stuff. Says it makes his roses grow. He's a financial guru who retired from some big investment firm in Boston. It's my guess he was better at pricing equities than horse poop."

"Speaking of finances, I'd like…"

"We're not speaking of finances," Charlie said.

"You started it when you bragged about selling animal excrement at an exorbitant price. And by the way, as Angel Warrior's owner, his nocturnal product belongs to me, but I'll let that pass, kindly soul that I am."

Charlie threw down the last of the straw, spread it evenly with the pitchfork, then wiped his hands on a camouflage rag dangling on the wall. "Did you come here to ride or to give me more unwanted financial advice?"

"Both."

"Would it be wise of me to take financial advice from a woman whose horse walks backwards?"

Charlie forked the wet straw he'd removed from Angel Warrior's stall into a wheelbarrow.

"You're not taking investment guidance from a recreational beast of burden, but from someone who over the years has owned seven businesses and in the process turned herself into a rich old broad. Maybe just for once you should listen. I'm convinced that if you were to rent the back pasture to a neighbor, sell twenty acres of woodland to a logging company and—"

"Not a chance," Charlie said, leaning on his pitchfork. "The farm's been in my family for generations, and I want to keep it intact. Besides, pretty soon I'll come into enough money to pay off the mortgage. And when I do, I'll buy you a horse that doesn't keep slipping into reverse gear."

"I don't want another horse."

"And I don't want your advice."

The Widow Bahr rolled her eyes, turned, and left.

Charlie sat on an overturned bucket and wiped the back of his neck with a red handkerchief. If things didn't work out as planned, he'd have to take The Widow Bahr's advice if he wanted to save the farm. He hated to think of how happy it would make the woman.

Charlie then turned his thoughts to Lenny and how he'd deceived him. It didn't look like he was going to blow the whistle, though. So that worked out okay. Still, he felt guilty about lying to the kid. Lenny's in his 30s, so he's not a kid, but he seems like one sometimes. So damn trusting.

Had I been him, I'd have punched the horse doots out of me.

Charlie stood up and tucked his T-shirt into his fatigue pants. He liked Lenny, liked him a lot. Kind of like the son he'd wished he'd had.

Was it time to tell him the whole story?

Charlie scratched his stomach with both hands. No, not yet. The kid wasn't quite ready for that much truth.

*　　*　　*

Sally ran into The Widow Bahr leaving the barn. "I'm glad to see you're wearing clothes today."

"I do own a few," The Widow Bahr said.

"Then why don't you always wear them?"

"Because I simply love the freedom of riding with nothing on. I feel close to my nature and to my natural self. Aren't there things that you do just because they feel good?"

Sally hesitated. "Yeah, but I don't run around bare-assed."

"When on occasion I ride without clothing, it is only here. If you want me to desist, I shall."

"Hell, I'm no prude. I've done things you couldn't imagine. As for Charlie, he doesn't give a damn one way or the other either. You don't turn him on."

"I have no intention," The Widow Bahr said, putting space between her words, "of turning your husband on."

"Good. Because you wouldn't succeed."

The Widow Bahr snorted and climbed into her black BMW.

Sally watched her drive off. Sally knew she'd behaved badly with the woman, but couldn't help herself. That smug bitch always annoyed the hell out of her.

Charlie stepped from the barn. "You look upset. What's up, Carrot Top?"

Sally didn't give him an answer, and Charlie appeared not to expect one. He pulled up a wooden chair, sat down and started to oil a halter, his movements jerky. That's how he behaved when something was eating at him, Sally knew. She would get nowhere asking him what it was because he'd just grunt or say something wiseass. She dropped onto a bench and watched him work.

He looked tired and fragile. Sally told herself she shouldn't get so angry with him. He deserved better than how she treated him. She loved him in spite of everything, and she knew he loved her just as much.

She recalled how sharp he'd looked in his army uniform the first time she'd seen him. They'd met at a craps table in Atlantic City. Just out of college, she hadn't found a teaching position, so she was dancing at a sleazy club on the boardwalk. They got to talking, to laughing. Three days later he proposed, and Sally accepted. They'd both won big at blackjack, both were buzzed on champagne, both said they'd live happily ever after.

Two months later, they flew to Las Vegas for a quickie wedding. Her parents—both surgeons—had objected to her marrying the corporal—they would always refer to him as 'the corporal.' Charlie promised he'd leave the Army when his current enlistment was up, then go to college or learn a trade. But he stayed in uniform for another twenty-six years. Sally followed him from one grim Army base to the next, teaching English when she could find a position, waitressing when she couldn't, dancing on occasion. It hadn't been an easy life. But now they had a home base, a place to grow old together—just as long as the damn bank didn't foreclose.

The tears came.

"Hey Carrot Top, what's wrong?" Charlie asked.

"It's just my allergies acting up again. Straw does that."

Charlie grunted and returned to oiling the halter.

"I'm going inside," Sally said. "I've got to get some rest. My job's killing me, but I sure as hell can't quit because we'll lose the farm if I do."

She started toward the house, hating herself for what she'd just said.

CHAPTER 13

Kopa ta na mem torwu.

"I'm on your side."

With great reluctance, Dean Sheepslappe agreed to see Juan Jorgenson for a working lunch in the stadium's big-donor lounge looking down on the fifty-yard line. It contained a bar, a double row of tan leather armchairs, six TV screens and one sophomore boy with tiny ears, who uncorked white wine and prepared crab-salad sandwiches for the dean and Juan.

They warmed themselves side by side in the sun's rays slanting through the floor-to-ceiling window. The dean loosened his necktie, kicked off his shoes and slouched.

Juan sat stiff and buttoned up. He said he wanted to discuss his tenure situation.

"I'm on your side," the dean said.

Juan bit into his sandwich. A glob of crab stuck moistly to the left corner of his mouth. "He did it on purpose, you know."

"Uh… who did what on purpose?"

"Sabotage Gerry Gerbil. Lenny Thorson hates the mascot, hates football and hates the college. It's a terrible shame."

The dean nodded and bit into his sandwich. Juan liked to accuse Lenny of everything that went wrong on campus. "Um... Juan, do you know anything about gerbils in the wild?

"No, I'm afraid not."

"I've heard they're tough little buggers."

"I wouldn't know," Juan said.

"Do you think one could kill a bobcat?"

"I'm sorry, sir, but that's not within my field of expertise."

The dean signaled the boy to refill his wine glass. "Thorson won't change the grades he gave the Sprocket brothers."

"It's a terrible shame."

"Without them, the team will lose half their games."

"A shame," Juan said, holding out his empty wine glass, but the boy ignored him. "I don't like telling tales out of school—no pun intended, sir—but I've heard that Doctor Thorson is responsible for the majority of the campus graffiti so unjustly accusing you of... uh... financial... um... misdirection with reference to the construction of this fine edifice."

Juan patted the arm of his chair.

The dean didn't believe Juan. If Lenny Thorson suspected him of kickbacks, he wouldn't have scribbled it with a Sharpie on the men's room wall, but would have told him so to his face. Lenny was soft spoken and polite, but he had balls, a straight-forward guy, always in control of his temper, always cool, always calculating. He'd somehow made that hitman from Chicago disappear, hadn't he? Likeable too, the dean thought. Not like this goofball in the sagging brown suit and argyle socks.

"It's a terrible shame," Juan added.

"What?" The dean said, turning to Juan. He wanted to knock the crab off Juan's face. Maybe knock Juan out of his chair.

"Undermining my chances for tenure," Juan said. "Stealing Elspeth too. He only won her over because he told terrible lies about me. But I shall win back the woman's sweet affection and all that goes with it."

"That's nice," the dean said. He laid his crab-salad sandwich down and started picking his front teeth with the toothpick that had held the sandwich together. He was somewhat put off his lunch by the image of a skinny-ass Juan naked and astride Elspeth.

"And of course, there's poor Gerry Gerbil."

The dean burped quietly.

"It's terrible of me to say," Juan said in the voice of someone who didn't think that what he was preparing to say was all that terrible, "but I must admit that, try as I may, I honestly dislike him."

"Gerry Gerbil?"

"No. Doctor Thorson."

The dean nodded. "I'm on your side."

"I know you are, and I appreciate your support."

The dean set his wine glass down, pulled on his left shoe and relaced it. He had to get away from this fool.

Juan dabbed his lips with a napkin that depicted a chesty model astraddle a beefy black Harley, but missed the clump of crab meat. "And I have reason to believe that Professor Thorson is responsible for all those letters the school newspaper receives, the ones claiming you personally receive payments for the ads on campus. I of course refuse to let those lies be printed."

The dean jerked on his right shoe but didn't lace it.

"It's a terrible shame," Juan said.

The dean bolted for the door. He had to get away from this peckerbreath in the argyle socks before he slapped him silly. "Don't worry," the dean muttered over his shoulder, more for his own benefit than Juan's, "Lenny Thorson won't trouble us much longer."

*　　*　　*

To cleanse his mind of Juan, the dean took the long way back to his office, avoiding eye contact with students and faculty by pretending to be lost in thought. He had enemies, he knew—few friends and lots of enemies. But what the hell, in a couple months he'd be promoted to college president and—better still—not long after that he'd somehow make Luther pay him the three million dollars in kickback for the stadium contract. He'd stick around just long enough to have the stadium named after him—he deserved that much—then he'd resign. Claim it was for health reasons. No more staff meetings, noisy students, tweedy professors, and no more Juan. Especially, no more Juan. Screw them all.

That had been his third wife's favorite saying: 'Screw them all.' Zelda said that about everyone—neighbors, relatives, coworkers, and finally the dean himself. He smiled to himself. Zelda had been a first-class bitch, and he'd admired her for that. Still grinning, he looked up and caught the eye of one of the Sprocket brothers. Titus, he thought. Or maybe Tom. Both had dangling lower lips and cretinous brown bangs. The boy wanted to stop and talk, no doubt to complain about his banishment from the playing field, but the dean averted his glance and kept on walking.

No, that wasn't Zelda's favorite expression, but Penelope's, his fourth wife. She was the most angry woman the dean had ever met and his favorite of the bunch.

The dean held the door open for the Sri Lankan girl who worked in the faculty dining room. Juan maintained that Lenny was helping the girl transfer to Brown, but the dean wasn't sure he should believe anything that Juan said about Lenny. Just the other day, Juan had claimed that Lenny had grown up in a junkyard.

The dean hadn't known his own father. Three aunts advanced three different fates for the man: killed in combat, died of drugs, fled to Finland. The dean's mother—penniless, badly educated, big-boned and cranky—engaged in shoplifting and check kiting, staging falls in public buildings and finding cockroaches in her Big Mac. In and out of jail for short spells during which the boy had stayed with one or other reluctant aunt, the mother had finally discovered religion and founded The Glorious Church of the Ever-Loving Lord. Her soul found solace while her corporeal self cleaned up financially. Thus they'd toured the Bible states, bilking believers in return for spiritual comfort and a promise of an assured passage to the Next World.

She'd be proud of me if she were still alive, the dean told himself as he pushed his office door open and stepped inside, and no doubt she'd approve of his plans for Lenny Thorson's assured passage to the Next World. He could hear her voice now: "Anyone in your position would do the same thing."

CHAPTER 14

Custolo ak Iopica

"Guardian from on high; angel"

Lenny sat at the Moon View Revolving Restaurant's booth number seven, sipped ginger citrus tea, listened at high volume to jazz on the college radio station and fretted over a thick stack of French quizzes. On the top one he circled *le* in *le table* and wrote *'la table,'* then scribbled a red "-1" in the right column and heard a *thunk*. He looked up just in time to see a large bird bounce off the window. Lenny jumped to his feet, hurried to the window and watched the creature corkscrew down, turning and turning, until at the last minute it pulled out of its spin and soared over a row of parked cars, now only lumps of gray in the evening fog.

With a sense of relief, Lenny returned to his quizzes. He hated to see animals suffer. When he was eleven, his father had given him a .22 rifle for shooting rats in the salvage yard. Instead, Lenny built traps. Twice a week he would lug his prisoners to a marsh two miles away. His father pretended not to notice. His father pretended not to notice many things Lenny did. They had gotten on well.

This afternoon, Lenny had driven home from the college through a thickening fog. Now floating ten stories above the ground, he felt as if he were all alone, as if he were the last person in the world, drifting on a gauzy cloud over an empty landscape. Was this what it would be like to be dead, to be an angel? Or was this how it would feel to be the last person on Earth? Perhaps he was.

If that were the case, then the fetching Judy Gleit—who this far into first-year French still couldn't correctly recognize *table* as of the feminine persuasion—had vaporized attractively into the ether, gone to that place in the universe reserved for the language-challenged. So why bother grading her dismal quiz?

Lenny reached into the aging tweed jacket lying beside him on the booth and retrieved a stack of lined 3x5 cards bound by a blue rubber band. He carried the packet everywhere. The upper left corner of each card contained a word inviting further study. *Pone, poontang, gecko* and *oenophile* were just four of the entries.

Lenny separated out a fresh card and wrote *angel* on it, then pushed the pile of quizzes aside and picked up an etymological dictionary.

Angel emerged from the Middle English *aungel* and from there either the Old French word *angele* or possibly the Old English *engel,* but then slipped diaphanously into the etymological fog of speculation: more Old French or Old English? Or Latin? Greek?

Angel's sole synonym appeared colloquially as *sponsor.* Fascinating, Lenny thought, and turned to *sponsor.* It came first from the Latin *spondere,* meaning *surety,* and Lenny felt lonely.

He'd been happy when Elspeth had stayed overnight in spite of how she moaned in her sleep, the way she rolled up in the sheets, and her many complaints about the restaurant's random roamings.

Lenny didn't like being alone, even though he was so often alone. He had spent too many long days by himself in a rickety salvage yard office with his dictionaries, his dog Studebaker and now and again a caged rat. He shuddered at the thought of being the only person left on Earth.

*   *   *

A short-legged and mustachioed man known as Bob Two slithered up the ventilation shaft from the Weeblecrank Life Insurance Company one floor below the Moon View Revolving Restaurant and climbed into the stationary kitchen that occupied its center. He wore floppy tan coveralls with many deep pockets and "Skammer's Air Conditioning Service" printed in red across the back.

Bob Two withdrew a long-bladed hunting knife from the leather sheath on his belt and tested its sharpness with his thumb. The voice on the phone had said he'd be paid $25,000 for this job and would at the same time get to avenge the disappearance—and presumed death—of his first cousin, who'd grown up only two blocks away in Chicago and was also named Bob. Neighbors had labeled them 'Bob One' and 'Bob Two.'

Bob Two nudged the kitchen door open a crack and spotted his victim seated at a booth, thumbing through a fat book and scribbling into a note card. Jesus, look at that guy! Shoulders like a horse. Not someone to go up against in hand-to-hand combat. Better to hide here until he's in bed and stab him in his sleep.

*   *   *

Lenny sipped tea from a chipped cup and shuffled through his 3x5 cards. He didn't particularly like ginger citrus tea, but had inherited 1,400 bags with the restaurant and was not going to let them go to waste. One does not grow up recycling radiators, back seats, hood ornaments, door handles, pistons and windshields without acquiring some sense of thrift.

Sponsor's only synonym turned out to be *angel*, which led Lenny back over a once-treaded trail. He strode his forefinger down the page until he reached *spontaneous*, whose convoluted etymology involved the word *spin*. That pleased him, and would surely please the Moon View Revolving Restaurant if it were reading over his shoulder.

Lenny favored books over the internet for etymological research, both for their greater accuracy and because he just liked holding books in his hands, which reminded him of his childhood back in the salvage yard.

Bob Two slipped into the kitchen's freezer room, where he grabbed a packet of frozen boysenberries, pressed it against his weaselly nose and sniffed.

Lenny discovered that a *spontoon* was a short pike carried by soldiers in the 18th century. Lenny was glad he'd never had to go to war, to shove a spontoon into another man's surprised belly.

Bob Two dropped the boysenberries and sneezed sibilantly into both hands.

Lenny was surprised to learn that *spoof* dated back only as far as the late 19th Century, its fabricator a British comedian named Arthur Roberts.

Bob Two was surprised to find himself standing before an eight-foot stack of wooden crates.

Lenny learned that an ancestor to the colloquial *spook* is the Dutch *spooc* ('ghost').

Bob Two jabbed his knife into a crate at eye level, twisted open a hole and withdrew a lobster tail glazed in ice.

Lenny assumed that s*poonfeed* appeared without etymological explanation because its formation was apparent.

Bob Two used the saw-toothed side of his knife to enlarge the hole.

Lenny found out that *sporadic* emanates from Middle Latin and thence from Greek. Another word applicable to an unmannerly ex-restaurant, Lenny mused.

Bob Two shoved a lobster tail into each of his six pockets.

Lenny lay his 3x5 cards down with a groan and pulled the pile of quizzes toward him.

Bob Two dropped a second lobster tail into each pocket.

Lenny sipped the last of his tea, and a warning *click-click-click* filled the air. He seized the booth's edge with both hands and held on tightly. Lately, his home had been bolting into motion with unusual enthusiasm. The night before, he'd tumbled from futon to floor. With a terrible jerk and roar, the room leaped into action. Lenny's pack of 3x5's slid from the table, hit the floor and fanned open to a perfectly formed hand of playing cards, and the crate started to topple.

Bob Two braced both hands against the weighty cases of frozen lobster tails. For a moment he and the stack achieved a perfect equilibrium, but slowly, ever so slowly, the mustachioed assassin started to lose the battle, began to lean backwards, at first in slow-motion, then faster and faster until the struggle turned into a tip and a rush and a horrific bang as eight crates of frozen Maine lobster meat crashed down onto the surprised killer.

Lenny heard a loud *thump* above the rumble of the rotating restaurant. Was his home breaking away from its mooring, metamorphosing into a flying saucer, carrying him cloudwards to Never-Never Land?

Bob Two groaned in pain, his shoulder had dislocated, his forehead was gashed. He crawled out from under the crates in disbelief and agony. He groped for his knife but couldn't find it.

Lenny associated *Never-Never Land* with J. M. Barrie's *Peter Pan,* and from there his thoughts drifted to the obscure expression 'Cloud Cuckoo Land,' which in some history books described the reality-denying final days of the Thousand Year Reich. The expression came from *The Birds*, a play by Aristophanes. Up there above the foggy world, all alone, Lenny felt as if he were in his own little Cloud Cuckoo Land.

Bob Two crawled from the freezer room and worked his way painfully across the kitchen with the hope of finding both a substitute killing instrument and a safe place to recuperate until his prey went to bed. Disoriented by his pain and the numbing cold, addled by the room's reorientation, slithering tenderly on knees and elbows, Bob Two cursed and groaned and tumbled through the ventilation shaft from which he'd earlier emerged, landing with a juicy splat atop the policy-strewn desk of a recently promoted assistant vice president of the Weeblecrank Life Insurance Company. There he lay, spread-eagle and broken.

Lenny pushed his cards and dictionaries out of sight, picked up his red pen and started into his stack of quizzes.

Another lonely and uneventful evening, he told himself.

CHAPTER 15

Cutkoske nat

"Lobsterman" (1) one who traps lobsters;
(2) an individual believing they are a lobster

Daniela stood at her office window and watched the rain streak the glass. A sucky day, a sucky week, a sucky next two years at WDRK.

Her desk phone rang. Probably Bradley with some new complaint. Or Nelson with another offer of marriage. Or worse, the station manager sending her off to another baking contest.

Or maybe Lenny.

Lenny. What a disappointment he'd turned out to be just when she thought she'd met someone smart and funny and cute and honest. He was smart and funny and cute all right, just not honest.

Skating had been fun. Dressing up as a pirate had been fun. Kissing him had been fun.

Daniela pulled her top desk drawer open, grabbed the pirate hat and eye patch and dropped them into her wastebasket.

She plopped down in her chair and took a deep breath. A few more calls, a bit more research, and then she'd have enough to go on TV with her exposé. It would hurt, but this was her job. She was a journalist.

Call Lenny and hear his side? She knew she should, but she wouldn't. She couldn't handle the pain. And what could he possibly say to clear himself?

Her cellphone chimed. Daniela picked up the phone and checked the caller. It was Nelson.

Should she answer? Daniela hesitated, then set the phone down.

Nelson was handsome, gentlemanly, wealthy and excruciatingly boring. But Daniela hadn't completely counted him out. After all, he wasn't unemployed or a druggie and didn't gamble or have any other known vices. Just boring.

*   *   *

'Skammer's Air Conditioning Services'—was that too many words to print across the front of a cheerleader's sweater? Dean Sheepslappe decided it probably was. Only people in the first rows could read the words. But the ad would fit just nicely across the door of a campus police cruiser.

The dean loosened his tie and shuffled through the pile of proposals on his desk from companies wishing to post ads on cheerleaders and cop cars. Most were from Luther Skammer's many questionable enterprises. Luther was a scary guy but a useful partner. He was the only person the dean knew who could pick up the phone and order up a Chicago hitman as easily as most people called out for a pepperoni pizza.

In addition to the air-conditioning service, Luther and Grace operated Skammer's Construction Company, Skammer's Wishy-Washy Laundry, Skammer's Ford Ranchero, Skammer's Happy Hour Bar and Grill, and a taxidermy shop (Skammer's Stuffings).

The dean thought back to college and how he'd first met Luther. The mobster had put him in charge of the football team's point-shaving scheme, then bought him a new convertible. Later Luther had financed the dean's successful run for state senate, and afterwards got him his position at Ghurkin College even though he lacked a background in education. Something to do with blackmailing the founder, the dean suspected, but never asked. The dean in turn steered college construction projects Luther's way.

The desk phone rang. Speak of the devil. The dean picked up and heard Luther's unhealthy breathing.

Luther said, "Okay to talk?"

"My secretary's not listening in today because she's out again, pretending to be sick," the dean said, swiveling his chair to look down at the stadium, a sight that always calmed him. He needed calming whenever he spoke with Luther Skammer.

Luther sniffled, wheezed, sniffled again. "Why'd you call me?"

"Just before noon," the dean said icily, "I happened to gaze out my office window and whom did I see? It was our man in perfectly good health, emerging from the college library and on his way to class. That's not the way it's supposed to be. Right this very minute, I should be sitting here composing a heart-wrenching press release, and your police chief brother should be staring into a row of television cameras to explain how some crazed football fan had killed Assistant Professor Lenny Thorson on account of the Gerry Gerbil incident at the parade."

The dean heard more insalubrious breathing, then Luther said, "Yeah, last night things didn't go exactly like we planned."

"Apparently not."

"Bob Two's in a head-to-toe cast. I just seen him in the hospital. He looks like a goddamn mummy. Some jerk came to work this morning and found him bleeding all over his desk. Bob Two told the cops he'd been servicing the air conditioner and somehow wound up on the guy's desk."

"They bought that?"

"Seems so. In any case, my brother can handle the situation. After the cops left, Bob Two told me he'd fought with a goddamn giant who's an expert at hand-to-hand combat and gets his strength from a diet of lobster tails and some kind of goofy berry. Bob Two says the guy's a fucking killing machine. Who the hell is he?"

The dean took a deep breath and let it out. "A linguist."

Long pause. "A lindwhist? What's a lindwhist? Is that some kind of martial arts pro?"

"Something like it," The dean said. He rotated back to his desk and picked up a photo of a shoddily taxidermized parrot submitted by Skammer's Stuffings as a candidate for the center of the basketball court.

"Yeah, well, you should've warned me," Luther Skammer said. "I'm in deep shit with my… uh… supplier in Chicago. Bob Two's gonna be in a full-body cast for six months, and Bob One is still missing. I've sent a couple of my guys out to look for him, or what's left of him."

"What did they find?"

"Nothing yet, so I told them to go back and look some more. And for now we gotta pay twice as much for help from the Windy City. They don't like messing with The Lobsterman."

"The Lobsterman?"

Luther sneezed mucously. "Yeah, that's what we call him on account of when they put Bob Two into the ambulance, a bunch of frozen lobster tails came sliding out of his pockets."

The dean set the parrot photo down. "Lobster tails?"

"That's right. I think it's some kind of symbol thing, you know? Like sleeping with the fishes. You seen the *Godfather*, right? Someone sends a fish to the Corleones to tell them their man sleeps with the fishes. Our guy's doing the same thing. We're dealing with a mean son-of-a-bitch who's not one damn bit afraid of anyone."

Luther sneezed twice and blew his nose. "Since Chicago's balking about sending anyone right now, I've contacted a local guy who's agreed to take on our problem. I've given him your number. He's a mean bastard, by the way. He calls himself Billy Butcher because he likes to chop his clients into pot roast. There was this one time in New Orleans when he—"

"I don't want to know," the dean said with a shudder and hung up.

Luther was vicious, a hothead and a big worry for the dean. At the beginning of their collaboration, Luther had wanted to kill Charlie, but the dean had talked him out of it. *Newsweek* did an article on the guy, the dean had argued, and his murder would bring national attention. Besides, they'd be the obvious suspects because they had the motive. Better to take out Lenny. Charlie himself had said in the *Newsweek* interview that he couldn't do the job without him. That made sense, since Sally once said that Charlie hadn't even finished high school. What would he know about documenting a language? Without Lenny, Charlie had no chance of meeting the year-end deadline. Get the blame put on some irate football fan for the killing, the dean had instructed Luther. Your brother's the police chief, after all. He could engineer that.

The dean shook his head. How in hell had he let himself get mixed up with mobsters, hitmen and murder? Last night he'd had that nightmare again about going to prison. Was all this worth it? Maybe he should forget about the three million dollars and go into hiding? No, because Luther would just track him down anyway. The dean shuddered at the thought of what would then happen to him.

He swiveled back to his window just in time to see his intended victim cross the courtyard, turn to greet a student and walk into a tree trunk.

Brilliant, the dean said to himself. What an actor. The college lindwhist—a.k.a. The Lobsterman. Who'd have ever guessed? The guy's brilliant.

CHAPTER 16

Skeenkont hoktea, skeenkont kucua.

"Naked ladies, naked truths."

Lenny was seated in Charlie's living room in front of a television set with the sound muted. Lenny leaned forward. "I think I just saw a naked woman on a horse."

Charlie's expression didn't change.

"No, I really meant it," Lenny said. "I saw her."

Charlie waved his Budweiser can. "It happens all the time."

Lenny didn't pursue this. He'd driven out to the farm because Daniela had left a chilly message on his answering machine the evening before, instructing him and her uncle to watch her noontime news show.

Charlie said, "So, my niece didn't say what's up?"

Lenny shook his head. "No, but she sounded serious."

"Daniela sounds serious too much of the time. She needs to lighten up, be more like you and me."

Lenny didn't feel like a lightened-up person, especially since the day he'd found out that Charlie's version of the Skalwegian language was ninety-eight-percent bogus.

The television set stood between two living room windows looking out on Charlie's barn and meadow. Lenny noticed a headless stuffed squirrel on the mantelpiece and on a nearby chair a crocheted pillow ("Show your Enemy Nothing but Love") speckled with what looked like bullet holes.

Lenny spotted the rider again, partway up the slope leading to the woodlands, and he was sure it was a naked woman.

When does one use 'nude' instead of 'naked' and vice versa? 'Nude' often takes on an artistic aura, Lenny knew, as in "a statue of a nude" or "a nude study." One wouldn't normally say 'a statue of a naked person.' In addition, 'nude' can serve as a noun, 'naked' only rarely.

He wondered how Daniela would look naked on a horse, and would he ever have the courage to ask her out on a real date? If so— and if she agreed—he'd take her somewhere nice but slightly out of the ordinary, maybe the restaurant at the Museum of Fine Arts in Boston. Lenny guessed that Daniela wouldn't be up for more lobster tails and boysenberries.

Yes, that was decided: As soon as her show was over, he'd call her and ask her out. It would take courage, but he would do it.

"You should ask my niece out on a date," Charlie said.

Lenny started. "Daniela?"

"That's the only niece I have."

"Uh… I hadn't considered it."

"Yeah, sure," Charlie said, and threw his empty beer can at one of the spinning wheels. "I saw how you two were getting on when we were on her show."

"Those were just her television manners. She's too successful to be interested in me—too smart and too pretty." Lenny picked up the remote just as Daniela's face filled the screen. She wore a maroon blazer with the station logo over the upper left pocket, a collarless black knit shirt, dangling silver earrings and the face of a Greek goddess. "Good afternoon. My co-anchor Bradley Noyze is off today."

She spoke of a new zoning law. Lenny half listened, all the time worrying about what would come next. Had Daniela somehow found out about the ersatz Skalwegian? Probably not. But even if she had, would that be remarkable enough to deserve air time? Not normally, but perhaps her recent interview with the two men responsible for faking the language made this a newsworthy event. Lenny glanced over at Charlie, stony-faced as usual.

Daniela said, "Stay tuned for a special report after the commercial break."

It seemed to Lenny that she'd looked directly at him when she said that. "She looks angry."

"Daniela looks angry too much of the time. That's why I want to get the two of you together. You're never angry. You'd be good for her."

Again Lenny contemplated what a disrobed Daniela would look like atop a horse, with her silver earrings glistening in the sun and her hair bouncing with the gait.

Charlie said, "Are you sticking with your decision?"

"Do you mean, am I not going to blow the whistle on you?"

"That's right."

Lenny picked up the pillow and examined it. Now he was sure those were bullet holes. "I'm staying with the project, at least for now."

"Do what you think is best."

Nothing seemed best—or better, to be grammatically correct.

After the dancing clean undies faded from the screen (Skammer's Wishy-Washy Laundry), Lenny released the mute button just in time to hear a snippet of *Greensleeves* before Daniela said, "If you remember your high school chemistry, you might have studied rare-earth elements. With such tongue-tying names as neodymium, terbium and dysprosium, these rare minerals are essential for the production of hybrid cars, wind turbines, cell phones, computers, and much more. The need for them is growing by leaps and bounds and their price is skyrocketing. Today over 90% of these minerals come from China."

Charlie said, "Uh, oh."

Lenny said, "What?"

Charlie shook his head.

Daniela paused to push the hair from the corner of her eye. "We here at WDRK have learned that an extremely valuable deposit of rare-earth elements was recently found on Skalvik, a tiny, barren island eighty miles off the northern coast of Norway. All its inhabitants left about 200 years ago and settled in this region, gave up their native tongue and learned English. The late Harvey Hanssen, a descendant of those immigrants and a lifelong resident of New Skalvik, purchased the island about ten years ago."

Charlie said, *"Oh, shit!"*

"Our investigators have learned that Mr. Hanssen cut his only child, Grace Skammer, out of his will many years ago. Instead, his fortune, which consists of the island of Skalvik and a large mansion here in New Skalvik, will go to the man who had assisted the late Mr. Hanssen in documenting the Skalwegian language."

Lenny's jaw dropped.

Charlie said, *"Fuck!"*

"And that," Daniela said, her expression fierce, "Is none other than Charlie Fox, my uncle and the man I invited on this show along with his partner, Dr. Lenny Thorson, an assistant professor at Ghurkin College, and one who is *insincerely* assisting in documenting the Skalwegian language, supposedly for scholarly purposes, but in fact, both he and my uncle are in this purely for the riches."

Daniela's glare faded, to be replaced on screen by a bowlegged man wearing long green shoes and gripping a purple bowling ball (Skammer's Lanes).

Lenny's stomach seized, his forehead heated up, and across the meadow he saw the nude lady on a large white horse.

Lenny wanted to be on a horse, or running free in the woods. Anywhere but here. Maybe Paris. Get a job tutoring English, rent a tiny place and…

And Daniela said, "As would be expected, Grace Skammer is contesting the will, claiming that her father was not of sound mind when he wrote it. At year end, she, Charlie Fox and their attorneys will appear before a panel consisting of a judge and a pair of mental health professionals. In addition, a team of language specialists will also be in attendance because the will contains the unusual stipulation that, for Charlie Fox to inherit the estate, he must have completed documenting the language and demonstrate that he is a fluent speaker."

Lenny's mind swam. So that's why Charlie was going to all the trouble to invent a new Skalwegian language, and that's why there was a deadline.

At least Daniela didn't know the language was phony.

Lenny sagged. He felt used.

And hurt. Daniela had said 'insincerely' with reference to him— 'who is *insincerely* assisting in documenting the Skalwegian language.' Lenny found the adverb awkward, but most of all he felt hurt.

Maybe he deserved it. He'd been naïve and a fool—so what's new?—but he hadn't behaved insincerely. He wasn't a schemer trying to get rich from mineral deposits.

Charlie said, "Maybe I should have told you earlier."

"Hell no, you shouldn't have told me earlier! Goddamn it, Charlie, you shouldn't have told me at all because you shouldn't have gotten me involved in your filthy scheme in the first place!"

"'Filthy' is a harsh term."

"'Filthy' is perfect for the job," Lenny said, jumping to his feet. "I'm the word guy, remember?"

Lenny wanted to put the gloves on again, climb back into the ring and punch someone. He hadn't been this angry in years. "You've cost me my reputation and my self-respect. And not only that, but you—"

"Hold that thought," Charlie said. He grabbed the remote and turned up the sound.

"Normally I wouldn't report on a story of such a narrow scope," Daniela said in a weary voice, "but I felt I should inform my viewers that I had no knowledge of the mineral rights on Skalvik Island or Harvey Hanssen's will when I invited my uncle and his partner on the show. They obviously appeared with the sole intention of swaying the judge with their false devotion to the Skalwegian language and culture. Although I am my uncle's only close relative, I want to assure you that, should he offer me any part of his immense riches, I will not accept a single penny." Daniela lay her hands palms down on her desk and scowled into the camera. "Good day."

Charlie turned off the television.

Lenny sagged. "Goddamn it, Charlie!"

"Cheer up, Lenny, it's not the end of the world. There's an old Skalwegian saying that goes, "Things that look bad at first glance often turn out to—"

"*Fuck!*" Lenny shouted. "*Fuck! Fuck! Fuck!*" He kicked a wooden spinning wheel. It somersaulted once, hit the wall and smashed to the floor.

Charlie chuckled. "Atta boy, Lenny."

CHAPTER 17

Rippahak

"Dilemma"

Lenny stepped outside, dropped onto the porch swing and tugged off his right sneaker.

Charlie followed. "We need to talk."

"No, we don't. I'm quitting. Use your millions to hire some other fool." Lenny massaged his throbbing big toe. "You agreed to work with Harvey just so he'd write you into his will. That business about a stolen car was pure bullshit."

"No it wasn't. Harvey never told me about the rare minerals, and I didn't find out about the will until after he died. What the hell do you take me for?"

Lenny looked up. "I'm not sure I know any more."

Charlie stepped off the porch. "I've gotta check on The Widow Bahr's horse. Come along. I have more to say."

Lenny hesitated, then shoved his foot back into his sneaker and followed.

The sun shone brightly, and the grass glistened from a passing shower. The pond stirred under a light breeze, ducks swam about,

The Widow Bahr's big white horse snorted from the corral.

No more Skalwegian, Lenny decided, and no more listening to Charlie's lies.

That meant no more worrying about his job. It was down the flusher, along with any chance he had with Daniela.

Surprisingly, Lenny felt calmer. The worst had happened. Deal with it.

Charlie leaned over the fence railing. Lenny joined him. Angel Warrior studied them for a moment, whinnied, then walked backwards. Charlie said, "Did you ever meet Harvey?"

"Once."

"Then you must wonder how a nice guy like that could have raised a daughter who would run off with a mobster."

"I suppose so."

"In fact Harvey didn't raise her," Charlie said. "Her mother left him when Grace was a baby. He didn't see either one for years, but supported them anyway. After the wife overdosed, Grace moved in with her father. She was seventeen, popping pills, getting into all sorts of trouble and fighting with Charlie. After a couple of years, she ran off and married Luther."

Angel Warrior trotted over, drool dangling from the corners of his mouth.

Charlie patted the horse's nose. "You still think I was working with Harvey for the money?"

Lenny shook his head. "I believe you."

"That means a lot to me."

Lenny reached out to pat Angel Warrior, but pulled his hand back when the horse showed its teeth. "What prompted Harvey to set a deadline for the end of the year?"

"I suspect that doctors told he didn't have much longer to live. He was afraid that, after he died, I'd let things drag on and finally give up. And I probably would have. It's in my nature."

"What about the island? Are you going through with his plan to develop it?"

"Not a chance," Charlie said.

"Don't you have to? Isn't it in the will?"

Charlie shook his head. "It was a verbal promise. And yeah, I do feel guilty for going back on my word, but the whole idea's absurd. So is the island. Just a couple weeks before he died, Harvey flew us there to show it off. The place is only about fifteen miles across, and it's a dump—chilly, windswept, barren, and overrun by rats the size of badgers. No one would want to live there. Or learn Skalwegian, for that matter. But Harvey kept planning right up to the day he died, sketching where roads should go, where to put the fire house, the school, the dock, humming to himself all the time, as happy as can be."

"Like you'll be after you get rich."

Charlie shook his head. "Nope."

"No? You won't be happy?"

"No, I won't be rich. I'm giving everything away. Well, not quite everything. I'll keep just enough to pay off the mortgage on the farm so Sally can quit her mindfuck of a job, then I'll turn everything over to that smart lawyer I hired. She'll set up a company or a charity or whatever to distribute the mineral rights among the descendants of Skalvik. At least the ones who can be found. It'll involve DNA tests, lots of investigating and no doubt hundreds of pretenders, but that's not my problem."

Lenny gave this some thought. "Should I believe you?"

"Why not?"

"You've lied to me before."

Charlie took out his phone, punched in a few numbers and handed it to Lenny. "Talk to my lawyer."

Lenny took the phone. A woman's voice said, "Bolt, Brown, Regan and Sanders. How may I direct your call?"

Lenny hesitated. "Uh… sorry, wrong number." He handed the phone back to Charlie. "I guess I owe you an apology."

Charlie slipped the phone into his shirt pocket. "You're damn right you do. But I don't want one. I want to hear you say you're staying."

"It's still a scam," Lenny said. "The language is still bogus."

"You want to make Grace and Luther multimillionaires?"

"No, but you don't need me," Lenny said. "You can hire some other linguist. We're a dime a dozen."

"Would that person go along with my little deception?"

Lenny shifted his weight to the other foot. "Uh… probably not."

"Without you, the Skammers will get rich, the money won't get divided up among the people who deserve it, I'll lose the farm, and you'll lose your job. Are you all right with that?"

Lenny shook his head. "I guess not."

Charlie punched Lenny's shoulder. "I'll take that to mean you're still on board."

*   *   *

Lenny went home, sat at booth number eleven and had second thoughts about letting himself be dragged into continuing to work with Charlie. What if someone found out that the language was bogus? Would he and Charlie go to prison?

Can inmates bring etymological dictionaries?

Lenny picked a dumbbell up in each hand and had reached forty-five reps when Daniela called. Lenny hesitated, then set the dumbbells down with a clank. "Yes."

"I wanted to talk to you face to face."

"This isn't face to face," Lenny said.

"You know what I mean."

With his free right hand, Lenny picked up a dumbbell and raised and lowered it twice. "No, I don't."

"You sound angry."

"I don't get angry."

After a long pause, Daniela said, "Well?"

"Well what?"

"I've called to give you the opportunity to explain how you got yourself into this mess."

"I don't have to explain anything. You accused me of something I'm not guilty of."

"Are you telling me," Daniela said in the same icy tones that she'd used on television, "that you're not involved in my uncle's scheme?"

Two more pumps of the dumbbell. "That's exactly what I'm telling you."

"Lenny," Daniela said, "not even *you* are that naïve."

"I am," Lenny said, "I really am."

But Daniela had already hung up.

CHAPTER 18

Shakensit di dunklont posat.

"Fear is a black cat."
(traditional Skalwegian saying)

The dean locked his office door from the inside, pulled open a desk drawer, took out a bottle of Jack Daniels and poured a drink. His hand shook. He gulped it down, poured another, drank that, then went to the window and peered down at his stadium. Usually this calmed him, but not this morning. He'd had that sweaty prison dream again the night before—a life sentence, a windowless cell, the loony guy in the lower bunk farting and beating off.

The nightmare had been coming more often lately—once, twice a week. He'd first had it after he'd visited his mother in prison, just before his freshman year in college. Seeing her had been a shock. Her eyes were hollow, her hair dirty, her breath toxic. She complained of the cold gray walls, of bland food, assaults from other inmates, the scratchy uniform.

I should be looking forward to the good life, the dean told himself. A sunny condo in San Diego, sleeping late, golf every day, swimming in the ocean. Instead, I'm facing a long prison sentence as an accomplice to murder. The nightmare had turned real.

And he felt he hadn't done anything really bad.

The dean closed his eyes and leaned his forehead against the cool windowpane. It was time to get out, to save himself. How in hell had he gotten mixed up with mobsters, with hitmen, with murder?

Well, Grace and Luther had pulled him in, that's how. If they'd paid him the $3 million when he had it coming, then he'd never have gotten caught up in their murderous scheme.

The dean finished his drink. Yes, it was definitely Grace and Luther's fault, not his. Someone else was to blame. It always was. Something his mother often said.

The dean took out his phone and called Luther.

It rang several times, then, "Yeah?"

"It's me."

Luther sniffed. "Make it fast. I got a miserable fucking cold."

"I know a way to save you a ton of money."

A pause. "Yeah?"

"It's about my birthday present."

"Huh?"

"My birthday present," the dean repeated. It was their codeword for the kickback.

"Yeah, okay. What about it?"

"I'm willing to cut it down by half."

No response.

The dean waited, the phone trembling in his hand. And waited. And waited some more. "Or maybe even by two-thirds."

"How come?"

"Things are proceeding so well that you and Grace no longer need my services, and for that reason I thought that it would make sense that the three of us just—"

"Get your ass out here."

"What?"

"Get out here. We gotta talk."

"But…"

Luther blew his nose. "Now!"

"Can't we handle this over the phone? Since you're not feeling well, and because my day is filled with so many important meetings, I—"

"My place!" Luther said. "Right now!"

The phone went dead. The dean stared at it for a moment, then lay it on his desk and poured another drink.

Now what?

Withdraw the little he had in the bank, sell whatever he could, pack a couple suitcases and drive west? Albuquerque, maybe. He had a cousin there who might help, a bookie with connections. Change his name, his appearance, get some kind of job.

And look over his shoulder for the rest of his life?

A couple years earlier, Luther's accountant had skipped an IRS interview and fled the country. Seven months later, his body was discovered in a dumpster behind a Tijuana brothel, a marinated pork taco jammed down his throat.

The dean shuddered, poured another drink, gulped it down.

He had no choice.

He pulled on his suit jacket and headed to the door, passing Sally on the way. "I'll be gone a couple hours."

The dean climbed into his car and drove slowly away.

How risky was it meeting Luther and Grace at their home? Usually the three got together in one of the construction trailers, with workers right outside and a door close by. But inside their house with no one else around except for a couple bodyguards? Was he driving into a trap?

Maybe not. After all, Luther did say he had a cold, and he sounded like it on the phone. Then again, Luther always sounded like he had a cold.

The dean stopped the car at the foot of Luther's driveway. He still had time to turn around. But what would that buy him? Luther would go ballistic and send one of his knee-breakers to drag him to the meeting anyway.

The dean turned up the winding drive. A massive stone building stood atop a hill overlooking New Skalvik. The judge in the inheritance case had let Luther and Grace move in temporarily to keep the place from becoming run down. Harvey's rich and eccentric father had built it a hundred years earlier to resemble a castle. People came from miles around to gawk. Locals joked about it. Children whispered it was haunted.

The dean parked at the edge of the circular driveway, turned off the engine, got out, leaned against the front fender and tried to work up the courage to go inside.

He'd never been to Skalvik Hall. Harvey's father had thrown noisy parties here, the dean had heard. Harvey himself had never given parties and lived alone with a family of cats.

A stone turret rose in front, its windows covered with ivy. Smaller turrets stuck up here and there. Gargoyles gaped. Greek statues poked their heads above the stone wall that enclosed a side yard. They reminded the dean of gravestones. Was that where Luther buried his victims? The dean shuddered.

He dragged himself to the front door, hesitated, then lifted the lion's head knocker. His hand trembled.

Go?

Stay?

No, go.

He eased the knocker down, turned and stepped away. The door squeaked behind him.

"There you are."

The dean turned around.

Grace held the door open. She was a plump woman of fifty hard years, with curly red hair, gray roots and plastic surgery that gave her a perpetually wide-eyed look. She signaled the dean inside and led him to the living room.

His legs weighed a ton.

The dean dropped into a soft lavender couch.

"Can I get you something to drink?" Grace asked.

"That's very kind of you, but no thanks."

The dean realized he already had a buzz.

Grace settled into a chair on the other side of the coffee table, crossed her legs and lit a cigarette. She wore a gold blouse, black slacks and gold sling-back heels.

A pretty woman at one time, the dean guessed.

"Luther will be down in a minute," Grace said. "He's got another one of his colds." She lay her cigarette on a glass ash tray and stood up. "I'm getting another cup of coffee. Would you like one?"

"No, but thank you so much for offering."

The dean watched her disappear down a hallway, glad to see her go. He was tired of grinning like a fool and trying to sound so goddamn polite.

He checked around for exits. There was just the front door, a long sixty-foot dash, and the room was filled with stuff to trip over on his way out: shields on low display tables, suits of armor standing here and there, three massive globes of the world, and a stuffed and snarling black leopard. Harvey's father had been a world traveler, a collector, an eccentric like Harvey, people reported, but an extrovert, noisy, rich and obnoxious. An adventurer. A guy afraid of nothing.

The dean was afraid, more afraid than he'd ever been. Until now he'd thought that fear was what he'd experience before a big football game. But that was just nervousness, a heightened sense of the moment, his mind crystal clear. He always knew exactly what had to be done, how to block, tackle, flop on a fumble. His mind wasn't clear now. He was sinking deeper and deeper into the garish lavender couch, frozen in fright, unable to lift his arms. A loose football would roll right through his legs.

Grace returned with a mug of coffee, took a sip and sat across from him.

A black cat hopped onto the dean's lap.

"Just push it off," Grace said.

"I like cats."

He ran his hand along its spine. When he was a kid, he'd brought home a stray white kitten that he'd named 'Fluffy.' His mother said he couldn't keep it because they had to be on the road so much, preaching. That evening he caught her drowning Fluffy in the toilet bowl.

"If you like cats," Grace said, "then you'd love it here. We had fourteen at last count. Luther hates them, but we haven't gotten rid of them because we wanted to give the impression to the judge and whoever that they keep the memory of my father alive. That's also why we moved into this goddamn museum," Grace said, scowling at a shiny suit of armor standing a few feet away. "The judge finally agreed, but only because an empty house is a target for thieves and vandals."

No thief or vandal in their right mind, the dean told himself, would go anywhere near the residence of Grace and Luther Skammer.

"If you're not bullshitting about liking cats," Luther said, waddling down the stairs, a box of tissue in one hand, a grocery bag in the other, "then they're all yours." He settled into a paisley armchair that squeaked in pain. Luther had short gray hair, drooping cheeks and a belly that bulged under a purple robe. "What's this crap about breaking our agreement?"

The dean leaned toward Luther in an effort to appear confident. "I don't think of it as breaking an agreement, but instead—as I said on the phone—I have found a way to save you a considerable amount of money. As I see it, you and Grace have managed things extremely well up to this point, and as such I'm no longer needed and just in your way. I'm sure that from now on you can handle whatever should—"

"You're fucking kidding," Luther said, then blew his nose, then twice more. He dropped the tissue into the grocery bag. "You're not going anywhere."

"But as I said on the phone, I would be more than willing to reduce what you owe me by half in exchange for my... uh... quietly withdrawing from our agreement."

"When you talked with Luther on the phone," Grace said, flicking ash in her empty coffee cup, "you said you'd go down by two-thirds."

There goes the new BMW he'd picked out. Also, he'd have to rent in

San Diego instead of buying. But anything was better than choking on a taco.

The dean nodded.

Luther grinned. "Then it's a deal."

The dean felt his shoulders slump, his mind clear, a load lift away. He was free of this murderous pair, of the nightmare of prison. He got to his feet and held his hand out to Luther. "It's been a pleasure working with you, and I'll never forget—"

"Sit your ass back down," Luther said. "By 'agree,' I meant we only owe you one million. I didn't mean you could shitcan our deal. Right, Grace?"

"That's right," she said. A white kitten crawled onto her lap, and she slapped it to the floor. "We still need you as a front man to go before the board and vouch for us. You've the dean of a college, after all, and an upstanding member of the community." Grace smiled sweetly at the dean. "You're also a crook, but no one knows that... yet."

The dean sank farther into the sofa. He'd just given up two million dollars and gotten nothing in return. Plus he'd raised Luther and Grace's suspicions. "I'll take that drink now."

Grace ignored him and lit a cigarette. "By the way, I saw Lenny the Lobsterman that time he was on TV. The guy looks more like a boxer than a professor."

A rumor was circulating on campus that Lenny had once fought professionally, but the dean assumed it had been started by Juan as a way to somehow discredit his rival.

"Quiet guys like that scare me," Grace added. "Look what he did to Bob One and Bob Two? Still, I keep asking myself why doesn't he go to the police or into hiding?"

"Because he's not afraid," Luther said and wiped his nose. "This is a game for the him. He's messing with us. I just wish I could hire the guy. Then Chicago and their overpriced hitmen could go fuck themselves. I'd tell The Lobsterman to take someone out, and he'd do the job, no problem." Luther turned to the dean. "Then I'd have him haul the body back here and bury it in the side yard with all the others."

The dean's gut seized. Is he kidding? Or is he toying with me? He likes to scare me, the dean knew. Yes, that had to be it.

Still…

The dean slapped his knees and jumped to his feet, sending the cat scurrying. "I guess we're done here."

Luther looked him up and down. "What's the big hurry? Have a drink, chat for a while."

The dean glanced at his watch. "I'm… uh… late for an important meeting with the college president."

"Oh, yeah?" Luther said. "What it's about?"

The dean started toward the door. "It's… uh… about buying new cheerleader's uniforms."

"New cheerleader's uniforms?"

"That's right," the dean said and hurried past the black leopard, its yellow eyes following him. "New cheerleaders' uniforms."

The dean dashed outside.

Luther and Grace's laughter followed him out the open door.

CHAPTER 19

Oolont nat

"Cad, bounder, rake, rascal, scalawag"
(literally, "feces man")

Lenny graded quizzes while Henri sat at his desk and lobbed paperclips into a corner wastebasket.

"I'll do some investigating for you," Henri said. "We need to learn as much as we can about that lovely newswoman so you can win back her respect. I'll even steal time from my genealogical pursuits, that's how much I'm on the side of all things amorous. Think of me as Henri LeBeau, Private Eyes."

"*Private Eye*," Lenny said, "in the singular. And your help isn't necessary."

"Believe me, partner, it is necessary. Otherwise, you'll let this goddess slip away. I'm doing this because you're my friend. Remember that passage in Balzac's *Père Goriot* when a famous Parisian criminal tells the young hero that a friend is someone you can call up in the middle of the night, ask him to help bury a body, and he'll come over, help you dig and not ask questions? I'm that type of friend."

"I don't have any bodies to bury."

Lenny's mind flashed to Charlie's brother Oscar, crammed inside his canned-ham crate.

Henri shrugged. "One never knows."

"I know because I'm a dull, tweedy assistant professor who by this time next year will be sorting bumpers and wheel covers in some salvage yard and living all by myself in a rusted mobile home."

"*Mais, non, pas du tout!* With my help you'll soon win the heart of this lovely info-baby."

"It's 'info-babe,' and Daniela told me not to use that term. And as I said, I don't need help."

Lenny knew he needed help.

Students had booed him that morning in the quadrangle. The Sprocket brothers had proffered matching middle fingers. Even the sweet Sri Lankan girl from the faculty cafeteria stepped off the sidewalk and pretended not to see him.

Coworkers also turned away, except for three seeking financial backing for their business ideas: A hirsute associate professor of sociology had invented a "semi-perpetual-motion machine;" a biologist who was preparing to market a mutual fund indexed to Red Sox standings; and a full professor of business administration—a gaunt and shifty-eyed man—had devised a leather chair that, at the press of a button (voice lowered to a wet whisper), granted its occupant "special pleasures."

The trio lost interest when Lenny told them no money was coming his way.

Having run out of paperclips, Henri started cobbling together a plan for his upcoming class. Henri never wrote a syllabus and never prepared classes more than a few minutes ahead of time—if at all. His vague sense of duty drove Lenny crazy.

But today Lenny sympathized because he himself had twenty-four quizzes to grade before his next French class, papers he would have finished the night before had he not wandered in search of synonyms for 'insincerely' and from there stumbled thirstily into the Endless Desert of Etymology.

Henri stuffed a folded yellow sticky—his class plan—into the back pocket of his jeans, picked up the morning's *Gerbil Bugle* and spread it across Lenny's desk. "This rag was leaning against the door when I arrived, open to this page. Some kindly soul wanted to dump a big bucket of *merde* over your head."

Henri tapped a photo of Daniela, then one of Charlie from the *Newsweek* article and another of Lenny as it appeared on his faculty ID.

Lenny read what turned out to be a recap of Daniela's broadcast. Fair enough, he thought. What annoyed him was the sidebar quotation from "an anonymous colleague of Dr. Thorson's who said that the language teacher had brought shame to the campus." The same source added that Dr. Thorson had deliberately sabotaged Gerry Gerbil during a recent parade, which not only endangered innocent on-lookers but again brought disgrace to the college. "It's a terrible shame," the source concluded.

"Have you read this?" Lenny asked.

"Yup."

"This smells of one Juan-Bjorn Jorgenson," Lenny said.

"Yup."

"Speaking of bad odors," Lenny said.

Juan stood at the door, holding open a copy of the *Gerbil Bugle*. "It's a terrible shame."

"I know," Lenny said. "The school's shabby rag brings shame to the campus."

Henri laughed.

Juan wiggled both ears. "No, I meant the predicament you've gotten yourself into. Although you and I were competing for tenure, I must say, in all fairness, that I didn't want things to end like this."

"You're making it sound as if I'm out of the running."

"I'm afraid you are. At least that's what the dean has been heard to say. It's a terrible shame."

Lenny felt the urge to tip Juan upside down and shove his head into the wastebasket.

He also considered sweeping the twenty-four unmarked quizzes off his desk and onto the floor, followed by his gradebook, the manila folder containing the semester's syllabuses, and the leaky, ersatz-gold pen that Elspeth had bought him at a thrift shop for his previous birthday.

Juan took on a look of false woe and shifted from one foot to the other. "I know we've had our differences in the past, but if there's anything that I can do, don't hesitate to ask."

Lenny pondered the offer. "Well, my Chevy needs its roof pounded out, and I'd like a date with Emma Stone."

Henri hooted and took a step toward Juan.

Juan stumbled backwards and disappeared into the hallway, to be immediately replaced by Elspeth. She carried an overstuffed paisley shoulder bag and a look of fury.

"Never," she said, "have I felt such humiliation."

As happened so often when Elspeth appeared, Henri bolted out the door.

Elspeth leaned over Lenny's desk. "You are more of a fool than I thought. It's bad enough that you live in that... that *place*, and that you dress so abominably, and that you so often disappear into your own world of definitions and derivations and I-don't-know-what. But now—now you have become an ethically compromised individual. What do you have to say for yourself?"

Lenny faked a yawn.

Elspeth's face reddened and her eyebrows twitched, first the left, then the right, then both.

Lenny reached for an etymological dictionary but changed his mind. *Eyebrow* wasn't a very interesting word, really.

He caught the tail end of something Elspeth was saying. She had switched from anger to self-pity, her favored mode. Lenny caught the words, "...and I keep asking myself if I should continue seeing an individual who is so ethically compromised."

"Okay."

"Okay, what?"

"It's okay that we shouldn't see each other anymore."

Elspeth took a step back from the desk. "Uh… well… perhaps you *can* defend your position, and we *can* work out our little differences."

Lenny hated the pseudo-British way she pronounced 'can' with a broad, back-of-the-throat 'a.' He picked up the French quizzes and started grading. Once more, comely Judy Gleit had tried to smuggle 'table' past him in men's clothing. Lenny scratched out the masculine 'le,' replaced it with the feminine 'la,' and this time took off two points. He didn't look up, but sensed Elspeth's confusion.

She said, "Decisions shouldn't be made in the heat of the moment."

"I'm sorry, Elspeth, did you say something?"

"Sometimes," she said with a quiver, "sometimes I say things I shouldn't say."

Lenny did a perfect imitation of Henri's two-shouldered, up-to-the-ears Gallic shrug, both hands lifted, palms up. "No, no, what you said was perfectly true: My living space is unconventional, my garments shameful, and I do have a propensity to wander into Wordland at the least-expected—but oftentimes most-needed—moments. No, no, you're perfectly right, Elspeth." Lenny turned back to his papers, scribbled a red "-2" next to a defective past participle and followed that with a dismissive gesture with the back of his hand, also on loan from Henri. "Get on with your life, good woman. Just try to remember me with warmth and understanding."

It surprised Lenny how much fun he was having. He wished Henri were here to share in it.

"Perhaps," Elspeth said quietly, "Perhaps if I took you to the faculty café and bought you a nice, post-birthday lunch, we would see things differently and…"

Lenny tuned out. Pretty Judy Gleit had answered the final six questions with unexpected fluency. Lenny guessed she'd copied from the boy who sat next to her, a loose-limbed kid from Maine who got A's in French and drooled in Judy's presence. Lenny would have to split up their seating.

'Split,' a satisfying-sounding word, either as noun or verb, crisp and businesslike.

In the hallway the week before, Lenny had overheard a boy offering 'splitted' as the past tense of 'split.' Lenny had suffered for the rest of the day.

"...and deep down I know that we're nevertheless quite possibly meant for each other after all."

Lenny looked up.

"All I ask of you, Lenny, is that you produce a reasonable defense for your actions."

Lenny shook his head sadly and he once more shrugged Gallically, "I'm afraid I can't. You've found out the truth about me: I'm a cad, a bounder, a rake, a rascal and a scalawag."

For a long time Lenny had wanted to use those words, especially strung together, and for a long time had wanted to rid himself of Elspeth.

Her lips vibrated, her firm full breasts heaved and quivered, and for a passing moment Lenny felt sharp longings.

He wrote "See me" on the top of Judy's quiz, and Elspeth disappeared from the room.

So, that was that.

Lenny felt clever and pleased with himself, free as a bird, and a bit lonely.

Had he done the right thing?

Henri returned. "She's gone?"

"Gone for good."

"Really for good?"

"Really for good."

"Ah, *mon ami*, that is *merveilleux*! Now you are free to devote your attention to this."

Henri opened *The Boston Globe* and tapped a photo. "It's her again."

Daniela stood in a clinging, low-cut black dress next to a tall and smug man with a sharp chin and frighteningly long teeth. He and Daniela each held a plate of shrimp and celery and each smiled attractively at the camera.

Lenny's heart sank.

Henri dropped into his chair, absently picked up the framed photo of one of the twins and peered at it. "As I said, we need a plan for you to sweep your gorgeous television person off her feet. That's the right expression, isn't it? Off her feet?"

"That's right, but I wouldn't know how to sweep a woman off her feet."

"Ah," Henri said, raising a forefinger, "What you need is a bit of advice from an expert and... *merde*! I just remembered I left my class halfway through. We'll talk later." He rushed out the door.

Lenny sat staring at the ungraded quizzes and let his thoughts turn to Daniela. Henri was right—he shouldn't give up. He wanted to see her, explain his innocence and ask her out on a date. Take her somewhere classy.

He reached for the phone, lifted it to his ear and lost his nerve. Besides, Daniela wouldn't answer. He decided instead to spend as much free time as possible at The Monsoon Mist, Daniela's favorite spot in Harvard Square. He'd just hang around and show surprise when she appeared. She couldn't ignore him then. He would suggest they sit together and talk things over. Maybe he'd pretend to want to get her opinion again on Charlie's mental state.

Pathetic, Lenny told himself. He felt like an *oolont nat*—a stalker, a cad, a bounder, a rake, a rascal and a scalawag.

CHAPTER 20

Ehotkekont nat

"Dangerous man"

Lenny felt out of place. Lenny felt out of place pretty much everywhere, but especially in Harvard Square with its privileged students and a faculty that floated on the upper clouds of academia. Ghurkin College—and he himself—existed more as ground fog.

Nothing about The Monsoon Mist suggested monsoons, mist, or the Far East to Lenny except for the six-foot palm next to the door, dying in an undersized clay pot. Otherwise, this was a typical fern tea shop: soft jazz through bad speakers, blackboards listing unpronounceable teas and coffees, brown cane chairs and circular faux-marble tables around which students complained about global warming, obscene salaries for Fortune 500 executives, and a roommate who leaves dirty socks lying all over the place. From behind the counter came clinks, hisses and bangs as ice was scooped, espresso steamed, and dishes dropped.

Lenny guessed he'd have to return the phone message the dean had left. He didn't feel like talking to the man, but he did feel it might give him an air of importance when Daniela walked in. If Daniela walked in.

The first thing the dean said was, "I'm on your side."

"Oh?"

"That's right. I tried to talk them out of it, but couldn't."

"Talk whom out of what?"

"Talk the Feds out of revoking your grant. It seems that word got to them about your involvement in the Skalwegian scheme."

Lenny had lain awake the night before, fearing just such an occurrence. But not this soon. How could an obscure agency in Washington, DC have heard the news so quickly? Juan's doing, he guessed.

The dean continued. "So, you have to pay them back."

"I was afraid of that. I haven't cashed the $3,000 check yet, so I'll just mail it back and you can send them the rest."

"I'm afraid it doesn't work quite that way."

"What do you mean?"

"I mean what I just said: You owe Uncle Sam $200,000."

"But you kept most of it," Lenny said. "I got only $3,000."

"True, but that's not the way things work."

"Are you trying to tell me you're keeping the $197,000?"

"Exactly. The college has strict rules about this sort of thing. Even I can't break them."

Lenny was stunned.

"That's just the way things work in the world of business, Thorson. You're an academic and have never worked in the private sector, never run a business."

"That's not true. I ran my family company for three years."

After a pause, the dean said, "What kind of business?"

"A salvage yard."

Another long pause. "If it were anyone but you, I'd say you were joking, but somehow I know you're not. But don't let this whole thing get you down. Just find the two hundred grand somewhere, write the Feds a check, forget about the whole thing and move on. And remember, I'm on your side."

"The hell you are. You're a goddamn—"

"Someone just came into the office. Can't talk."

For the next hour Lenny sipped chamomile tea, nibbled on a crumbly low-cal lemon scone, graded his backlog of French quizzes and steamed. A hundred and ninety-seven thousand dollars! How in hell could he ever pay that back?

He glanced up to see Daniela at his elbow.

"Are we still friends?" she asked and sat down.

"Were we ever friends?" Lenny said, turning back to his grading.

Daniela broke off a corner of one of Lenny's scones and popped it into her mouth. "Ah, so you're still mad."

"I don't get mad."

"You should," Daniela said. "It would do you good."

"I'll keep that in mind."

"What are you doing?"

"I'm writing the great American novel in Skalwegian. It's the only way I can pull my career out of the toilet."

Daniela took more scone. "I'm really sorry I got you into so much trouble, Lenny, but as a journalist I'm responsible for getting the truth out to the public."

"It's not the truth, goddamn it! It's…"

Lenny stopped talking. A tall and startlingly handsome man hovered over the table. Lenny recognized him as the toothy guy from the charity function photo that showed Daniela in that delicious black dress. "May I join you?" he asked.

Daniela nodded, then gestured with a chunk of scone toward Lenny. "Lenny, this is Nelson Scuttlewood."

"The Third," Nelson said and eased into the chair next to Daniela.

"And Nelson, this is Doctor Lenny Thorson. He's a friend of my uncle and teaches at Ghurkin College."

Lenny hesitated, then held out his hand.

Nelson ignored Lenny's hand. He turned to Daniela. "Is this the individual you told me about? The one who's getting rich off those rare minerals?"

"Uh… well…"

Nelson's long teeth reminded Lenny of the rats he trapped back in the salvage yard. Lenny wanted to push this creature into a large trap and haul him to a marsh. "My involvement in this business has been misinterpreted."

Nelson waved irritably at a waitress. She hurried toward him, then at the last moment veered away to deliver lattés to a love-struck young couple speaking Chinese.

Nelson turned back. "Are you pretending you're not embezzling?"

Lenny went back to the paper he was grading and for effect made a large and meaningless red check next to one of the answers. Without looking up, he said, "You've grossly mishandled 'embezzling.' It means 'to appropriate the property or money of others who have placed their trust in you.' Were I to profit from the extraction of rare-earth materials, it would not be embezzling. But I'm not in that particular situation and never will be. In fact, I'll probably lose my teaching job and in a few months will end up sorting through greasy engine parts in a salvage yard somewhere, and I'll be happier."

Lenny knew he wouldn't be happier, but didn't want to sound self-pitying.

Again Nelson waved at the waitress, who skillfully looked in all directions except his.

Lenny decided to double her tip.

Daniela pinched off a bit more of one of Lenny's scones. "When life gets gnarly for Lenny, he retreats into Wordland."

Lenny shifted the plate of scones out of Daniela's reach. "We all have our havens, our hiding spots, our tree houses. As for riches, some people make their money through hard work or soft luck, whereas others dumbly inherit a fortune from a father who owned eight slummy apartment buildings in Baltimore."

Lenny silently thanked Henri LeBeau, Private Eyes, for researching this jerk.

Nelson folded, then unfolded his long arms.

Daniela gave Lenny a wry look.

Lenny continued. "I'm not involved in any scheme to profit from mining and never was. In fact, I'm nearly broke. I didn't choose a high-paying profession such as slum landlord or something in the media, where an attention-craving television personality must make... what? Five times more than an assistant professor? Ten times?"

Daniela said nothing, and Lenny immediately regretted what he'd said.

But he was also proud for defending himself.

And slowly it dawned on Lenny how angry he was, really angry, that he was reacting to long-toothed Nelson's snarky attitude, Daniela's remark about Wordland, the dean's theft of his grant money, Elspeth's accusations, and the bathtub-sized dent that Gerry Gerbil had stomped into the roof of his sad old Chevy.

He had fought with anger in the ring—anger about his mother's early death, about his oversized body, about living in a tilting trailer sitting on concrete blocks, about going to school in bib overalls covered in rust and grime, and about how other kids called him 'Junkyard Dog.'

His anger felt good now. It had been away for too long.

Lenny told himself that the moment had come for a grand exit. Depart stage left to the admiration and silent applause of the stunned spectators. He was proud of himself, proud of how he'd put down Nelson, proud of how he'd stood up to Daniela even though he'd gone too far and knew she'd never talk to him again. And he was especially proud that he'd taught long-toothed Nelson the proper use of 'embezzle.'

Coolly, without acknowledging his tablemates, aware of their swelling admiration and growing respect, Lenny slowly and stagily gathered up his French quizzes, slipped his red pen into the breast pocket of his tweed jacket, half rose, banged his knee against the table, and toppled a pot of hot chamomile tea down the front of his trousers.

CHAPTER 21

Zeebont Zaknak

"Cute fool"

Lenny drove home, tugging at the spot where his wet slacks clung to his crotch. What a clumsy oaf, he thought. What was the third of the fanged Nelson clan telling lovely Daniela right this minute? Did he have his tanned hand on her shoulder? Had he slipped his chair closer to her? Had his hand dropped under the table and onto her knee?

What an idiot I am, Lenny thought, pulling again at his soggy britches. I'm an idiot, an *idiote* in Old French, an *idiota* in Latin, an idiot in all of the world's languages.

Henri would howl when Lenny told him of his folly. He'd tilt his head far back and shudder with great bursts of Gallic laughter.

Picturing this made Lenny smile, then chuckle, then laugh out loud until tears filled his eyes. He steered to the side of Massachusetts Avenue and parked. Pedestrians stared. Lenny laughed and slapped the steering wheel with both hands. Things were so awful they were hilarious.

Once he reached home, Lenny changed into bib overalls—the

outfit of his childhood—and started restacking the lobster boxes inside the freezer room. Before leaving for work that morning, he'd noticed they'd toppled, probably during the restaurant's latest cranky spin. Physical labor took him back to the simpler years in Jake's Salvage Yard, stacking used tires, sorting hood ornaments into buckets, removing the bumper from an elderly Oldsmobile to give to a thankful senior, or replacing a stained rear seat for an embarrassed teenage boy.

Lenny found a knife on the floor of the freezer room. An ugly tool, the blade sharp on one side, saw-toothed on the other. Left by some workman, he figured.

Lenny had the last of the crates restacked when his phone chimed. To his surprise it was Daniela.

She said, "You were cute this afternoon."

Lenny didn't know quite how to respond. "*Cute*?"

"Right, cute."

"I behaved like a clumsy oaf and said things to you I shouldn't have said."

"That too," Daniela said, "but sometimes clumsy oafdom is cute."

"In that case, I've been cute all my life."

Daniela giggled. "You probably have. Why do you sound out of breath?"

"I'm rearranging my furniture. I just didn't like the way the zebra-skin couch looked next to the Tiffany floor lamp, and the oriental rugs simply begged to be shifted because they were beginning to fade unevenly in the sunlight, and esthetically, I felt that—"

"Okay, okay, Lenny. I get it. It sounds like you're still annoyed with me. But listen, I called because Charlie phoned to assure me that you'd known nothing about Harvey's will and the minerals until my broadcast, and that you've refused to take any money from him after he inherits the island."

"Did you expect anything different from me? If you hadn't spoken with Charlie, would you still think of me as a cheat?"

"I guess not, and I apologize."

"You just 'guess not'?" Lenny said. "And why in hell didn't you talk to me before you went on the air and ruined my reputation?"

Long pause. "I'm sorry, really sorry," Daniela said, her voice small. "But I was just so disappointed in who I thought you were that I wasn't thinking straight. I should have known you would never, ever get mixed up in something illegal."

Something illegal?

Like helping someone fake a language so they'd inherit a fortune? "Uh... right."

Daniela hesitated, then said, "Did you mean that remark about my needing attention so much that I had to go on television to get it?"

"Uh... a little, I suppose. Just a little. But it was cruel, and I shouldn't have said it."

"Well, there's probably a bit of truth in it. I've always received extra attention because I'm perhaps somewhat... uh..."

"Drop-dead gorgeous," Lenny contributed.

"I was going to say perhaps a bit better-looking than average. And it's affected my outlook on life."

"I understand perfectly. I have the same problem, but I've discovered correctives. For example, right this minute, in order to conceal my manly attractiveness, I've donned blue bib overalls with the knees blown out and a Ghurkin College T-shirt with armpit stains."

"Are you really wearing overalls?"

"Of course. Do I make up stories?"

"Never," Daniela said. "Oh, I forgot to say that I'm reading a retraction over the air tomorrow. I'll say that I wrongly accused you of complicity in Charlie's scheme."

"Don't bother. First of all, no one pays attention to retractions, and secondly, you don't want to damage your reputation as a journalist."

"What about your reputation, Lenny?"

Lenny picked up the knife he'd found earlier. He wondered what the saw-toothed edge was intended for. "That doesn't matter. It's too late for me. I'm fucked already."

Lenny liked how 'fucked' sounded in conversations and vowed to use it more often.

Daniela said, "I'm very sorry, Lenny. I really, really am."

"I'll survive."

What Lenny really wanted to say was, 'Can we get together again?' But he was drained of confidence. He was no Nelson Scuttlewood the Third. Aim lower than Daniela, he thought. "Your boyfriend seems okay, I guess."

"He's not really my boyfriend. We go out some, but it's not a serious relationship. Sometimes he lurks around the Monsoon Mist coffee shop just waiting for me to show up."

Lenny ran his thumb across the knife blade. What a wicked object. "Guys do that sort of thing? I'm shocked."

"You probably are because that's not something you'd ever do. You're a nice guy."

"Nice? No man wants to have that word hurled in his face. We all want to think of ourselves as a bit dangerous. By the way, 'nice' descends from Middle English, back when it meant 'strange, lazy, foolish.'"

"Not when I use it. I don't speak Middle English."

"I can teach you some."

Daniela giggled. "I was actually thinking of you as dangerously nice, as Lenny the Dangerously Nice."

Lenny laughed. He wanted to ask her out. Instead he said, "Did I spill any chamomile tea on you?"

"No. But if you were intending to, you need more practice," Daniela said. "Say, the weather's supposed to be beautiful this Saturday, and I... uh... was wondering if you'd want to do something outside?"

Did he? Or course he did. "What about hiking up Great Blue Hill?" Lenny said. "It's only an hour's drive, and the view is great."

Lenny and Elspeth had often hiked there. She loved hills and mountains and often spoke of her climbs. In high school she'd spent eight weeks studying in Munich, where she climbed the Alps as often as possible. One sunny morning she was happily deflowered on a dewy bed of edelweiss by a Hungarian lad who'd lost an arm in a duel and who called himself Count Adolph Holstein-Schmidt, but who later turned out to be Hans Schmidt, postal clerk and auto-accident amputee.

Elspeth often spoke fondly of edelweiss, hikes and dark-eyed counts.

"Sounds great," Daniela said. "I'm looking forward to the climb and seeing you again. You're a nice guy, Lenny."

"And dangerous," Lenny added, flinging the knife against the wall where—to his surprise—it stuck, the handle quivering back and forth.

"Of course," Daniela said. "Extremely."

Lenny could tell that Daniela didn't think of him as all that dangerous. He just wished she'd have seen him throw the knife.

CHAPTER 22

Oponayetu

"To deceive, cheat on"

The dean stood at his office window, coffee cup in hand, and gazed down at the stadium. Luther had sent six workers for today's repairs, but there they stood, chatting and smoking and burning up Lenny's grant money. The dean turned away and dropped into his desk chair. Complain? Yeah, sure. No one complained to Luther Skammer and stayed healthy for very long.

The dean was terrified of Luther. Otherwise he wouldn't have let himself be pressured into serving as front man—finding a Boston law firm that would contest the will and then convincing a psychiatrist to testify that Harvey had been mentally unfit to write it.

The dean's cellphone rang.

"It's me, Billy Butcher. I'm the guy your friend hired for a little job."

"Uh… okay."

"They found Bob One," Billy said. "Luther's guys searched the woods near the college and found him dead, his head bashed in and half his trigger finger missing. It looked like it'd been bitten off. That's why I called you. The Lobsterman's a crazy killer, and you're gonna have to double my fee if you expect me to whack the guy."

Dead? A finger bitten off? The dean rotated back and forth in his seat. "I'll have to talk to Luther."

"You do that."

"You're clear on the plan?"

"Of course I am. I'm a pro," Billy Butcher said. "Like Luther told me, I gotta follow The Lobsterman and some woman named Elspeth when they go hiking, find an isolated spot and take care of them. Nothing's simpler."

"No, it's not, dammit! I told you to chase the woman away first!"

"Uh… okay, but I don't mind servicing her too. No extra charge."

The dean shuddered. "No. Just him."

"You're the boss. Anyway, I'll need a couple of days to get ready. I'm gonna need a chainsaw," Billy said, his voice taking on a happy cadence. "Also some sharp knives and a hatchet so I can—"

"Just do the job and spare me the details."

*   *   *

Competing without acknowledging it, Lenny and Daniela climbed straight up Great Blue Hill's steepest ski run and reached the top in fifteen minutes, where they sat huffing and puffing, enjoying a seat on the warm afternoon grass. To their left, the less fit glided up the hill in a chair lift. To their front stretched wooded suburbs, a curving Interstate highway and a dozen single-story high-tech buildings. In the distance to their right rose the Boston skyline.

Daniela wore tan shorts and a baggy blue work shirt that she'd pulled out of her waist band and tied in the front to reveal a patch of trim tummy. To avoid fans, she'd tucked her hair under a Red Sox cap and wore oversized, reflective sunglasses. Lenny had on jeans, scruffy green Nikes and an unauthorized T-shirt depicting Gerry Gerbil drunk on a barroom floor.

Daniela said, "Do you come here often?"

"Is that a pickup line?"

"Yes, but not in this instance."

"I've hiked here a dozen times in the past couple years."

"Good—we won't get lost."

Lenny stood up. "Of course not. Just follow me. Guys like to lead, to blaze trails, to impress members of the fair sex with their outdoor skills and woodsy cunning, their instinctual ability to confront nature in its most terrifying manifestations and emerge unscathed and triumphant."

"This is a park, Lenny, not the Yukon."

Lenny reached down and pulled Daniela up, letting his eyes glide warmly across the swath of skin above her waist band. "That's what you've heard, but it's a jungle back there in these woods, teeming with killer gerbils. You're extremely fortunate that you have me here to protect you."

"Uh huh."

They circled halfway around the crest of the hill, then Lenny took Daniela's hand and the two plunged down a narrow side path through scrub oak.

"Do you know where you're taking me?"

"Of course not," Lenny said. "This is uncharted territory. Before we go home—if we survive attacks by bears, Big Foot and cranky gerbils—I'll take you to the visitors center. Their map labels this area 'The Dark Quarter.' It's apparently some kind of local black hole that sucks everything in—sunlight, poodles, lottery tickets, iPads—and doesn't let anything out. Scientists at MIT have studied the heck out of the place, but aren't getting any results because researchers go in and never come back out."

Daniela clutched at Lenny's elbow, then tapped his temple with her forefinger. "I sometimes wonder what goes on up there."

"So do I."

They walked deeper and deeper into the woods, brushing shoulders from time to time, exchanging looks, laughing. They didn't encounter bears or Big Foot, but they did come upon a couple engaged in noisy bondage.

The man lay on his back, arms and legs tied to four saplings at four compass points. The woman worked on top, rhythmically emitting high-pitched animals noises, her sweaty bare shoulders glistening in the sun, her knees digging into the pine needles. The man groaned and moaned, keened and wailed.

The only items of clothing worn by either were his argyle socks.

Unnoticed, Lenny and Daniela backed away.

"Well," Daniela whispered after they were farther down the trail, "*That* was interesting."

Lenny said, "I wasn't expecting to come upon anything like that."

"No, I imagine you weren't," she said, glancing up at him. "Hey, why the long face?"

"I'm… uh… shocked to see such goings on. I have a puritanical nature."

Daniela stepped around in front of Lenny, pressed her hands against his chest and forced him to stop. "You're a terrible liar. What's really going on?"

"Well, I guess I was a bit surprised."

"To find a couple going at it in the woods?"

Lenny started walking again. Daniela fell in beside him and took his elbow. Lenny said, "When I said I'm shocked, I meant it. I'm also relieved, I guess. You see, the woman was my… uh… my little friend who left her mascara wand in my bathroom."

Daniela stopped. Lenny stopped too.

"Oh," Daniela said. "I'm sorry."

"I'm not. It's okay because we'd already broken up. In fact, I feel…"

And then Lenny stopped talking. What did he feel? Relief that things were really over with Elspeth? Sure. But he also felt sad, betrayed, even somewhat jealous, possibly angry. He'd wanted Elspeth out of his life, but he didn't want to see her joyfully astraddle Juan Jorgenson.

Lenny also felt horny, and he pictured himself lying nude and spread-eagled in the pine needles with Daniela over him, her bare breasts jouncing.

She asked, "Do you know the man?"

"It's Juan Jorgenson, the creep I told you about who's competing for the same tenured position I am. Or I was—I'm pretty much out of the running now."

Daniela put her arm around Lenny's waist and pulled herself close to him.

"I'm sorry about that."

"Don't be. It's not your fault."

"Are you sure it's him?"

"Of course I'm sure."

"Does he have a different name?" Daniela asked.

"Actually, he does. His first name is 'Bjorn,' but after he started studying Spanish, he called himself 'Juan.'"

"Is he from some aristocratic European family?"

Lenny snorted. "No. The little bastard is from a St. Louis suburb. Trust me, he's no aristocrat."

Daniela gave Lenny's waist a hard squeeze. "Okay, okay, I believe you. It's just that I'd swear I heard her call him 'Count Holstein-Schmidt.'"

CHAPTER 23

Ekaketu, nehatu, entahetu

"Leap, lie, look"

Seated on a folding chair behind his barn, Charlie watched the sun go down while he oiled a halter that didn't need oiling.

He knew he'd treated Lenny badly—borrowed his savings, lost him tenure and ruined his reputation. Instead of messing around with this damn halter, Charlie knew he should be in the study, working on Skalwegian. Easy to put it off. After Lenny had learned that the language was bogus, Charlie asked him to start making up verbs and nouns, but Lenny had refused. Charlie couldn't blame him. He hadn't been honest with the kid.

Charlie glanced up at the pond, the meadow, then the slope leading up to the woods. What had he gotten Lenny and himself into?

He poured more oil on the rag—a strip of the "So Are You!" T-shirt that Sally had ripped to pieces—then set the can down and went back to rubbing the leather. Right this minute he should be working on common L-verbs: *lather*—no, that's not common, so hold off on that for a while. Instead start with *leap*, then *lie*, *light*, *limp* (no, skip *limp* for now), *look* (had he made up a word for *look* already? He bet he had. He'd better check his notes), *love*, then…

"You look lost in thought."

Charlie looked up. The Widow Bahr had ridden up on Angel Warrior without his noticing. She was naked.

"Lady, if I didn't know better, I'd say you were trying to seduce me."

"Then you'd have it wrong, Mr. Fox. After my Morton died, I gave up sex. And good riddance."

Trying to keep his eyes on his work, Charlie said, "Suit yourself" in a way that he hoped ended the subject. He wasn't used to discussing sex with naked ladies—well, not in barnyards, anyway.

The Widow Bahr watched Charlie working. "I hope you know what you're doing."

"I've oiled halters before."

Angel Warrior decided to take two jolting steps backwards. The Widow Bahr pulled hard on the reins. "You know perfectly well what I meant."

"Sally uses that expression on me a lot."

"I'll bet she does, and I'll bet she finds you just as stubborn and irritating as I do."

"That she does," Charlie said.

"Can I give you some advice?"

"If it's about selling the woodland, I don't want to hear it."

The Widow Bahr's horse took several more steps backwards. "It's not about the woods, it's about this business with Luther Skammer and his horrible wife. You're playing with fire."

"I've been in tough spots before."

"Not like this."

"Worse than this. I've had guys with Kalashnikovs shoot at me. Now that's a tough spot."

Charlie kept on rubbing the halter. Although he didn't look up, he could sense The Widow Bahr glaring at him. Her horse too.

"Well, I just thought I should warn you."

"I'm warned. And why don't you put on some clothes? The neighbors are starting to talk."

"Since when did you care about what the neighbors say?"

Charlie stood up and looped the halter over a nail, where he knew it would remain unused until he oiled it again, probably pretty soon. "Never, I guess. So just keep riding around here bare ass. I don't give a damn one way or the other. And don't think you're going to seduce me, because better women than you have tried and failed."

The Widow Bahr pulled on Angel Warrior's reins and turned him around. "You're a stubborn and irritating man, Charlie Fox," she said over her shoulder, "and I don't know why I even bother giving you advice."

Charlie watched her ride away, her plump white buttocks bouncing to the rhythm of the gait. He wasn't worried about himself, but wondered if he should be concerned about Lenny. The guy was smart and funny, but smart and funny weren't worth diddly when it came to a fight. Luck would help, but Charlie didn't think Lenny was the lucky type. He sure as hell was no fighter. Still, he didn't think that Lenny was in any real danger. Who would try to hurt a harmless professor?

A diaphanous, waist-high fog started to roll off the pond as Charlie began his evening stroll across the meadow and up the slope to the woods. He passed towering clumps of out-of-control rhododendrons, a headless frog statue, and an oxidizing sundial set in concrete without heed to daylight savings time.

Charlie sat on the slope overlooking the pond, where here and there a cattail poked through the low gray layer of ground fog, and he asked himself if he were doing the right thing. Should he forget about the will? Quit fussing over nouns and verbs and go back to his old life?

No, he wouldn't. If he did, the bad guys would win. As for danger, well, he was a warrior. If they killed him, they killed him. Charlie patted the ground beside him, where six feet below, his brother lay tucked into a Gallahad Ham crate. "Get ready, Oscar, I might be joining you here earlier than expected."

CHAPTER 24

Ekomo mumutan ank ceme?

"Did the Earth move for you?"

After his last class of the day, Lenny picked up Daniela at WDRK and drove her to the Irish Clover, a pub near Quincy Market on the Boston waterfront. It was a noisy and happy place of dark wood, clan crests, county flags dangling from the ceiling, three different soccer games on three screens above the bar. At the next table sat an actual Irish couple attacking seafood platters. Lenny wondered if they'd been hired by the management or were actors faking the accent. Fakery was on his mind a lot lately.

The pub was so dark that Daniela couldn't read the menu without removing her sunglasses. As soon as she did, two tipsy blonde women rushed over to pose for selfies with her.

"I'm glad to accommodate you, but you're missing a unique opportunity," Daniela said, gesturing across the table at Lenny. "Don't either of you recognize this gentleman?"

The two forty-ish women gave Lenny a look of nonrecognition.

"That," Daniela said in her most dramatic of television voices, "Is Pierre Sherpa, the most famous mountaineer in the world, recently returned from scaling Great Bondage Mountain. Certainly you want your picture taken with him too."

The puzzled pair took a quick selfie of themselves with Lenny.

In his best imitation of Henri's French accent, Lenny said, "For zee lovely ladies like you, I would scale naked zee tallest mountain in zee Alps."

They left, frowning and doubtful.

Lenny said, "I like a woman who can make up stories on the spur of the moment."

Daniela reached across the table and patted Lenny's cheek. "I've been studying with the master."

They ate fish and chips and drank beer. Daniela talked Lenny into dancing, but only once, and that was off in a corner. Lenny said he danced like Gerry Gerbil, and Daniela said yes, but he had better hair. At the end of the evening, without discussing the matter, they returned to Lenny's revolving restaurant.

Lenny had not expected the evening to end with the two of them naked atop his futon, and he guessed that Daniela was equally surprised. What had begun as a low-key fun date ended up as a beery roll in the hay.

Lenny found Daniela less experimental than Elspeth and less of a hot gallop than his Albanian barebacker. But Daniela was sweet and surprisingly shy, and it was a relief to make love without having lectures on self-improvement whispered in his ear or listening to the animal groans of a depressed circus lady.

Lenny and Daniela took a break, lay side by side on their stomachs and watched the darkened world ten stories below. With one hand, Lenny stroked Daniela lightly between her smooth shoulder blades, and with the other, he pointed out the place where he'd spotted the doe.

She said, "I love it up here."

Lenny was working up the courage to say something like, 'There's room enough for two,' but the restaurant went *click-click-click*. He hugged Daniela, and twenty seconds later, the room jolted into motion.

Still in embrace, Lenny and Daniela rolled off the futon, onto the leather seat of the adjacent booth and from there thudded to the floor, Daniela on top.

Lenny said, "Here's where one of us is supposed to say, 'Did the earth move for you?'"

A half hour later, they were seated naked across from each other on the floor and drinking ginger citrus herbal tea from Lenny's inherited stash of 1,400 bags. Daniela said, "I hate to break the mood of the evening, but I think you should know that WDRK is doing a follow-up investigation on the Skalvik story."

"Is it that important?"

Daniela shook her head. "It's Bradley's idea. He wants to embarrass me."

Lenny held out a bag of lemon scones.

Daniela took one, then a second, and balanced each on a bare knee. "Because Charlie's my uncle, I've been pulled off the story, and Bradley's been put on it. He's doing okay, I have to admit. He's found out that Luther and Grace are using the dean as a front man to hire the lawyers and expert witnesses and to appear at the hearing about Harvey's will."

Lenny had a scone halfway to his mouth. He lowered his hand. "You're kidding? The dean?"

"Right."

"That explains why the dean had pressured me to give up the Skalwegian project. He must have figured Charlie couldn't make the deadline without my help."

"You said '*had* pressured me.'"

"He stopped."

"Why?"

Lenny thought about this. "Good question."

Daniela eyed Lenny for a few seconds. "Is there something about the project you're not telling me?"

Of course there was, but even at this tender moment, Lenny wasn't ready to betray Charlie by telling Daniela that the language was bogus. Also, he was well aware of Daniela's high standards and was afraid that the truth would send her into a righteous huff and right back into her clothes.

"Nope," Lenny said weakly.

"You're a terrible liar," Daniela said.

"But I'm good in the sack. Which reminds me, shouldn't we get back under the covers? You have to be at the station early tomorrow, and we still have important things to take care of before we can go to sleep."

As they were climbing onto the futon, Daniela said, "Why does this thing always smell so strongly of perfume?"

"Uh… it's a fungus fighter, a perfume-like substance imported from France. I put it on my feet to prevent toe erosion."

"I've never heard of toe erosion."

"It's quite rare."

"Have you seen a doctor?"

Lenny shook his head. "The only cure for the condition is amputatory."

"Is that a real word?"

"If it wasn't before, it is now. I'm a language professional, and as such I get to make up new words whenever I feel like it. If it weren't for people like me, everyone would just stand around pointing and grunting."

Daniela pulled the sheet over them. "And the world might be a better place."

CHAPTER 25

Posat poletan hotulu.

"The cat that ate the canary."

"For English speakers, the distinction between the French simple past and the *imparfait,* or imperfect tense, is a source of great confusion," Lenny said as he stepped from around behind the lectern and noted great confusion on the face of his two dozen English speakers. "But once one realizes that the French imperfect tense parallels the English use of 'was' plus the present participle, as in 'was residing,' then the proper use of that tense becomes evident."

Twenty-four blank faces stared back at Lenny at 9:15 on a Monday morning. Apparently, the proper use of the *imparfait* wasn't all that evident. Lenny wasn't bothered, though. He was in a terrific mood. Today he didn't give a rat's ass whether or not his charges ever learned to handle French tenses, nor did he fret over tenure, the $197,000 he owed the government, his questionable loan to Charlie or the alarming new engine clank his Chevy had developed during the drive to work. Daniela had stayed a second night with him, and there was nothing in the world that could get him down. Nothing.

He draped his left arm across the podium and smiled at his

students. "Think of what we mean when we say, 'He used to live in Paris,' or 'She used to dye her hair the color of parsley.'"

No one smiled back except for the fragile girl in the front row with hair the color of parsley.

One of the troublesome back-row nappers—Freddie Cooper—raised his hand and said, "Is that why the French are so weird and lose all their wars is because their tenses are so messed up?"

Freddie liked to jerk Lenny's chain. Today, Lenny's chain was unjerkable. "The French are no more confused than we are, perhaps in many ways less," Lenny said. "And they haven't lost all their wars. Have you ever heard of Napoleon?"

Freddie nodded vaguely.

The girl with the green hair said, "Dr. Thorson, you're in an especially good mood this morning. You look like the cat that ate the canary."

Lenny smiled.

Again Freddy raised his hand. "My mom says you're going to get rich and stop teaching here."

"I'm not taking a cent for my work on the Skalwegian language project. I want everyone to understand that."

The parsley-haired girl said, "You should write a letter to the school newspaper and let everyone know."

Lenny started to tell her that he'd written a letter on that subject, several in fact, but they'd not been printed. More of Juan's work. "Good suggestion," Lenny said. "I'll keep that in mind."

Then a boy in a fraternity sweatshirt spoke up: "I think Dr. Thorson should take the money. He has every right in the world to get rich if he so chooses. After all, we live within the framework of a capitalist system."

A business major chimed in. "Right on. This is a free country, and as long as Dr. Thorson operates within the framework of the legal system, pays his fair share of taxes and acts responsibility toward society and toward the business community, he can and should get rich. Good for you, sir. Right on."

Lenny didn't respond. Nothing bothered him today.

'Right on' was slang from the '20s, Lenny knew, taken up again in the '60s, and apparently still in use by business majors. Why hadn't the antonym arisen? Why does no one say "Right off?" Perhaps because the expression comes from 'right on target?' Something to research.

Although Lenny didn't enjoy being the subject of an ethical debate, he was glad that his students—so often apathetic—were engaged in one. He let them carry on.

Lenny loved teaching, loved his students (most of the time, anyway), loved watching them learn and mature and think for themselves (some of the time, anyway). Unsure of himself in social situations, Lenny always surprised himself by the confidence he displayed the moment he stepped in front of a class. It all came down to role-playing, he concluded. Here's Lenny Thorson, teacher and actor, and here you are, students and ticket holders. You have your part in the play and I have mine. Enjoy the show.

Teaching wasn't just a job for Lenny but a calling. He ached to get tenure and teach for the rest of his life. He never wanted to quit. He never wanted to retire. He never wanted to leave the profession. He loved the life.

Immediately after class, Dean Sheepslappe fired him.

The two men stood face-to-face in the hallway, Lenny bracing himself against a noisy herd of students charging east, the dean pushing back against the stream thundering west. Both had to shout, and from time to time Lenny lost sight of the dean's peculiar little head.

"I'm on your side," the dean had shouted. "And you're fired."

"Suspended?"

"No, fired! Pack up your office. You've just taught your last class at Ghurkin College. You won't be coming back."

"Why?"

"It's because you compromised yourself by engaging in a secret scheme to get rich by documenting a dying language."

"I've told you a dozen times that I knew nothing about Harvey's will."

"It's the president's orders, not mine," the dean said, "and I'm as upset by this as you are, Thorson, probably even more so, but I have to let you go. Hand your gradebooks over to Elspeth and leave campus."

"Are you serious?"

"I'm on your side," the dean said.

"You said that already."

"Moral turpitude."

"What?" Lenny asked.

"What?" shouted the girl with the parsley hair.

"Him," Lenny said, pointing at the dean, "I'm talking to him."

"I thought you were talking to me."

"Moral turpitude," the dean repeated in a louder voice.

"No, I'm talking to him," Lenny said.

A redheaded boy in a khaki tank top said, "What?"

"I'm not talking to you," Lenny said. "I'm talking to him."

"Have you finished your math homework?" the parsley-haired girl said to the redhead.

"Nope. I was hoping you had. I was going to copy yours."

"I fell asleep watching *The Daily Show*."

"Shit," the boy said.

"Right. We're both in deep shit."

"Moral turpitude," Dean Sheepslappe repeated in his loudest voice,

"That's a redundancy," Lenny said. "*Turpitude* on its own means 'baseness, depravity.'"

"I know what the word means," the red-faced dean said, his eyebrows twitching into an inverted V.

The second bell rang, the hallway cleared, and Lenny and the dean found themselves alone.

Lenny lowered his voice. "It comes from Latin through Middle French."

"What?"

"'Turpitude.'"

"Oh."

"'Turpitude' alone would do the job, although 'moral turpitude' is so often heard in everyday conversation that we—"

"You're fired," the dean repeated, his little head re-reddening. "Don't you understand? You're out of here. Gone. Dumped. Kicked to the curb."

This started to sink in. Lenny realized that he'd never again stand in front of his first-year French class and attempt to explain the subtleties of French past tenses to business students and pretty girls with colorful hair. He was shocked, disbelieving.

And, to his surprise, relieved, free, turned loose. It was all over. Done and decided. He was out. Gone. Dumped. Kicked to the curb.

The dean said, "You'll be paid through the end of this month."

Lenny said, "You're an idiot."

"What?"

"An idiot. The term descends etymologically from the Latin through Old French and then Middle English."

"What?"

"But I could be wrong. Not about your being an idiot, but about Middle English. It could be Old English."

"I don't believe we're having this conversation," the dean said, waving his arms. "I've just fired you, and you're carrying on about word derivations. Do you even understand what I've just said?"

"Of course I do. I'm the language expert, remember? And what in hell is the real reason you're firing me? And don't use the word 'turpitude' again in my presence, and certainly not the offensively redundant 'moral turpitude.'"

Lenny took a step forward.

The dean took a step back.

Lenny was enjoying himself in a perverse sort of way and could see that the dean definitely was not.

Two skinny boys with matching nostril rings sauntered past—cheerfully late for class.

The dean pointed at the boys, "What would the parents of those two young men say if they found out that a member of our faculty—a man responsible for shaping minds and morals—has obtained a $200,000 grant supposedly to preserve an obscure language, whereas in fact he was involved in an odious scheme to make Charlie Fox— and himself—fabulously rich."

"Goddamn it, how many times do I have to tell you that I didn't find out about Harvey's will or the mineral deposits until after I'd started working with Charlie! In any case, I've refused to take any money!"

"I have a hard time believing that," the dean said.

"Because you're a goddamn first-class idiot," Lenny said.

Lenny turned and walked away feeling shocked and disappointed and surprisingly light on his feet.

CHAPTER 26

Koretu

"To dump, dispose of "

Sally kicked the dean's office door open, leaned with her fists on his desk and shouted, "You're a flaming asshole!"

The dean said into his phone, "I'll get back to you," and laid it down. "You haven't lost you sailor's mouth, have you, Sally?"

"We have to talk."

"Give me a minute," the dean said, fumbling inside his desk's pullout filing cabinet. "I have some important matters to attend to."

Sally sat down. She doubted that the dean had important matters to attend to. He just wanted her to know her place. She guessed that she'd interrupted one of his many secretive phone conversations. Well, she'd wait. She got paid no matter what. So screw the dean.

Which she had. Many times. Long ago.

He'd been her first serious love.

She watched him remove files, replace files, and rearrange files, and she wondered how she could have ever spent more than five minutes with this bastard—pompous, greedy, deluded and dangerous— now gone plump and rosy-faced. She'd met him back when he was number 87 on the University of New Hampshire football team. He was a senior, she was a freshman. He was much sought-after and much experienced. She was a virgin (sort of). She'd thrilled to his disregard for rules, and he liked the bad girl in her, the chance-taker, the rebel. He'd seduced her (sort of). They spoke of marriage, but never followed up.

Years later, they met again when she took a summer-school course at Ghurkin College in the hope of strengthening her teaching credentials. They'd run into each other on the quadrangle, and he'd offered her a job right there as the replacement for his departing administrative assistant. The pay was higher than what she'd get as a teacher, suspiciously high for someone with no experience. Right from the start, Sally guessed that, from the way the dean had eyed her up and down, he was after more than office skills. But she accepted the job anyway—Charlie's horse-stabling business was barely breaking even, and they were behind on mortgage payments. She knew she could fend him off. And she had.

She never told Charlie or anyone else about her earlier relationship with the dean.

Sally knew the man was a crook, even back in college. Once, when they were going at in the back seat of his yellow convertible, he'd bragged that he'd been given the car for shaving points on the playing field.

How could she have ever fallen under the spell of such a man?

Should she threaten to tell the police about the point-shaving, and use that as leverage to save Lenny's job? No, the crime had taken place too long ago and would be too hard to prove. And to tell the truth, she was afraid of the dean.

What luck she'd dumped the guy. One of the smartest things she'd ever done.

She started to say something wiseass about the bronzed football shoes on the dean's desk, then remembered that she'd come to ask a favor.

Finally the dean closed the folder and set it next to his battered purple football helmet. "So, Sally, what brings you bursting into my office?"

"You know damn well why I'm here."

The dean shook his head, twitched his eyebrows and pushed his three football photographs closer together on his desk. "If I knew, I wouldn't have asked, would I?"

"Henri just told me you fired Lenny."

"Moral turpitude."

Sally wanted to sweep the dean's football photos to the floor and club him over the head with his goddamn cleats. "Bullshit!"

The dean leaned back in his chair and tented his fingers. "Through his involvement in this Skalwegian business, Lenny Thorson has compromised the good name of our school. A college is a place for learning, not a launching pad for riches, for vulgar commercial pursuits."

Sally pictured the Skammer Ford Ranchero banner above the library entrance and 'Skammer's Harley Heaven' spelled out in white lime in the middle of the football field—just a few examples of how the dean earned money under the table. Could she blackmail him to get Lenny's job back? No, it would be too hard to prove. "Put Lenny on probation but rehire him."

The dean swiveled to look out the window and down at his stadium. Nodding to himself in confirmation that it hadn't gone missing, he swung back. "It's out of my hands," he said, lifting both of them to show they were empty. "It was the decision of the college president."

"The college president doesn't take a dump without first asking your permission."

"The trustees"—the dean added hastily—"the trustees handed down the decision. As much as I like the lad, I had no choice."

"That's bullshit."

"That's the truth. And even if it weren't, do you think you could change my mind by bursting into my office like this? Did you think that I'd reverse my decision just for old time's sake?"

Sally's shoulders sagged. He was right. What had she been

thinking? Of course he wouldn't give in. The dean never gave in. He enjoyed a fight.

She'd liked that in him back then. She remembered the good times, and for just a moment, it passed through her mind that she could probably seduce the jerk right here in his office, right on the circular red rug. For Lenny. A sacrifice for her former student, her protégé. Just that.

But she slapped her knees, stood up and walked away. Before slamming the door, she turned and said, "You've got shit for brains."

It was Charlie's favorite saying.

*   *   *

The dean shook his head. Such language.

Was it worth putting up with her swearing and bitching just for the tidbits she revealed about Lenny and Charlie's progress with the Skalwegian language? Or should he replace her with someone younger, someone who'd put out?

He'd dumped Sally right after college, a smart decision, but one he still somewhat regretted. She'd been cute as hell with those wide eyes and all that frizzy red hair. A virgin too. And then there were those dancer's long legs and her great ass. Even now, she looked terrific as she stomped out of his office.

He'd have liked to have banged her right there on the rug. Promise to rehire Lenny. That would be a lie, of course, and later there'd be a fierce argument, which would be fun. His four ex-wives had been scrappers, but none as good as Sally. If he'd married her as she'd begged him to, she'd have kept him on his toes. But with her foul mouth and bad manners, she'd never have fit into the world he had planned for himself. Too bad, because he still felt a little something for her.

It was too bad he had to kill her husband.

CHAPTER 27

Yopaka and bleefuma

"Slackers and crooks"

The dean stood at the front window of the stadium's VIP lounge and watched two of Luther Skammer's construction workers finish spreading fresh concrete over a section of the stadium's inner wall where, during the night, they'd incorporated Bob One's body, minus its trigger finger.

It angered Dean Sheepslappe that his partner was cheating on repairs. He was also mad at Lenny, although he had to admit that the man hadn't in any way lied or misled him. What really irritated the dean was how Lenny had taken his firing. Why hadn't he begged, even a little? It was fun when underlings begged. The year before, he'd merely hinted to Juan that he might not be rehired, and the dickwad had turned into a pleading, blubbering, flattering rag doll. But not Lenny. Lenny was tough. Lenny had killed one hitman—biting his finger off in the process, for Christ sake—and left the other in a head-to-toe cast. The dean admired Lenny. Lenny The Lobsterman. A guy to fear.

The dean feared Luther Skammer even more, a dangerous man as were the thugs who worked for him. The dean would be glad when he'd be free of this Skalwegian business, when he could pocket the kickback, serve as college president just long enough to get the stadium named after him, then claim health problems and retire to San Diego. The dean hated New England winters, and he hated New Englanders, all of whom were out to cheat him.

A pickup bounced into the stadium and parked beside a big red cement truck. The dean picked up his binoculars. The truck's door read *Skammer's Construction Company.* Behind the wheel sat Luther himself, his chief engineer beside him. In the bed of the pickup, propped up against the cab's rear window and facing backwards, stood a figure in a full-length cast that shone bright white in the sunlight.

"Jerks," the dean said aloud. Had it been his call, the second hitman would also have gone into concrete. Instead, Luther took him wherever he went, maintaining it built employee loyalty. What a dickbrain.

The dean wondered if he could borrow the guy as a casualty for the upcoming Revolutionary War reenactment. Thinking about the event lifted the dean's spirits. Over the years, he'd taken part in all the battles and enjoyed every minute. He loved the action, the noise and the smoke, the scramble, the sweaty bright uniforms, the gritty camaraderie. Many of his fellow reenactors were military veterans. When asked about his own service—which was nonexistent—the dean would shake his head and say, "Too painful to talk about."

The dean lowered the binoculars. A Chicago hitman had been taken down by a professor of languages and linguistics. The dean shook his head. Getting rid of Lenny just wasn't working out. He was tough, canny, unpredictable. But maybe Billy Butcher could do the job. Luther says the guy has never failed.

The dean watched Luther drive away in his pickup—the killer in the body cast bouncing in back—but leaving behind a gangly engineer with three rolls of drawings squeezed under his right arm.

A polite coughing came from the dean's left. He turned to see Juan standing there. The dean hated Juan and his argyle socks.

Juan said, "I dropped by to inform you that I've been honored with the vice-presidency of the Gerry Gerbil Hill Toppers."

"The what?"

"The college hiking club."

Right, the dean thought, that climbing bunch that Elspeth can't stop jabbering about. Juan dropped by every day or two to report on a new task that he'd assumed in his quest for tenure. "That's nice."

"Elspeth is president. This weekend we're again scouting out Great Blue Hill as the venue for the group's next outing."

"That's nice."

The dean guessed that Juan was trying to win Elspeth back. The dean wasn't supposed to know about this liaison between a department head and her underling, but he did and didn't give a damn. But he could use the information as leverage should the need ever arise. Hell, he'd thought about trying to pork Elspeth himself, but decided against it because of how she'd babble on and on in her phony British accent.

Juan shifted to the other foot and cleared his throat. "I have it from a reliable source that Dr. Thorson deliberately sabotaged Gerry Gerbil."

"Oh?" the dean said without interest. He'd heard this before from Juan.

"It's lucky no one was hurt," Juan said. "Also, I'm now absolutely convinced that he's the one sending those vicious, unsigned letters to the *Gerbil Bugle* about your business dealings. Since they contain nothing but lies, I of course refuse to print them."

The dean had heard all this before too. The dean turned to look down at the stadium.

Juan was saying something. The dean turned around. "What?"

"I said, I have it on good authority that Dr. Thorson regularly entertains two young women, both reportedly models for an undergarment catalog. And by *entertaining*, I mean… well, something that I'm not ready to put into words."

A panty-model naked sandwich! The dean eyes went unfocused, and his ears hummed. How did Lenny Thorson pull that off?

Juan added, "And I know for a fact that Dr. Thorson is the one behind that petition to recombine the faculty and student dining facilities, and he's also—"

"You haven't heard?"

"Heard what, sir?"

"I fired Lenny."

Juan brightened, scratched the tip of his pickle nose, then took on a woeful look. "I'm sure you had the best of reasons, Dean Sheepslappe. I have to say that, although Dr. Thorson and I had our disagreements, I hope you will find it in your heart to give him a sufficiently strong recommendation that he can find another teaching position somewhere else."

Somewhere else far away, the dean figured. Far enough for this little turd pile to get another shot at shapely Elspeth.

"I'd like to add," Juan said in a sober tone, "that although I am now the sole candidate for the tenure track position, I get no joy in…"

The dean waved his hand to cut Juan off, who fell silent, then backed away. Most of his conversations with the dean ended with Juan backing away.

CHAPTER 28

Oofala!

*A Skalwegian expression uttered when surprised
by fortune's fair turnings. No close equivalent in
the English language.*

"You drive like a Parisian," Lenny said, bracing his hands against the dashboard of Henri's massive red Ford Excursion.

Henri glanced left before rolling through a stop sign. "That's because I learned to drive in Paris."

"You never learned to drive," Lenny said. "And watch out for that FedEx truck!"

Henri slipped his SUV between the truck on the left and a Boston taxi on the right. Lenny exchanged startled looks with the cabbie, his nose inches away. Henri drove too fast, cut off cars, ignored stop signs and exhibited a race car driver's skill behind the wheel. He had once told Lenny that the less accomplished had died long ago on the broad Darwinian boulevards of Paris.

Normally Lenny avoided riding with Henri, but he was being taken out for a belated birthday lunch and felt he couldn't refuse. Also, now that he was without work, he was getting lonesome and was willing to take a chance with Henri behind the wheel. Daniela spent most nights with him, but he had the rest of the day alone to reread the dictionary, fret over finances and search online for teaching jobs. So far, he'd found none for which he was qualified.

Henri turned to Lenny and grinned. "I'm days late with your birthday present, but it's *superbe*."

Lenny thought of the sweating stripper, the vomitous balloon trip. "You don't need to get me anything."

Henri bumped both of the right-side wheels onto the curb as he passed a bus on his left. He was driving east on Memorial Drive toward the Longfellow Bridge and then Boston Harbor.

"How could I not celebrate the birthday of my officemate—uh... my former officemate—and my best friend? I will buy you lunch and then give you a birthday present that you will find *superbe* and truly *extraordinaire!* It will change your life."

"For the better," I hope.

"Mais, oui!"

Henri parked in a restricted space near the harbor, then he and Lenny walked to Quincy Market, a restored 18th-century marketplace, now home to a block of eateries and shops. They passed a Victoria's Secret, an Urban Outfitters and a women's clothing store with a vowel-rich Italian name. In a shop window, Lenny spotted a pair of swooshy, wrap-around sunglasses that sold for $250. Lenny wondered who'd buy them. Well, Bradley the info-boob would, Lenny decided. Also the toothy Nelson Scuttlewood the Third.

The air smelled of French fries and fried clams, and Lenny was hungry.

Henri chose an outdoor table near a pushcart that called itself "Everything Pink." Four prepubescent girls were trying on oversized pink hats, examining each other, then squealing and jumping up and down. The proprietress—a buxom forty-something in a shiny black sleeveless blouse—traded lusty looks with Henri.

Normally Lenny wouldn't eat at the faux Cheers Bar in Quincy Market, but it was Henri's choice. Henri said it reminded him of

Paris. Lenny thought the pushcart lady had more to do with his friend's dining decision. The bar's interior sported the requisite Red Sox, Bruins, Celtics and New England Patriots uniforms tacked to a wall, along with a rifle of Colonial vintage and black-and-white blowups from the old TV series.

Lenny ate fish and chips. Henri had a dripping double cheeseburger, fries, and a glass of beer. Today he wore faded jeans, cowboy boots and a blue work shirt, his most American of outfits. Lenny wore a white dress shirt, jeans and scruffy black running shoes. Diners glanced over whenever the cowpoke spoke too loudly in his French accent.

Throughout the meal, Lenny worried about Henri's birthday gift. He peered about for exotic dancers, balloonists, a Bavarian in lederhosen leading a flock of gift goats. Halfway through the meal, a heavy-set man with a badly broken nose lumbered toward the table. He looked familiar. Did he have something to do with the birthday present? The man pointed at Lenny. "I remember you. You're Tommy Johnson."

Uh, oh, Lenny thought. That's the name he'd fought under. He now recalled the protruding jaw that had presented such an easy target, the fear-filled eyes. "Sorry," Lenny said, "You've made a mistake."

"You don't remember me? I'm Eddie Holmes. Down in Jersey, you and me, we fought once. I was way over-matched. You could've pounded the crap out of me but you held back and took it to a decision. I appreciated that. You was good. I always figured I'd hear about you fighting for the title, but never did. What happened? You stop boxing?"

"I'm sorry," Lenny said. "I'm a teacher—or I was a teacher—and I've never been in the ring."

"Yeah?"

"Yeah."

Eddie rubbed his knuckles. "Maybe I took too many punches to the head, or maybe you took too many punches to the head. One of us sure as hell did."

He walked back to his table, sat down and stared at Lenny.

Henri wiped a brown streak of cheeseburger grease off his chin. "Is there something about your past that you've been holding back?"

Lenny said nothing. He remembered Eddie Holmes as a clumsy kid, also underage and boxing with a made-up name. Lenny was glad that Eddie looked healthy.

But Lenny wished it had been his final opponent who'd shown up just now, that there'd been a terrible mistake. (An extended hand: "Hi there, Tommy. Remember our fight? You knocked me out cold for half an hour. Jeez, I'd never been hit so hard. I had it coming for taunting you like that about your dad's beard. You were good, man. The best. What you been doing with yourself? You've been teaching college? Sweet. Me? My wife and I own a bakery—four fingers displayed—and we got four kids.")

But Jimmy Smith was dead and buried. No wife, no bakery, no kids. Dead and buried.

Lenny had cried in the pickup all the way home. He told his father that he'd never fight again, never hurt anyone again, never get angry again. "If boxing's so important to you, why don't you put on the gloves and get back into the ring?"

Lenny had expected a sharp response, but instead his father peered over the steering wheel into the night. Finally, he said, "I'd go back if I could, even at my age." Then without looking, he reached over and squeezed Lenny's shoulder. "Sorry kid. Sorry about what happened tonight. You don't have to fight no more."

The day Lenny learned that his opponent had died, he opened his dictionary to *Aardvark* and read for the rest of the day, the rest of the week, the rest of the month, trying not to see his unconscious opponent lying at his feet while the referee held up Lenny's gloved fist in victory.

Some victory.

Somewhere between *moccasin* and *monospermous*, Lenny discovered that he could carry entire pages about in his head. Reporting this fact to his father, he had been advised that his time would be better spent trapping rats.

"You're not hungry?" Henri asked.

Lenny realized he'd been staring at his plate. "Uh, I had a big breakfast."

"Then let's blow this joint," Henri said, a favorite expression.

They walked to the harbor, where sailboats rose and fell at anchor. To Lenny's right hovered the lofty blue derricks of the container port, to his front a Lufthansa airliner settled fatly onto a runway at Logan airport, and to his left stood the Bunker Hill Monument.

Lenny looked at his watch. "Don't you have a class?"

Henri shrugged.

They dangled their legs over the end of the pier. A Pepsi can and three plump jellyfish bobbed gently past, and two seagulls quarreled over a chunk of something purple floating in the water. Henri pulled a bottle of Dom Perignon and two glasses from his briefcase. He said, "It's getting warm, so we'll have to drink it fast."

"I don't think alcoholic beverages are allowed here."

Henri puffed up his cheeks and blew out his breath just as the cork popped into the harbor. "We Americans need to stop being so... um... tight ass. Is that an appropriate expression?"

"Yes, and thanks, Henri. Lunch and champagne make a great gift."

Henri shook his head, apparently disappointed that Lenny had thought his birthday celebration consisted of mere food and drink. Or possibly he sensed that Lenny wanted his birthday present to consist of mere food and drink. Henri clinked Lenny's glass. "You are aware of my little preoccupation with genealogy."

Lenny was aware. Many times he'd helped Henri cobble together a last-minute class plan because he'd spent the previous weekend in libraries and town halls tracing ancestors, either his own or the Skalwegians settlers that Harvey had asked him to find before his death. Lenny said, "And?"

"And you once told me you had a grandmother you'd never met."

"She left Quebec for California, abandoning her husband and daughter—my mother—who was eleven at the time. We never talked about her."

"Are you curious about your grandmother?"

"I suppose so."

Henri looked extremely pleased with himself—the cat that ate the canary. He reached into his briefcase, whipped out two pieces of paper and jiggled them in front of Lenny's face.

"What are these?" Lenny asked.

"One must read them to find out."

Lenny read both papers twice. Then a third time. One was a photocopy of his grandmother's birth certificate, the other a DNA report. He looked up at Henri. "Are these real?"

"*Mais, oui!* Of course they're real," Henri said with a broad smile. He raised both hands, turned them palms up and lifted his shoulders in a great, Gallic shrug. "I'm an expert on this sort of thing. Of course they're real. That time you had me over for lobster and boysenberries, I swiped your toothbrush to use for the DNA test."

"I always wondered where it went."

"Want it back?"

Lenny shook his head. "Do you know what this means?"

Henri finished his champagne, poured himself another glass and refilled Lenny's. "Of course I know what this means. Your grandmother was a full-blooded Skalwegian. That makes you one-quarter. As confirmation, the DNA report traces some of your ancestors to Skalvik. Congratulations: You're in line for a piece of the action. That's what one says, right? 'A piece of the action?'"

Lenny was too stunned to reply. A quarter Skalwegian? No one would believe he hadn't known this all along. If his reputation was crap before, now it would be something worse. Lenny wished Henri had given him another session with the chubby stripper, or another balloon ride, or even a herd of goats. Lenny wanted to rush home, sequester himself behind his crates of frozen lobster tails and never emerge. Daniela would tend to his needs, bring him fresh vegetables, the *New York Times* and the occasional traveling dentist.

Daniela?

What if they were close cousins?

Lenny watched a seagull swoop down and grab a pizza crust off the pier. "Am I related to Daniela?"

"No."

"You're sure?"

"I checked back several generations. At most you'd be something like fifth cousins."

Lenny let his breath out. What if Daniela had turned out to be a close relative? How would he have handled that? Would he have stopped seeing her? Or lied to her?

'Sequester' came from the Middle English 'sequenstren,' with its ancestor probably some word from Middle French and Latin before that.

Henri said, "You look lost in another world."

"Huh? Oh, I guess I was."

Henri raised his glass. "Is there a word in Skalwegian for when one is struck by great luck?"

"Yes… in fact there is one, and I just learned it from Charlie. It's *oofala*."

Henri nodded several times, pursed his lips and said, "*Oofala*. That's a fine word." He clicked Lenny's glass. "*Oofala!*"

Lenny was stunned, shocked and dismayed.

He wasn't sure this qualified as an *oofala* moment.

CHAPTER 29

Zaknak hocak memut domalopa.

"The fool loses his head."

Lenny sat atop his futon with his phone to his ear and a third mug of black coffee in his other hand, watching the morning raindrops streak the windows, slanting first left and then right at the whims of the wind. Finally Charlie answered.

Lenny took a deep breath. "Did you know my mother's mother?"

"I don't think so. Did she live around here?"

"No, Quebec. She ran away to California and died there many years ago."

"Why do you want to know?"

"Because Henri researched my ancestors and found out she was a full-blooded Skalwegian."

"No kidding?" Charlie said. "That's great. Hey, maybe we're related?

"Not according to Henri."

"Too bad," Charlie said.

"Right, too bad. It would be great having you for a cousin, even though you're a fraud and a cheat and owe me $22,000."

Charlie chuckled, "That's the spirit."

Lenny watched the rain splash across the windows. "Actually, I'm proud to be a quarter Skalwegian."

"It's your best part."

*   *   *

Lenny lifted Daniela by the waist, set her on his futon and said, "I'm one-quarter Skalwegian."

Daniela tugged his left earlobe. "Is this a little game we're playing?"

Lenny shook his head. "No, it's true." He reached into his jacket pocket, pulled out the copies of the DNA report and his grandmother's birth certificate, unfolded them and handed them to Daniela. "Henri gave me this."

Daniela read the papers, then looked up. "Welcome to the club. I... uh... just hope we're not—"

"Related? No. Henri checked."

Daniela looked relieved.

Lenny wondered if she was thinking what he was thinking: children who were part Skalwegian, angelic and beautiful if they were girls, big and clumsy if boys. He hoped so, but doubted this would ever happen. Daniela could do a lot better than him.

Lenny didn't fall asleep until 4:00 A.M., wondering what Daniela really thought of him, and trying to recall the derivation of *clumsy*. He woke twice, once when the restaurant came alive with a clank and a shudder, and again shortly after dawn when he opened one eye to watch Daniela pull a sleeveless blue top down over her head, her lovely shoulders, her sky-blue bra and her trim tummy. He felt her coffee-scented kiss on his forehead as he drifted back to sleep. He woke a few minutes before noon and lay thinking about the past few months. First came the golden chance to work with Charlie on the Skalwegian language, followed by an inside track at tenure and finally the miraculous $200,000 grant. He had felt—if not on top of the world—at least on top of the junk pile.

Then everything went to hell: He'd flunked the Sprocket brothers and lost favor with the dean and much of the student body. Then there was that incident with the Gerry Gerbil statue, followed by the crushing revelation that Charlie's Skalwegian was bogus. Soon afterwards, his reputation went down the toilet with the news of the mineral deposits on the island, and then the dean confiscated the grant money. Finally, he was fired from a job he loved.

The only good thing to happen to him was Daniela. And that was very, very good.

How did he now feel about the Skalwegian language? For the first time since learning that it was ersatz, Lenny was recharged. Fake or not, it was—sort of—the tongue of his ancestors, and he wanted to preserve it. This was illogical, he knew. But from time to time it did one good to be a little illogical.

Lenny clicked on the television. It wasn't the news that interested him, but the newscaster. Daniela appeared on the screen, introduced herself and smiled. Lenny smiled back. He had the satisfaction of knowing that, of the tens of thousands of drooling men watching her, only he that morning had seen her pull her top down over her sky-blue bra.

Lenny microwaved four lobster tails during the first advertisement. He returned to the television set, chewed slowly, and half-listened as Daniela reported on some change to a local zoning law. Partway through, a hand slid a sheet of paper across her desk. "This is just in," Daniela said, picking up the paper. "WDRK has learned from the Massachusetts Highway Patrol that a body was found this morning on Great Blue Hill."

Daniela crinkled her face. Lenny knew how much she hated reporting on death and violence.

"Officer Milton Cooper, in charge of the investigation, stated to our reporter on the scene that, in his eighteen years of law-enforcement work, he had never seen such a grizzly slaying. According to Officer Cooper, the decapitated corpse was deposited in the seat of a descending chairlift shortly after the killing. Officer Cooper stated that the victim, a man believed to be in his late thirties or early forties, sat upright with... with... his severed head in his lap and..."

Daniela swallowed and looked off to her right. Someone said, "Keep reading."

Daniela grimaced, then said, "The beheaded victim wore nothing except for one brown-and-gold argyle sock and a... uh... ribbed lavender protective device. The police are looking for a man carrying a chainsaw and dressed in a park uniform. A spokeswoman for the Blue Hills Reservation told our reporter that none of their people had checked out a chainsaw in the past few days, but that a park uniform was recently stolen from an employee's car."

Daniela took a deep breath and continued. "The victim's hysterical companion at first identified the headless man as Count Holstein-Schmidt, but calmed down later and identified the murder victim as Dr. Juan Jorgenson, an assistant professor of languages at Ghurkin College."

Lenny ran to the bathroom and threw up in the toilet, then washed his face in the sink, rinsed out his mouth with a glass of water, and once more threw up in the toilet. Looking up at himself in the mirror, he wondered why in the world anyone would do such a terrible, terrible thing. And why to Juan?

Poor Juan, he thought. Poor Juan and poor Elspeth.

CHAPTER 30

Yeksliss

"Drizzle"

Dazed and saddened, Lenny riffled through a gradebook from two terms back. Toss or keep? Keep, he decided, purely for sentimental reasons. He filed it in a cardboard carton among syllabuses, course plans, tests and other teaching material, sorted by semester.

Would he ever reopen these cartons? Lenny didn't know. Would anyone ever hire him again? Lenny doubted it. There were few positions open in his field and, with his blemished record—he was ethically compromised and had also been fired in mid-term—he'd be at a disadvantage against fresh PhD's. Was all this sorting and filing just a waste of time? Probably.

What would happen to Juan's teaching materials? Straight into the dumpster, Lenny supposed.

He glanced out the window. The sun shone bright and warm, but Lenny wanted drizzle. He was in a drizzly mood. *Yeksliss* was the noun.

Poor Juan.

Lenny guessed that Juan and Elspeth had made the Blue Hills a regular trysting spot.

Lenny dropped a handful of old tests onto the floor, bent over to pick them up, then straightened up and shouted, "Fuck it!"

He rummaged through a kitchen cabinet until he found four green trash bags, stuffed his teaching materials inside, dragged the bags to the elevator, rode down to the ground floor, and hurled everything into the dumpster behind the building.

He stood for a moment, fighting the urge to climb in and retrieve his teaching career and all his dreams. But he didn't. Life had taken a new direction.

Lenny punched the elevator button to the top floor and said 'drizzle' a couple times in his mind. He liked words that sounded like the action they described. If he were to invent a language, he'd make as many words as possible onomatopoeic.

Then it occurred to him that he was inventing a language, or at least assisting someone in inventing a language.

'Drizzle' emanated from the Middle English, but from where beyond that, Lenny didn't know. He would research the term when he got back upstairs. Something to do.

As a second breakfast, he'd eaten four ice cream bars and drunk three cups of black coffee. Once back upstairs, he retrieved another bar from the freezer. He'd gained eight pounds since his firing.

Poor Juan, Lenny thought. He'd never again eat ice cream, teach a Spanish class, make love with Elspeth.

Lenny settled into booth number four, bit off a big crescent of ice cream and thought about running away. He'd sell the Chevy—probably just for junk—and everything else he owned, then take off for Europe and try to contact Sasha. He'd start with the circuses. How many could there be? Certainly not many that employed an Albanian lady bareback rider.

That summer was the only time he'd ever felt really free. The two of them would wake up each morning, brush their teeth—Sasha bathed infrequently but insisted on sweet-smelling breath—and then they'd tumble together, her muscular legs locking him in place. Afterwards, they would decide whether to hitchhike to another city, to another country even, or just to remain in bed until noon, doze, sweatily recouple and then drop down to a corner café for coffee and sandwiches.

They'd first met on the Paris subway when Lenny felt Sasha's hand in his back pocket. Lenny had grabbed her wrist, which caught the attention of a plainclothes policeman, who tried to arrest her. Sasha looked terrified. The cop looked cruel. Lenny put his arm around Sasha's shoulders, gave them a squeeze and said it was just a little game they played. After the cop left, Sasha hugged Lenny around the waist and said no one had ever been that kind to her. He took her to a restaurant, bought her a nice meal and made her promise to stop picking pockets.

Perhaps finding Sasha again would be a long shot. And would she still be unattached? Unlikely.

But Lenny knew he could never leave Daniela, no matter what.

He went for another ice cream bar and reformulated his thoughts, substituting Daniela for the barebacker and fashioning a brighter fantasy of running away, one that fell within the realm of the possible.

He was still thinking about Daniela when she called. He had an etymological dictionary open on his lap, turned to 'drizzle.'

She said, "I'm horrified at what happened to Juan."

"So am I."

"How are you doing?"

"Not so good," Lenny said. "I can't get the image of Juan out of my head. And poor Elspeth must be in shock. I tried to call, but only got her answering machine."

"I wish I were there with you."

"I wish you were too," Lenny said.

"I called in part to ask if Juan had a nickname."

"Would you like to run off to Europe with me?"

"Of course I would, Lenny, but I can't get away for a couple of months at least. Why do you ask?"

"I want to forget everything, run off to Europe with you and live on black coffee and croissants."

Daniela paused. "Sounds romantic, if not nutritionally sound. Maybe we can take a vacation together in the fall. And I asked you a question."

"Uh... which was?"

"Did you or any of your chums—I'm thinking of Henri in particular—give Juan Jorgenson a snarky nickname?"

"Not that I know of," Lenny said. "Why are you asking?"

"Because the killer referred to him as 'The Lobsterman.' That's what Elspeth told the police after she calmed down enough to be coherent."

"I didn't give Juan that nickname or any other. Maybe the dean did. He liked to make fun of Juan, sometimes right to his face. The dean is pond slime."

"You don't need to tell me. I know from experience."

Lenny hesitated. "How?"

"Because he once talked me into accompanying him to a charity ball and tried to get me drunk."

"Oh. I see," Lenny said, dragging out his words. "Then you've *dated* the jerk."

"Not in the sense that you're thinking. Not in the way we're dating, the way we dated twice last night."

"Why didn't you ever tell me you knew him?"

"Why should I? I meet a lot of people in my line of work. Besides, we only went out that one time. Okay?"

"I guess."

Lenny closed the dictionary, set it aside and flipped the ice cream stick against the window only to watch it bounce back onto his lap. "I heard you get out of bed this morning. I meant to get up, but I fell back asleep. I've gotten fat and lazy since I was fired. I've worked all my life, starting with the salvage yard at age six and later on at countless part-time jobs that supported me in college."

Lenny didn't mention the only break in his working life, his steamy European summer with Sasha.

Daniela said, "Some things you are, Lenny—dreamy, word-obsessed, and of course cute and cuddly—but not lazy. Anyway, let's meet for coffee at the Monsoon Mist, around 5:00."

"Could we make that Prague? I know of a great little café there."

"See you at 5:00, Lenny. Kisses."

Bantering with Daniela had kept him from thinking about poor, headless Juan. But now he was puzzled. What's this Lobsterman business? He doubted that the nickname applied to Juan because he'd once thrown a hissy fit at a faculty party when the only protein was lobster. So who did eat lobster?

Who had eight crates of frozen lobster tails?

New Skalvik's chief of police, Bart Skammer, had speculated during a press conference that Juan's killer was a random madman who'd watched too many chainsaw movies.

Lenny wasn't so sure.

Not sure at all.

He pulled himself to his feet.

Did Juan die in my place?

Am I The Lobsterman?

Horrified, Lenny drifted to the window and stared at the parking lot below. Two thoughts throbbed side-by-side in his skull: Someone wanted to kill him, and someone had killed Juan in his place.

Lenny felt a chill.

Calm down, he told himself. After all, the only proof is a stupid nickname. Besides, Elspeth was rattled and could have misheard the killer. He could have said 'Lockerman' or something like that.

But Lenny couldn't quite convince himself, couldn't drive the guilt from his mind. If someone wanted him dead, it must have something to do with this stupid Skalwegian business, because why else would anyone want to behead a linguist?

*   *   *

Daniela made a loop around the inside of the stadium, a second, a third. Usually she jogged on the college track, but there was a meet today. Construction workers shouted things at her she couldn't make out and didn't want to. If Lenny were here, the men wouldn't dare to even look in her direction.

It had been a tough afternoon. She'd almost thrown up during her 3:00 newscast, reporting again on the details of Juan's death. After she was off the air, she fled the station without telling anyone. Bradley would be happy to do the 6:00 o'clock show alone. He'd love to describe in great detail how Juan had ridden the chairlift with his head in his lap. The prick.

Daniela had never met Juan but felt sorry for him, not just murdered but murdered and humiliated. And she felt sorry for Lenny—broke, unemployed, and upset over Juan's death, much more than Daniela had expected considering how much Lenny had disliked the man. Something's going on there, she guessed, but she knew she'd get nothing out of Lenny. He could be so open at times, so closed at others. Well, everyone has their secrets. She'd held off telling him about that time she'd gone out with the dean—more of a pity date than anything—and she'd never quizzed Lenny about this Sasha person he sometimes talked to in his sleep.

She slowed down and smiled to herself. Lenny. She'd never met anyone like him, his obsessions with etymology, his wit, kindness, vulnerability and honesty. Plus his tight muscles and flat tummy. If she and Lenny had children, she hoped at least one would be a boy, large and clumsy and cute and clever.

Daniela stopped walking. Who was she kidding? Lenny wasn't the marrying kind. If he were, he could do a lot better than her.

Enjoy the situation as long as she could, she told herself. Who knew what the future could bring? Think of what happened to Juan—alive one minute, dead the next.

So what was she doing here, sweating through her T-shirt and flipping the bird at jeering construction workers, when she could be rolling around with Lenny on his perfumed futon?

She jogged through the exit and raced to her car.

CHAPTER 31

Rimenum

"Poetry"

Following Juan's death, Elspeth draped herself in black, stopped exercising, put on twelve pounds, fainted gracefully in public, and penned a 1,922-line poem to Juan's memory. She hinted to Lenny of suicide but never followed up. She declared herself miserable but appeared quite cheery, and to be thoroughly enjoying the attention.

After Sally had assured Lenny that the dean had flown to Colorado Springs to play golf with a rich contributor to the school's athletic program, Lenny agreed to attend the memorial for Juan at Elspeth's blue-shuttered cape in central New Skalvik. It was an Anglophile's abode: A bust of Shakespeare on a pedestal eyed Lenny and Daniela as they stepped through the front door, posters of British poets filled the hallway, and under glass on the coffee table lay a Wimbledon roster autographed by an obscure tennis player with a shaky hand. Lenny and Daniela found Elspeth standing next to the kitchen table upon which sat a lopsided cake shaped like a tombstone and smeared with black frosting and tiny white writing: "Juan Jorgenson: 'The Valiant Never Taste of Death But Once.'"

Daniela slipped away to leave the two former lovers alone.

Elspeth said, "Lenny, I know what you say about me behind my back. You've described me as a self-absorbed, second-rate poet."

This was how Lenny sometimes thought of Elspeth, but he would never have told anyone. "I never said anything of the kind."

"Yes you did."

"Who said so?"

"None other than the late Juan Jorgenson, that's who."

"He lied."

Elspeth pressed the back of her hand against her forehead in pre-swoon but stayed on her feet. "Do you feel no guilt, accusing a dead man of lying?"

"Trust me, Elspeth, I have more than my share of guilt."

Lenny turned and caught Daniela's eye. He waved at her, hoping she would come and rescue him. She didn't.

Elspeth glanced over. "She's attractive in her way, although I can never get over how all TV newswomen look alike. They're all are so blonde and busty."

"Daniela has dark hair, and she's… well… pleasantly average in that particular department."

Elspeth wasn't listening. She bent over the cake and squinted as if reading the Shakespeare quotation for the first time. "Women like that aren't real journalists. They know nothing about the world, about anything. They're just attractive. Well, sort of attractive if you go in for that type of woman. All looks and no brainpower."

"Daniela graduated with honors from Wellesley College and got her master's degree at Harvard."

Elspeth picked up a knife and started to hack the cake into black squares. "It's easy to get into Harvard if one has a rich and influential parent, an ambassador or a Fortune 500 CEO."

"Daniela's father returned from Afghanistan with PTSD and a head wound that kept him from holding a permanent job."

"See what I mean?" Elspeth said, slicing an angry cut between *Juan* and *Jorgenson*.

Elspeth heard only what she wanted to hear, one of her many traits that drove Lenny batshit.

He watched her cut *Jorgenson* between the *r* and the *g* and then cleanly between the *n* and the *s,* and he felt sickened by the death of his former rival.

Had things gone the other way—or at least how Lenny suspected they were intended to go—right at this moment Elspeth would be slicing *Thorson* asymmetrically between the *r* and the *s.*

Lenny said, "I know this is a terribly painful subject for you, but could I ask you a couple of questions about the... uh... incident?"

Elspeth lay the knife aside, assumed her saddest look and without prompting started telling her tale in a voice that carried far beyond the perimeter of normal conversation between two people. She and Juan had climbed the hill to picnic and pick edelweiss, but were fallen upon by a killer who stripped off all her clothes before chasing her far into the thicket. From the distance where she crouched under a dwarf oak and slapped at meddlesome insects, she heard an angry chainsaw rip the air but luckily for her the roar of the infernal machine covered the cries of the martyred victim.

It was her theory that aged, leftover followers of Spain's dead dictator had dispatched Juan in payment for his classroom outspokenness against all forms of fascism. Many parts of her 1,922-line poem touched on Juan's bravery, she declared. Yes, she'd be reading it later that afternoon. All of it. Probably twice.

Lenny said, "It doesn't require an inordinate amount of bravery to criticize the regime of the long-dead Franco, nor does it seem possible that any of his doddering followers would travel this far to knock off some obscure detractor."

"You have no shame, Leonard Thorson, no shame at all!"

"I have more than my share," Lenny said. He watched Elspeth flop pieces of the black-frosted cake onto paper plates, carefully concealing the Harleys. "Do you have any idea why the killer referred to Juan as *The Lobsterman?*"

Elspeth nodded.

"Well?" Lenny said.

"You'll have to wait for the reading. But for now, I can tell you that, somewhere between verses 1,100 and 1,130, I draw a parallel between Juan's hatred for fascist dictatorships and his deep dislike for that particular variety of seafood."

Lenny doubted he'd be able to pay attention past line five. "Final question: Can you think of something that you haven't told anyone, something that seemed particularly unusual?"

"Well, there is something."

She said nothing more.

Lenny groaned. Was it in her poem? Would he have to pay attention through all 1,922 lines? He said, "What was that something?"

"Well, what struck me as odd, in addition to everything else, of course, was that the horrible man called me by name. His exact words were, 'Elspeth, get the hell out of here and stay away!'"

"Did you recognize him?"

Elspeth shook her head.

"Did you tell the police he knew your name?"

"I guess I forgot."

"Don't you think that's something they'd want to know?"

Elspeth started folding black paper napkins that read, 'Juan, We All Loved You Dearly!' "Maybe, but will it bring the poor soul back? Now that's enough talk. You've made me tebbly upset."

When Elspeth turned to open the refrigerator, Lenny slipped away. As he'd suspected, it wasn't a random murder. Elspeth had led the killer to the wrong man.

Lenny felt sorry that Juan had died, and he felt even more sorry that Juan had died in his place. This was something that he'd have to live with for the rest of his life. Add that to the sight of Jimmy Smith, lying on the canvas, his left leg twitching, twelve hours to live.

Lenny joined Daniela, who was standing with Henri and Joan or Jane. They'd been laughing, but stopped when they saw Lenny's expression. Everyone else in the room was eating and drinking and having an inappropriately good time. No one had liked Juan.

Daniela took Lenny by the arm and steered him into a corner underneath an out-of-focus color photo of a raven pecking at corn kernels in front of the Tower of London. "Are you okay?"

"No, I'm not okay."

Daniela stroked Lenny's cheek with the back of her hand. "You're a sweet man."

"I'm a guilt-ridden man."

"I don't know why you should be. Do you want to talk about it?"

"No."

"Maybe you will later," Daniela said. "By the way, I just spoke with Charlie on the phone. He's sorry you lost your job."

"How did he find out? I didn't tell him because I didn't want him to worry."

"I told him."

"You shouldn't have."

"Well, I did, so that's that," Daniela said and tapped Lenny in the chest. "You might want to call him."

Elspeth pinged a knife on the side of a wine glass for silence and climbed on a kitchen chair in the middle of the living room. "Join me at this terrible and somber moment when we all fight back our tears like waves from the ocean deep, and share with me the joy and sorrow of my 'Ode to Juan Jorgenson.'" Lenny stopped listening.

He slipped into the kitchen, phoned Charlie, told him everything he knew about his role in Juan's death and the danger they were both in.

Charlie said, "*Ool!*"

Good word choice, Lenny thought. The two of them were in *ool* up to their necks.

CHAPTER 32

Cokeka nad fastoua

"Freaks and perverts"

Dean Sherman Sheepslappe stepped into Boston's Old North Church and glanced around: A young couple sat with their fidgety toddler between them, a bearded old man dozed on a bench, and a sparrow flew from one window to the next, banging its head to get out. No one matched Billy Butcher's description.

The dean wondered if it was such a good idea to meet the killer face to face. The guy might get violent. Still, the dean wanted to let him know just how upset he was about the botched assignment. Who whacks the wrong guy? What's this world coming to when you can't trust people to do their jobs? The dean felt cheated.

He plopped down in one of the boxes reserved for wealthy parishioners. It was a wooden cubicle topping out at a seated man's eye level. Women wouldn't be able see over, which the dean guessed was intentional, considering those times. He pictured a Colonial family crowded into the box, shivering, listening for hours and hours as the preacher droned on and on about the fate that awaited sinners. The dean shuddered.

Buildings of an ecclesiastical nature reminded him of that period in his childhood when his mother was into religious scams and traveled the country as a tent preacher. The dean remembered his white suit, how quickly it got dirty and how quickly his mother would scold him. They traveled from one small town to the next, setting up their tent, unfolding chairs and laying out hymnals. His mother would stand behind the pulpit and promote a shortcut to the Promised Land as he in his white suit went from one shaky, blue-veined hand to the next as coins and bills dropped into the offering plate. His mother had instructed him to say, "The Lord blesses you and keeps you."

After the service, the Reverend Mother Sheepslappe would dump the collection plates onto their motel bedspread. She counted bills, and he sorted coins. On the alert at first for the disappearance of dimes and quarters, she eventually came to trust him. She would tussle his hair and say he was an honest young fellow. She warned him that the world was full of crooks and cheats. She hated crooks and cheats.

By age nine, he'd accumulated over two hundred dollars in bills that he kept hidden in his stack of comic books. He never stole from his mother, just bills from the collection plate. Stealing directly from his mother would be a sin. She said sinners went straight to hell.

He last saw her when she was in prison and he was eighteen years old and heading for the University of New Hampshire on a football scholarship. Over the next four years, Luther Skammer bought him a Chrysler convertible for point shaving, he met Sally, his mother choked on vomit in her cell, and he graduated with a C-minus average. Luther found him a job in the city government, where old-timers taught him how to shake down paving contractors, electricians and construction companies. He started speaking at political rallies, praising the basic American values of hard work and honesty. Luther marked him as an up-and-comer, and the two men formed a silent and profitable alliance.

The dean stood up and stretched. He guessed that a wealthy

congregation attended services here and that the collection plates would fill up. He wondered if anyone stole from them.

The dean heard the couple with the toddler gasp. He swung around to see a man shamble inside who fit Billy Butcher's description: squat and angry, greasy brown hair down to his shoulders, a black leather jacket and black leather pants.

The couple jumped up and rushed out the door. So did the old man. So did the sparrow.

The dean whisked Billy outside to a tiny memorial garden and out of sight. They sat on a stone bench next to a life-sized statue of St. Francis of Assisi. Vandals had broken off the fingers, which made the dean think of Bob One's chewed-off digit. He shuddered. "You hit the wrong man!"

"Uh… yeah, I read about that in the newspapers."

"Why didn't you find out where the guy lived so you could make a positive ID?"

"Shit man, you told me not to get near The Lobsterman until the hit. You said he'd spot me on account of he was so smart. You told me to follow the woman, and she'd lead me to him."

The dean hesitated. That was true. He had warned the hitman away from Lenny. "I'm not paying you."

"No?" Billy Butcher said with a wide smile.

The dean jerked his head back. Billy's two front teeth were sharpened to points. Was he born that way? Did he do it himself? Certainly no dentist would.

The dean slid to the far edge of the bench. "You'll get paid, but you have to do another job for me."

"Another chainsaw gig?" Billy asked brightly.

"No, nothing like that. It's a black-bag operation. You can pick locks, can't you?"

"Of course." Billy Butcher said, disappointment in his voice.

*   *   *

Nightmares kept Lenny up until after midnight, and he didn't wake up until 9:00 the next morning when his phone rang just as the Moon View Revolving Restaurant went into action. He rolled over and watched the stadium slip out of sight and the arboretum roll into view. He picked up the phone. "Yes?"

"Dr. Thorson?"

"That's me."

"This is campus security. Someone broke into your office last night and messed the place up. We don't know if they took anything."

Lenny groaned and sat up. "I'll be right down."

Sally had called him twice during the week to say that the dean wanted him to clean out his office. Lenny had ignored the dean's order because he didn't want to show his face on campus.

Lenny found Henri showing off the graffiti on the wall to a blond man and a blonde woman, both thirty-ish and somewhat translucent. Henri introduced them by their first names, which Lenny guessed meant that Henri hadn't bothered to learn their last names. They were Lenny and Juan's replacements. The man shook Lenny's hand and stammered something about how sorry he was to take over under such circumstances. Lenny assured him it wasn't his fault. The man—Bruce Something-or-Other—had thin fingers and a thin face, as did his sister, Lana Something-or-Other, and both smelled of the same cheap soap. Bruce struck Lenny as the type of person who'd do anything to avoid trouble. The dean would have no problem getting him to give retroactive A's to the Sprocket brothers.

The bell rang, and the brother and sister scampered off.

With a sweep of his hand, Henri said, "I told the janitors not to wash the walls. This will keep your memory alive."

In a large and shabby scrawl, the graffiti instructed Lenny that he was a freak and a pervert who hated Gerry Gerbil and who should die a horrible death.

Lenny said, "A freak, maybe, but not a pervert. Do I hate Gerry Gerbil? You bet."

Henri gathered materials for his class. "You're not worried?"

"If someone wanted to kill me," Lenny said, dropping into his desk chair, "they wouldn't announce it ahead of time."

"You're sure?"

Lenny pictured Juan riding the chairlift, his bloody head on his lap. "I'm sure."

Henri looked up. "You're doing okay?"

"I'm doing okay."

"Enjoying all your free time?"

"There's too much," Lenny said.

"When rehearsals for the grand and utterly *comique* reenactment of the Battle of Ghurkin Hill begins, then you'll have something to do."

"You're joking, right? Getting fired spared me that humiliation."

Henri smiled and slapped Lenny on the back. "You're not off the hook, partner. At yesterday's faculty meeting, the dean passed around the list of participants. Your name was right at the top: Lenny Thorson, Captain of the British artillery."

"No kidding?"

"Nope."

"Why has he given me a role, especially as an officer?"

Henri turned down the corners of his lower lip and shrugged grandly. "Maybe this is his way of keeping up the pretense that it wasn't his idea to fire you."

"Maybe."

"Are you going to play soldier?" Henri asked.

"Of course not. The dean can take his stupid battle and shove it."

"That's the right attitude," Henri said and headed out the door.

It puzzled Lenny that the dean had kept him on the list of reenactors.

The results of his searching the office also puzzled him. The intruder hadn't been a thief because he—or she—would have stolen his laptop, but there it sat in the middle of his desk, right next to the 3x5" black-and-white photo of himself and Sasha hugging at the waist in front of the Eiffel Tower. Lenny had kept the picture front and center because it annoyed Elspeth so much.

He picked up the photo and let his thoughts drift to Sasha, to the joy of that summer and the melancholy of their parting. The night before he was to fly home, he'd awakened around midnight in their Prague hotel room to see Sasha standing near the door, fully clothed, her backpack at her feet. Through half-closed eyes, Lenny watched her lift his trousers off the chair, take out his wallet, remove the bills and stuff them into her jeans. She stood watching him for a while, then nodded to herself and disappeared. Lenny didn't try to stop her. Appropriate, he thought as he rolled over to face the wall. She'd tried to pick his pocket when they'd first met and succeeded when they parted.

Lenny set the photo back down on his desk, then reread the graffiti scrawled on the wall. Could this be the work of the Sprocket brothers? Unlikely, Lenny decided. Even those two wouldn't write "freke" and "pervurt."

CHAPTER 33

Ceho di flekont

"Love is blue"

Lenny bent over, reached inside a green trash bag, retrieved a stack of French exams, straightened up and surprised himself by saying, "I love you."

Daniela sat on the restaurant floor and rummaged through another bag. Withdrawing a handful of class plans, she sniffed them and wrinkled her nose. "These will dry out, I suppose, but they'll always smell bad."

A little louder this time, a little braver, Lenny said, "I love you."

"I'll spread them out over there," Daniela said and pointed across the restaurant, not meeting Lenny's eye. "On top of booth number five, because it's getting the morning sunlight, or at least it will until this place gets it into its head to start moving again."

Lenny watched Daniela, seated cross-legged, the bulky trash bag on her lap, as she pawed through the moist archives of Lenny's academic life. Lenny had given into her urgings to retrieve his professorial past and had dug his exams and syllabuses out of the dumpster. Unfortunately, he hadn't sealed the bags, and now their contents were humid and scented, corrupted by their proximity to coffee grounds and hollowed grapefruit halves, high heels in singles, mystery boxes sealed with duct tape, a three-legged chair, and a headless store dummy of the male sex.

The teaching papers could be rescued, but not Lenny's pride. By declaring his love, he'd embarrassed Daniela and he'd embarrassed himself. He should have known better. Dating him was a lark, he guessed, just a lark, something Daniela could tell people about later in life at parties or at the station during commercial breaks, of the brief time she'd been involved with this goofily distracted ex-prof who lived on frozen seafood, boysenberries, and sterile etymological pursuits.

But now at least he knew where he stood, and with that knowledge came the peace that sometimes accompanies disappointments. No more worrying about where their relationship was going. It was going nowhere.

Just enjoy the moment.

Lenny lay a dozen sheets of class plans ("French 2, sessions 1-12") across the faded red leather of booth number seven. Enjoy the moment, he said to himself.

'Enjoy.' One of its archaic meanings was to have sexual intercourse, and Lenny guessed that perfectly defined his situation. The word in all its joyful connotations dated back several hundred years, arriving through the Old French *enjoir* and back to a word in Latin that Lenny couldn't remember but suspected he would if he weren't so preoccupied by the puzzling nonresponse to his recent confession of love. He didn't enjoy that.

Hurt welled up in him, and he felt like a fool. Lenny gazed down at Daniela seated on the floor, so self-contained, so sure of herself. He couldn't hold back. "Why in hell did you wait so long to tell me you'd dated the dean?"

"That again? It was only once."

"What else haven't you told me?"

Daniela looked up. "What's this all about?"

"Lying."

"I didn't lie? I just didn't tell you something of no importance, that's all."

"That the same as lying."

"No it's not," Daniela said. "And aren't there things about your past that you haven't told me about?"

Lenny thought about the dying boxer, the fake language. "Uh…"

"What about this Sasha person you talk lovingly to in your sleep?"

"Uh…"

Daniela pushed the bag off her lap, jumped up and stomped away.

"I'm sorry, Daniela. I'm in a pissy mood."

She stopped, turned around and put her hands on her hips. "And that gives you the right to put me in a pissy mood?"

"Uh… I guess not."

Daniela padded barefoot to booth number twelve, sat down, shook the *New York Times* open and disappeared behind it.

While a fresh pot of coffee was brewing and Daniela had her face buried into the newspaper, Lenny folded one of the drier exam masters into a paper boat and wrote across it in red, "Let's sail away to Tahiti." He pushed the boat under the *Times*. He heard a quiet giggle, but the newspaper didn't come down.

Lenny said, "I've been stressed out since I got fired."

"I know."

"It's not much fun to lose one's job."

Rattle of newspaper. "I know."

"Have you ever lost a job?" Lenny asked.

"No, but I soon might. Some capitalist pig is buying WDRK and bringing in his own people, so I'll probably get the boot as soon as the deal goes through."

"I'm sorry. How long have you known this?"

"About a week," Daniela said, lowering paper and then raising it again.

"Why didn't you tell me?"

"You have your own troubles. I would be losing a job that I don't like, but you've lost a job you loved and possibly your whole career along with it. It's different."

Lenny pulled the newspaper down, leaned forward and kissed Daniela on the forehead. "You should have told me."

She dropped the paper, stood up, put her arms around Lenny and kissed him.

He said, "I think I know exactly what'll cheer both of us up." He sat down, pulled Daniela onto his lap and cupped her left breast.

"Not yet," she said, pulling his hand away. "Let's talk first."

"That's exactly what I was thinking," Lenny said. "Guys hate to get into a sweaty, intimate situation before they've had a nice long heart-to-heart with their partner."

Daniela pinched Lenny's nose, then ran her fingers through his hair. She picked up the paper boat and reread the invitation to Tahiti, then set the boat on her head as a hat. "Let's run away to Tahiti."

"Let's run away to France and join a circus," Lenny said. "Can you ride a horse bareback?"

"I've never tried. Why do you ask?"

"I'd like to see you on a horse, bareback. Also naked."

Daniela shifted her weight on Lenny's lap. "There's hard evidence that you are indeed picturing me naked. It seems we've moved out of the long, heartfelt conversational stage and have progressed to the next one."

"Yup."

Lenny carried Daniela to the futon, swept the papers to the floor, lay her down, and the restaurant began to rotate.

It started out with a jolt, then spun with fury, faster and faster.

They heard a thump and rumble from the freezer room.

"What was that?" Daniela asked.

"No idea."

The restaurant slowed, then jerked to a stop with a grinding of gears.

Lenny and Daniela hurried to the freezer room. Boxes of frozen boysenberries had tumbled to the floor and broken open. Ripped bags lay everywhere.

Lenny bent over, scooped up a handful of cold berries and put them into his mouth. "We have our work cut out for us."

"What work?"

"The berries."

Daniela hesitated. "You mean we have to put them back?"

Lenny shook his head and ate another handful of berries. "Not the broken bags."

"So?"

Another handful of berries. "So, we can't let them go to waste. Start eating."

"Sure," Daniela said, getting into the spirit of things. "I'm guessing there are maybe a hundred torn bags. We'll divide them up. I get fifty, and you get fifty, minus those three mouthfuls you've already eaten."

Lenny shook his head. "Sixty/forty. I'm bigger than you."

Daniela put on her angry look, which Lenny recognized as the one she so often applied to her co-anchor. "No way. It's fifty-fifty or nothing."

"Okay, fifty-fifty," Lenny said, examining his blue fingers, his blue T-shirt, his bare blue toes. "The stuff stains."

"Yup," Daniela said, and stripped off her clothes. So did Lenny.

She ate a big handful of berries, then a second, then a third, but had to spit out the fourth.

By now Daniela's lips and chin were blue, and so were both her hands, her knees, her feet. She reached out and painted Lenny's nose with her forefinger.

He did the same to her.

Daniela drew wavy blue lines across Lenny's forehead.

He did the same to her.

She picked up a handful of berries and rubbed them across both of his shoulders. He shivered from the cold.

He did the same to her, but included her breasts.

Then each grabbed a handful of berries, stepped back and threw. Lenny missed, but Daniela hit him squarely in the mouth.

He wiped his lips, scooped up berries in both hands and slathered them all over Daniela's body, concentrating this time on her tummy and thighs. Especially her thighs.

She slapped boysenberries into his hair.

Lenny grabbed a double handful of berries with the intention of giving Daniela a total-body boysenberry-wash, then slipped and fell. His butt hit a pile of half-frozen bags with a *whoosh* that sprayed their contents in all directions.

Daniela paused, arms raised, both hands filled with ammo. "Rule number 43.5.1: Any berries sat upon while naked go into the sitter's own mouth."

"Fair enough."

Then Lenny pulled Daniela off her feet, and they made messy and shivering love in the melting pool of pulp, packaging and blue juice.

Again Lenny wanted to tell Daniela that he loved her, but thought the time and place inappropriate.

Enjoy the moment, he told himself. Enjoy the moment in the archaic sense.

Blue from head to foot, chilled to the bone, they stumbled to Lenny's futon, skimming slush off as they went, and climbed under the covers.

Daniela said, "This is going to turn your sheets blue."

"That's okay. The stuff will wash out."

The stuff didn't wash out—not from the sheets, not from Lenny and not from Daniela. They showered together for a half hour, rubbing soap onto each other, sometimes cursing and sometimes laughing. Finally they gave up on de-bluing their bodies, went back to bed and fell into a deep blue sleep.

Lenny awoke a couple hours later, rolled onto his stomach, looked down at the dean's ugly stadium and remembered that just a few hours earlier he'd told Daniela that he loved her. He remembered her response, which had been no response at all. What had he been thinking? Daniela was hanging out with him just for the sex and laughs. Years later, she and her friends would giggle about boysenberries and frozen lobster tails. What an idiot I am, Lenny thought. *Idiot, idiota, idios.*

He slipped back to sleep and dreamed he was searching in desperate slow motion through circus tents for Daniela-the-Bareback-Rider, but he couldn't find her anywhere.

When he awoke, Daniela was sitting upright beside him. She said, "Are you ever going to tell me why you keep that pair of torn boxing gloves hanging by your bed?"

Lenny grunted. Of course he wouldn't. He didn't want to chase away the woman he loved.

Who didn't love him back.

He slipped off the futon, pulled on his jeans and padded barefoot to the window. The college band was marching on the city's baseball field, which had rotated into view during the night. Lenny was hurt, frustrated, humiliated. But he was mostly angry now, both at Daniela and himself. He turned back toward her. She looked so contained, so sturdy, so sure of herself. The beautiful got special treatment, floated above ugliness and strife and rejection, lived on a fleecy white cloud. Lenny wondered how many men had fallen in love with Daniela, how many had confessed their love, how many she'd ignored, disappointed, humiliated, angered.

"The gloves hanging over the futon are the ones I wore that night twenty years ago when I killed a man in the ring."

There, he'd said it.

Daniela's jaw dropped.

"I sliced them up afterwards."

Daniela didn't move.

"I didn't mean to hurt him."

Daniela blinked twice. Opened her mouth, closed it. Blinked again.

Lenny turned back to the window and watched the college band form a 'G' for 'Ghurkin,' then a 'C' for 'College.'

Lenny swung back to Daniela. "I lied just now. I did mean to hurt him. He taunted me and made fun of the junkyard and my father's bushy beard. He got laughs from ringside. Dad toweled me off and said the jerk was just trying to distract me because he was over-matched. So just ignore him. But I didn't ignore him. As soon as the bell rang, I jumped up and hit the guy harder than I'd ever hit anyone. He..."

Lenny turned back to the window. The band was dispersing.

'Disperse' came from the Latin *disperses,* which was the past participle of *dispergere* ('to scatter'). Lenny wanted everyone in the world to disperse. He wanted to be alone. Well, not completely alone. Daniela could stay.

But he wanted her to say something. He wanted her to stand up and hug him, to tell him that everything was all right, that she understood, that he'd been just a teenager, that she loved him.

But she didn't.

"He died the next day," Lenny said, turning back to Daniela.

She picked up her clothes and carried them to the bathroom. When she came out, she was dressed, her hair a tangle, tears streaking her face.

"Do you want to talk about it?" Lenny said and held his arms out to hug her.

Daniela shook her head and hurried to the elevator.

Lenny heard the door open and close, the elevator whine. And that was that.

He went to the window and watched the clouds pass by. He tried without success to remember the derivation of 'window,' then 'cloud,' but his mind kept coming back to what had just happened. Why had Daniela reacted so oddly? Why had she said nothing? Was she angry? Shocked? Disappointed?

In any case, there was one thing he was sure of: Daniela would never want to see him again.

A half-hour later he dragged himself to the bathroom, splashed water on his face, wiped his cheeks and chin and then looked into the mirror. In neat letters at the bottom of the mirror, penned by a finger dipped in boysenberry juice, the message read, "I [heart] U 2."

CHAPTER 34

Nikken di hacha

"Fate is chance."

Billy Butcher eased into the parking lot and shut off the engine. In the dim street light, he could just make out a sign reading "Moon View Revolving Restaurant, A Revolution in Dining!" He reached into the glove compartment, pulled out a microfiber cloth and ran it across the dashboard. He loved his silvery new BMW—V8 engine, soft leather seats, every gadget and gizmo you could imagine. He'd earned the down payment from a hit on the owner of a pizza restaurant, some bumblefuck caught boinking the wife of a Cleveland underboss. Make the guy suffer, Billy had been instructed, so he'd wrapped him in duct tape and, with a pizza paddle, pushed him inch by inch into the oven.

Billy spotted a light in the restaurant. It was already past midnight, but The Lobsterman must still be awake. Is he looking down? Can he see me? Billy slipped lower in his seat. He'd made his employer double his fee, but was that enough? This was The Lobsterman, after all. Billy tossed the cleaning cloth back into the glove compartment.

He'd eaten here once, that time when he'd met a man from

Providence about a hit on a bookie. But all the guy had offered was a shitty two grand. Billy had turned it down. The food had been shitty too. The menu bragged that the lobster arrived daily from Maine, but Billy was pretty sure it was frozen. The asparagus was soggy and the baked potato hard in the center. But the cobbler was tasty, some kind of purple berry.

Billy glanced at the bomb on the seat beside him. Normally he didn't mess with explosives, but orders were orders. The blast was supposed to be a hit from some pissed-off football fan. Billy didn't know how the hell his employer would get that information out to the public, but it wasn't his worry. He guessed it had something to do with how he'd been ordered to break into The Lobsterman's office and scribble death threats on the wall.

The job's paying pretty good, Billy told himself, but he was disappointed he wouldn't get credit within his professional circle for killing The Lobsterman, for turning him into lobster meat.

Lobsterman to lobster meat—Billy liked that. He smiled to himself and slipped lower in his seat.

*   *   *

The restaurant started to rotate, and Lenny braced his hands against the sides of the shower stall. For the past fifteen minutes, he'd been scrubbing at the berry stains on his face and neck. No luck, but what the hell. Nothing could bother him tonight: the berry stains, the gyrating eatery, his lost job, his lost reputation. What did all that matter? Daniela loved him. He saw a great future for them together—kids, grandkids, traveling through Europe, a sweet old age.

The restaurant slowed, and Lenny went back to scrubbing, his mood shifting. Life was almost too good now. Whenever something positive happened to him, something worse soon followed. He thought in particular of the old Plymouth from the salvage yard his dad had fixed up for him, and how his first outing in it—driving with no license—had been a date with a highly cooperative cheerleader. Just two days later, he killed his opponent in the ring.

The good, then the bad, the very bad.

Lenny closed his eyes, let water run down his face.

'Opponent' had arrived in the English language from the Latin *opponentem*, with the present particle *opponere* meaning "to object to, to oppose."

*   *   *

Billy looked up at the restaurant turning around and around. He shook his head. If The Lobsterman wasn't awake before, he sure as hell was now. For the next hour, Billy kept his eyes on the windows but saw no sign of the guy. Time to get moving, he told himself. He picked up the bomb—gently, because these things had to be treated with respect—eased the door open, stepped outside and waited.

Again, no one appeared at the window.

Billy slipped across the parking lot to Lenny's Chevy, knelt on the blacktop, set the bomb down and picked the lock on the driver's side. He pulled the squeaking door open an inch, waited, an inch more, waited again. After the door was fully open, Billy leaned in and set the bomb on the driver's-side floor. It was a crude device, built by a man Billy had used once before to blow the windows out of a laundromat to warn its owner to pay his gambling debts. But this explosive was much bigger, wrapped in gray duct tape and with wires sticking out all over the place. Billy thought it looked like a cartoon bomb. Still, it would do the job—Lobsterman to lobster meat.

Billy chuckled.

He took several deep breaths, then eased the switch to ON. Holy shit! The damn lever almost came off in his hand! What a piece of crap! Gently, an inch at a time, Billy slid the bomb under the driver's seat. The bombmaker said it would take a pretty hard bump in the road to set the thing off, but Billy wasn't taking any chances.

He closed the door as quietly as possible, then scurried in a crouch back toward his BMW. He smiled at the way the street light reflected off the long silver hood. With this job, he could either head out for a week in Vegas or pay off the car.

Vegas, he decided. Take your fun while you can.

He climbed into the driver's seat, put his finger on the starter, then let his hand drop. Why miss all the fun? Sure, they'd show all this on TV, but by the time the camera crew got to the scene, the Chevy would be just a smoldering wreck, with doors and chunks of scorched metal scattered all over hell. Body parts, too, but they wouldn't film them, which was a shame. So sleep in the car and tomorrow morning drive a safe distance behind the Lobsterman until he hit the first big bump, watch the car and driver blown sky high, then do a quick U-turn and get the hell away.

Billy backed the BMW into a dark corner of the parking lot at the space reserved for Milton Mickelson, Vice President, Weeblecrank Insurance Company. Billy wondered if that's the outfit that insured The Lobsterman's car. That would be a nice irony. Billy loved irony.

*   *   *

Lenny stepped out of the shower and toweled himself off in front of a floor-length mirror. Although he'd gained a few pounds, he was still in good shape. He wasn't happy about the size of his head, though. Still, Daniela had twice called him handsome. Ruggedly handsome, in fact. 'Rugged'—what's the source of that word?

*   *   *

Billy Butcher was fighting back sleep when he noticed two large figures coming toward him. Billy came alive fast and pulled his pistol from his belt. Holy shit, was one of them The Lobsterman? No, neither was big enough. A beefy pair, though. Wide shoulders like football players. Goofy brown bangs. Looked like brothers.

What in hell are they doing here?

Uh, oh!

Both carried knives. Had The Lobsterman sent them?

Holy shit!

Billy raised his gun. Shoot them?

No, just get the hell out of here.

He reached for the starter, but then the pair veered off and headed for the Chevy. Billy guessed they hadn't seen him. He leaned back and tucked the pistol into his belt.

One guy knelt at the front left tire, the other at the rear. They jabbed their knives into the sidewalls.

Billy heard them laugh.

What the hell!

They hurried around the car, apparently to slash the tires on the far side, then ran giggling out of the parking lot.

Billy watched the Chevy settle onto its rims. It was lucky for those two dipshits that it took more than that to trigger the bomb.

Who the hell were they, anyway?

And now what? The car wasn't drivable. The Lobsterman would have to call a truck to cart it to a garage for new tires. The first big bump, and the Chevy would explode and take out the truck driver too. That would be fun to watch, Billy told himself, but he didn't want to waste a bomb.

He checked the restaurant windows, saw no one, then eased himself out of the car and scurried in a crouch to the Chevy. He pulled the door open and carefully, very carefully, slid the bomb out from under the seat and flipped the loose toggle switch to OFF.

He let out his breath, picked up the bomb in both hands, tiptoed back to his car, lay the bomb on the floor of the passenger side, started the engine and drove away.

What a clusterfuck.

*   *   *

Lenny sat in his shorts at booth number three, a book open on his lap. The first mention of 'rugged' that he could find dated from about 1300, when the word meant 'shaggy' and usually referred to animals. Later, 'rugged' came to mean 'robust.' Lenny flipped to 'robust.' It came into English in the mid-16ᵗʰ century from the Middle French term *rubuste*, and farther back to the Latin *robustus*, which literally meant 'strong as oak.' Lenny liked that. A massive oak had stood in the middle of the salvage yard. Lenny thumbed to 'oak' and found a note card with 'poontang' scribbled across it, left over from Lenny's first meeting with the Sprocket brothers.

Lenny looked up. He wished now he'd reported them to the authorities for sabotaging Gerry Gerbil's ropes. Didn't they know they could have hurt someone? He was glad he'd seen the last of the troublesome brothers. A mean-spirited and worthless pair, he told himself, and a menace to society.

*   *   *

Billy drove out of the parking lot and turned toward the center of town. He was a bit disappointed that the bomb hadn't blown the Chevy to pieces along with the two giggling delinquents. Still, it was better this way. Later on he'd find a way to use the device on The Lobsterman. Besides, now that he thought about it, the blast might have spattered his new car with chunks of metal and blood and guts. He'd feel like shit if something ever happened to it.

Billy passed under a street light and noticed a streak of dust on the dash. He reached into the glove compartment, grabbed the cleaning cloth, then glanced at the floor.

Holy shit!

The toggle switch was jiggling like a stripper's ass!

Billy dropped the cloth, eased the car to the curb, turned off the engine and stared at the bomb.

The switch was halfway between OFF and ON.

Hop out and haul ass? No, his fingerprints were on the bomb. And the car was registered to him.

And if the damn thing explodes, there goes his silver BMW!

Billy held his breath, reached down, squeezed the toggle switch between thumb and forefinger, and gently, very gently, moved it to OFF.

The switch came free.

Billy held it up at eye level.

"HOLY SHIT!!!"

*   *   *

Time for bed, Lenny told himself. He lay his etymological dictionary on the edge of the booth and climbed onto his futon.

KA-BOOM!

A bright orange flash rattled the windows. The room shook.

Lenny rushed to look outside.

Something was burning just a few blocks away.

He grabbed his binoculars off a shelf and focused on the blaze.

It was a car burning, its roof peeled back, the doors blown open. Something lay in the middle of the street. A body? No, not a body, more like a sack of something. He refocused.

But the thing had arms and legs! It was a body!

With no head!

Lenny stumbled to booth number six, dropped into the seat and called 911. His fingers shook.

When he was about ten, a tow truck had pulled a scorched Lincoln Continental into the junkyard, still stinking of smoke and burned flesh. Gas fumes had triggered the explosion. A family of four had perished. Probably what happened tonight, Lenny reasoned.

The operator said the incident had already been called in.

Lenny set the phone down. Who had died tonight? A guy driving home after working late? A teenage boy coming back from a date? Someone with the munchies on their way to a convenience store for a bag of potato chips?

Lenny thought of the dead boxer and the headless Juan, of the scorched Lincoln sitting in the salvage yard next to the big oak tree.

Lenny pulled the etymological dictionary toward him and opened it on his lap. The origins of 'oak' were uncertain, with a string of unpleasant-sounding candidates: Proto-Germanic *aiks*, Old Norse *eik*, Old Frisian, *ek*, etc.

The oak in the salvage yard had been beautiful, strong, soothing. Lenny pictured himself back there as a kid, climbing the lower branches covered in the first leaves of spring, watching Studebaker bark at squirrels. Lenny had driven past the yard a few months earlier. The junk cars with their flat tires had been hauled away, the rows of bumpers and fenders removed, the mobile home missing. The oak, too. Not even its stump showed. A sign out front displayed a gleaming row of garden apartments. Lenny guessed that was the way the world worked. Everything changed.

Lenny thought of the person who'd just died, how their life had changed and the life of their loving family and friends. It brought tears to his eyes.

CHAPTER 35

Cutkoske bleefuma

"Lobster thieves"

Lenny lay awake for the rest of the night, haunted by the image of the burning car and the headless figure sprawled in the street. He rose late and turned on his television in preparation for News at Noon. A commercial appeared for Skammer's Wishy-Washy Laundry and its dancing undies. Lenny circled the booths, fingering exams and lesson plans. The dry ones went into file folders, the damp ones he turned over. After his circuit, he returned to the television, picked up a dumbbell and started pumping.

Bradley's hair stuck up in back. Daniela said the makeup woman deliberately spiked his cowlick.

Daniela looked troubled. Also a bit blue.

The paper shook in her hand. "Police Chief Bart Skammer has just released a statement stating that last night's car explosion resulted in a man's death—"

"A man's decapitation," Bradley said, then added in explanation, "He lost his head."

Daniela glared at him. She'd told Lenny that, as senior anchor,

Bradley had it written into his contract that he chose which stories he got to report and which went to her. As retaliation for her not sleeping with him, he gave her anything dealing with violence and gore.

Daniela continued where she'd left off: "Dental records have identified the victim as Jeremy Hepplesworth III, also known as Tommy Slash, Fred Gunner and Billy Butcher. Chief Skammer has stated that his department is pursing the matter as a mob hit in light of the victim's long criminal record and the nature of the killing."

A dead mobster!

A bomb!

Lenny dropped the dumbbell with a clank and stood up.

Meant for me?

*　　*　　*

Dean Sheepslappe watched the television news from the luxury box in the empty stadium. He liked to hang out there when he had something to work through. Also, the place reminded him that the season's first conference football game was this Saturday, a much-anticipated event.

With the obstructionist Lenny Thorson off the faculty, Tom and Titus Sprocket were both credited with A's in French for the previous semester and thereby ruled eligible to compete on the gridiron. Lenny's replacement was unbelievably compliant, the dean thought, but also a weenie and—in spite of everything—not nearly as likeable as Lenny.

Who nevertheless still had to die. No more screwing around after last night's fiasco. Get rid of him and later on Charlie and Daniela. It was a shame to whack a babe like that, a real shame, but did he have any choice? Certainly not. Anyone in his situation would do the same.

What had gone wrong? Had the bomb detonated by accident?

Maybe. But where was Billy Butcher going when he was killed? The police report said he'd been driving away from Lenny's place when the blast went off. Had the idiot gotten lost?

Or had The Lobsterman somehow set Billy up to blow his own head off?

The dean let out a low whistle. That had to be it. The Lobsterman was a genius.

At least nothing can be traced back to me, the dean assured himself. Luther either, because his police-chief brother will handle the investigation. It'll cost a few thousand but was well worth it.

Dean Sheepslappe's phone buzzed.

It was Luther, who cleared his throat and mumbled, "That didn't go so well."

"It sure as hell didn't. Does your brother know what really happened?"

"Nope. But I'm thinking Billy screwed up. He wasn't the brightest bulb," Luther said, then chuckled mucously. "I guess we could say he didn't have much of a head on his shoulders."

The dean waited for Luther to stop snorting, then said, "More likely the Lobsterman sabotaged the device. I don't know how he did it, but he did."

A long pause, then Luther said, "You're probably right."

"I know I'm right, which means it's time to put my plan in operation."

"Yeah, I know. I've already briefed my guy who just got back."

"Just got back from where?"

"Concord," Luther said.

"The prison?"

"Where else? He stole a truck and got caught fencing the stuff to a bunch of restaurants. It was frozen seafood, crappy wine, bags of tea and some kind of weird berry."

"You're pitting a loser like that against The Lobsterman?"

"Okay, you tell me," Luther said, his voice filling with menace. "Who you got for the job? Some bearded old fart of a history professor with horn-rimmed glasses? Or maybe a lady librarian with bad ankles? For now, it's my guy plus a couple men from my construction crew along with the two shooters I'll hire from Chicago if they let me. If so, it'll cost a bundle, because Chicago's still pissed about the two Bobs. Anyway, you got a problem with that?"

"None. None whatsoever."

The dean pocketed his phone. He knew better than to argue with Luther when he was angry. Or not angry.

The sun had slipped behind a bank of gray clouds. More rain, the dean thought. At least the long-range weather report predicted dry skies for the reenactment.

The dean rode the elevator to the ground and walked to the center of the field. He took a deep breath and felt himself back in his glory days on the gridiron. Last summer he'd come here a couple times late at night to do wind sprints, but the next day found himself falling asleep at his desk. And they'd been more like wind shuffles than sprints. Only forty-eight and he felt like an old man, but after he'd pocketed what Luther owed him and moved someplace warm, then he'd take up jogging, buy a bike, swim in the ocean. The dean touched his stomach. Maybe lose a bit of weight.

He circled inside the stadium, and on his last trip around, noticed a long crack in the north wall, directly below the luxury boxes and wide enough for his hand to fit inside. He reached in and pulled out a fistful of chalky material that crumbled in his fingers like a stale lemon scone. Rotten cement, the dean said to himself. Rotten cement from a rotten contractor. The world was full of crooks.

CHAPTER 36

Omukoo

"Anger"

Lenny turned on his television, pressed the mute button and circled the restaurant, testing exam papers and syllabuses for moisture. Every minute or two he glanced at his watch because he didn't want to miss Daniela on the noon news. The night before, they'd shared a pizza, had a tumble on the futon, then she'd gone home. Lenny missed her.

But he had renewed doubts. Should he really get involved with a woman that beautiful and ambitious and who would always make so much more money than he did? As her fortunes increased and his at best stagnated, would she outgrow him? If they stayed together—got married even—and if he ever succeeded in returning to teaching, would the day come when he'd return home in his jacket with the shiny elbows and the unstylish wide blue necktie with the tartar-sauce stain, wearing glumphy shoes and carrying a briefcase filled with ungraded French quizzes, to find her giving him the same look his mother had given his father when he came home coated in rust and grime from a long day at Jake's Salvage Yard? Would she yearn for toothsome Nelson Scuttlewood the Third? Lenny feared so.

And did he really want to spend the rest of his life escorting an überbabe who'd be asked for a selfie wherever she went? All his life, Lenny had wanted nothing more than to be invisible. He'd spent a lot of time alone in a salvage yard surrounded by incurious piles of car parts.

Noon. Lenny pressed the mute button to bring back the sound. "Good afternoon. I'm Bradley Noyze, and this is today's news. Daniela, my junior assistant will not be with us today."

Lenny dropped into booth number three, picked up a slice of pizza left over from the night before and smiled at what Daniela's reaction would be when he told her that Bradley had referred to her as his junior assistant.

Bradley said "Iran" when he meant "Iraq" and twice referred to White House Press Secretary Anna Hiller as "Hanna Miller." Lenny heard off-camera laughter, probably from the hair girl who hated Bradley. Today his coif was particularly spiky, and again Lenny smiled.

Then he distinctly remembered that Daniela had said she'd be working today, and he stopped smiling. He hoped she wasn't sick. Lenny looked at his half-eaten pizza slice. She'd had two pieces last evening before driving home. He hoped the mushrooms weren't bad.

He was taking out his phone to call Daniela just as it dinged a snippet of Beethoven's Fifth. It was the WDRK station manager. He apologized for disturbing Lenny, but said Daniela had given him this number to call in an emergency. Was she there? No? Do you know where she is? No? She wasn't answering at home either, the man said.

Lenny called Daniela's cell, then her home number. No answer. He pulled his jeans over his boxer shorts and again phoned Daniela, hopping on one foot as he did. Again no answer. He tugged his drunken Gerry Gerbil T-shirt over his head, grabbed a bagel and hurried to the elevator, chewing as he ran.

Lenny pushed the Chevy with its four new tires to shimmying speed and well beyond, but it still took eighteen minutes to reach Daniela's apartment at the far side of New Skalvik. He circled her block twice for a parking spot, found none, and steered his Chevy up onto the sidewalk in front of a Starbucks, exchanged looks with a startled customer, and jogged up the hill to Daniela's apartment.

He arrived out of breath and scared.

He pressed her buzzer once, twice, three times and then leaned on it for a full minute. No response.

He tapped the top button of the list of occupants. The name *Tom Smith* sounded friendly, but its owner wasn't. "If the lady's not home," Tom Smith said, "then why the hell do you need to get into the building? Get lost, dickhead."

Melinda Davis in the top-floor apartment told Lenny that he was a crackhead trying to break in and steal her Hummel figurines, and he had just ten seconds to leave or she'd call the police.

Lenny buzzed G. T. W. Ogglethorpe and claimed to have a flower delivery. G. T. W. Ogglethorpe said he was allergic to flowers and asked they be returned to the florist. At least he was polite.

Fuck it. Lenny leaned back, then rammed his shoulder into the door. Wood splintered, glass flew and the door banged open. Lenny scrambled inside and raced down the hall to Daniela's apartment. He would break that door down too.

He didn't need to. The molding around the lock was cracked.

Lenny pushed the door open, bent down and picked up a woman's pink slipper.

A few feet farther, a broken blue mug sat in a puddle of coffee. Lenny leaned down and touched the liquid. It was lukewarm.

A wooden chair lay upside down in the living room. Books and a tulip vase had slid off the coffee table, but Lenny saw no other signs of a struggle and—to his relief—no blood.

He pulled out his phone to tap in 911 just as Daniela's landline rang. Lenny hesitated, then answered.

"I seen you break down the front door, big guy. Pretty impressive for a professor."

"Who the hell are you?" Lenny shouted.

"I've been watching from across the street to see if some neighbor had heard the commotion from earlier and called the cops. It looks like they didn't, or maybe they did hear and didn't give a flying fuck. Anyway, you'd better not call the cops either, because my boss will know about it in ten in minutes. He's got contacts all over."

"Hurt her and I'll kill you!"

The man whistled. "Tough talk. But you'd have to find me first."

"What the fuck do you want?"

"What I want—or what the party I work for wants—is for Charlie Fox to cooperate with us. Then you'll get the lady back, and we'll all go on our merry way and forget about this little incident."

Lenny doubted it would be that easy. "Cooperate how?"

"He's gotta give up his inheritance and let the island go to Grace Skammer, the rightful party in the first place. By the way, Charlie's gonna get a couple hundred thousand for his effort. The people I represent play fair."

"*Play fair!* You just kidnapped an innocent woman!"

"Yeah, well, we all have our little failings, don't we? Anyway, we'll have a lawyer draw up the paperwork for Charlie to sign. Then he can live happily ever after, just as long as he and you and the lady keep your fucking mouths shut."

"How can I trust you bastards? The minute Charlie signs the paper, how do I know you won't shoot the three of us and dump our bodies in the ocean?"

"Because the switch will be made—your little lady in exchange for the inheritance—right in front of a couple thousand witnesses."

"What in hell are you talking about?" Lenny said.

"You're gonna take part in that jerk-off battle out at that college where you was fired from, right?"

"No," Lenny said.

"Well, you are now. After the shooting ends and everyone goes into the stadium to watch the Red Coats surrender, that's when we'll make the switch, right there on the fifty-yard line, with a couple thousand spectators and a half dozen TV cameras."

"Why there?"

"Because my boss don't trust you not to go ape shit and start killing our guys like you've gotten into the habit of doing."

"Killing your guys? What are you talking about?"

"I'm talking about Bob One and Billy Butcher and how you busted up Bob Two."

"I don't know what in hell you're talking about."

"I figured you'd say that, professor. Anyway, like I said, keep your mouth shut and don't go to the cops, or your lady will disappear forever. We'll have some of our people all dressed up like soldiers, and they'll handle the exchange, right there at the surrender table in the middle of the stadium. We'll all have a swell time. You know— floats, marching bands, fancy uniforms, cannons firing, ladies in historic costumes. I can hardly wait. I love stuff like that."

"Who the hell are you?"

"You asked that before."

"I'm asking again, goddamn it," Lenny said.

"Just someone doing his job."

"For whom do you work?"

"'For whom?' That's classy. I don't deal much with guys who say 'whom.' You must be real smart—or real stupid if you think I'm gonna answer you."

The phone went dead.

It had been a stupid question and an unnecessary one. Lenny didn't need to be told for whom the goon worked. He already knew.

In fury and frustration, Lenny grabbed a ceramic table lamp and hurled it against the wall. Shards flew. He pushed the television set off its stand, kicked the coffee table and broke its glass. He punched a hole in the wall. He picked up a laptop and was ready to hurl it through a window when it occurred to him that everything he was destroying belonged to Daniela.

This made him even angrier, angrier than he'd been in years.

CHAPTER 37

Kuchin

"Pain"

Lenny roared down the road to Charlie's farm, the gas pedal to the floor, the Chevy rattling and shaking and smoking. He thumped the steering wheel with the side of his fist. "*Shit! Shit! Shit!*"

He was angry and hot and out of control.

He could hear his father shouting from the corner of the ring: "Get ahold of yourself, Lenny! He's just trying to get to you!"

But Jimmy did get to him, and a minute later he lay dying.

Again, Lenny pounded the steering wheel. "*Shit! Shit! Shit!*"

'Shit' was first used in the 14th century, taken from the Old English nouns *scite* (dung) and *scitte* (diarrhea). Others insist that the word derived from the days of sailing ships when…

Lenny looked up to see that he'd drifted to the side of road. A mailbox loomed. He knocked it over.

"*Shit!*"

He cranked the wheel to the left.

The Chevy slid sideways and uprooted another mailbox.

Lenny steered the car back onto the road, lifted his foot off the accelerator and glanced into the rearview mirror. He had to turn around and leave groveling apologies and a promise to reimburse the owners.

It was the right thing to do.

But he wouldn't do it.

He was in too much of a hurry, and too much was at stake. He wanted to get to the farm as soon as possible to comfort Charlie, who'd choked up on the phone when told of Daniela's abduction.

Besides, Lenny felt that he'd gone through life apologizing and doing the right thing too much of the time, backing away from conflict, giving in too often—to his dad, to Elspeth, the dean and everyone else.

Lenny took careful aim at the next mailbox. He hit it dead center. It flew end over end. He swung to the left side of the road and rammed another mailbox, then turned back to the right and slammed into a fourth, a fifth, a sixth.

After five minutes and five more mailboxes, Lenny swung into Charlie's driveway. Sally's car was gone. At work, Lenny guessed. Good. He wanted to talk to Charlie alone.

Lenny stepped out of the smoking Chevy and walked around to its front. The grill was bashed, the bumper twisted, and Lenny felt a great sense of accomplishment.

His phone chimed. "Yes?"

"It's a nice sunny day, isn't it?"

Lenny recognized the gravelly voice of the man who'd called him in Daniela's apartment. "How did you get my number?"

"Does it matter? I just called to say I hope you're enjoying the fine weather. Oh, yeah, and also to say you're real smart not to go to the cops. But don't change your mind, you or Charlie. Otherwise... well, use your imagination."

"You bastard! If you hurt Daniela, I'll—"

"Have a nice day."

The phone went dead.

Lenny found Charlie in the barn, slumped on a bench, oiling a halter.

Charlie didn't look up. "I remember her from when she was just a little girl, her hair in pigtails, her knees always skinned. I taught her how to whistle and…"

Charlie stopped talking and shook his head. He took out a red handkerchief, dabbed his eyes, blew his nose, then looked up. "I want to kill someone."

"So do I."

"Still think we shouldn't go to the police?"

"The goon who snatched Daniela called again. He says he'll know if we do."

Charlie looked up. "Luther's got contacts all over, and his brother's the chief of police."

Lenny sat on a folding chair. "We need a plan."

"Damn right we need a plan. What've you got in mind?"

"Not much yet. I'm too pissed to think."

"You look it," Charlie said. He stood up and hooked the harness over a nail. "Let's go up the hill to Oscar's grave. A walk will calm you down."

"No, it won't."

"Then it'll calm me down."

Charlie led Lenny away from the barn and up the grassy slope to where Oscar was buried under a massive old oak. Charlie and Lenny sat in the shade and watched the neighbor's sheltie chase a pair of squawking Canada geese around and around the pond.

Charlie patted the ground beside him. "I'm glad Oscar's not here to know the trouble Daniela's in. He worshipped her. He always said she…"

Charlie stopped talking.

Lenny tried to say something to soothe Charlie but couldn't. His throat had closed tight, and his heart was pounding the way it had before a fight.

But he wasn't in the ring. He was on a sunny hillside overlooking a calendar version of the perfect farm scene: pond, puppy, geese, cattails, meadow.

After a long silence, Lenny said, "Even if you cooperate, they plan on killing us—you, me, Daniela."

"I know."

"It'll be at the surrender ceremony, after you've signed the paper and they've turned Daniela over to us. They can't kill us in front of all the spectators and TV cameras, but will later, after they've hustled us out the stadium. They'll make it look like an accident."

"I know that too," Charlie said, then added, "I'll get Andy to help us. He took a bullet through the butt in Iraq, and I dragged him to safety. So he owes me. Besides, his job at the courthouse bores the living *ool* out of him."

"Good. I'll bring in Henri because he's on the reenactment planning committee."

"I can't hide this from Sally. She'll insist on coming along."

"Sign her up," Lenny said. "I'll talk to The Widow Bahr."

"Why her?"

"She pays for the rented horses and wagon for the reenactment."

"So?"

"She told Henri that the dean asked for a second wagon this year, a covered one. I'll see if she can find out what it's for."

Charlie was quiet for a moment. "I'll bet it has something to do with how they plan on sneaking us out of the stadium."

"That's my guess too," Lenny said and got to his feet. "You brief Sally. I'll talk to everyone else and tell them to get here at 8:00 sharp tomorrow morning. So let's get moving."

Charlie stood, gave Lenny a sloppy left-handed salute and followed him to his car. He pointed at a foot-long chunk of wood protruding from the grill. "How in hell did that get there?"

"Just a little accident," Lenny said. "*Ool* happens."

*   *   *

Lenny drove home, microwaved four lobster tails, tossed a spinach salad, sprinkled a half cup of boysenberries across the top, sat at booth number nine, ate one mouthful and pushed the plate away.

He stared out the window for a half hour, drank cup after cup of coffee, then grabbed pen and paper.

Where to start?

He'd felt bold and authoritative when talking to Charlie, but was now scared and irresolute.

'Irresolute' derived from...

Lenny reached for a book on etymology, hesitated, then pulled his hand back. Don't get distracted, he told himself, and don't panic. Just treat this like planning a new course. Take it step by step and everything will work out.

Except this was a case of life and death, not an effete survey course on the 19th century French novel. Plus, there was a good change nothing would work out.

List with each problem and its solution, Lenny told himself. He drew a line down the center of the paper, decided it looked crooked, crumpled the sheet, tore a fresh one from his notebook and drew a straighter line. But he scrunched that one up too and tossed it behind booth number ten.

This was much harder than planning a new course. Lenny got a third piece of paper, and the restaurant clicked and clanked and shuddered and turned.

Lenny gripped the edge of the table. It seemed that the place had been spinning faster lately, but maybe that was just his state of mind. He grabbed his coffee cup before it could slip off the table. His uneaten meal slid sideways and crashed to the floor.

The room rotated once more, jerked twice, then stopped with a clanking of gears.

Lenny leaned back and looked out the window. It was evident that Daniela had to be rescued sometime after Luther handed her over and before his goons forced the three of them into the back of a wagon. How long was that? Five minutes? Ten minutes?

Create a diversion? Fake a fight at the surrender table? Get other reenactors involved? But what would that accomplish? Luther's thugs would just turn the diversion to their advantage.

Henri might have an idea. He had a great imagination. Also, he'd be playing a British surgeon in the medical tent during the surrender ceremony.

The medical tent!

Lenny jumped to his feet. Of course! As soon as they released Daniela, he would make a noisy fuss about her health, sweep her up in his arms and rush her to the medical tent. The TV cameras would zoom in, unable to resist such drama. It would look like part of the act. Luther would be helpless to intervene. Lenny felt clever.

He got a broom and a dustpan, swept up the broken plate, leaned the broom against the booth, sat down and no longer felt so clever. Once he got Daniela into the tent, how was he going to smuggle her out the stadium? She couldn't just slip away unnoticed. Everyone knew her face from TV. People would crowd around and ask for selfies. Besides, Luther's men would be guarding the tent and the exits.

Start a riot? Maybe renew the fighting between the opposing armies? But how could he engineer that?

A helicopter rescue? No, the crowd would be too thick for a chopper to land. And where in hell would he get one?

Dig a secret tunnel ahead of time?

Yeah, sure.

Stupid ideas. Stupid, stupid ideas.

Lenny pondered the origin of 'tunnel.' He grabbed his etymological dictionary and thumbed to the T's. 'Tunnel: Probably early 15th century, from the Middle French term *tonnelle* ("net") or *tonel* ("cask") but some authorities maintain that...'

Lenny hurled the book across the restaurant, grabbed the boxing gloves off their hook, and pulled them on for the first time in twenty years. He hit the wall. The covering split, stuffing flew. Lenny kept punching. The wallboard creaked, cracked, caved. Lenny struck with wild fury. Pain stabbed up and down his forearms, and it felt good.

CHAPTER 38

Kurvaka

*"A life-size female figure used during the
Ceremony of the Return of the Summer Sun"*

The next morning, Lenny arrived at Charlie's barn with a sense of trepidation about the mission ahead of them. He also had a pounding, sleep-deprived headache. It wasn't yet 8:00 A.M. but almost everyone was already seated in a circle of folding chairs: Charlie, Sally, Andy Deezel and The Widow Bahr. Henri was late as usual. Lenny and Charlie had briefed everyone the evening before.

Angel Warrior kicked his stall to the rhythm of Lenny's thumping headache. Rain beat on the barn's metal roof. Thunder boomed, lightning flashed. Everyone had arrived drenched.

The barn smelled of hay and horse manure.

Sally poured Lenny a cup of coffee from a vacuum bottle and pointed at his sneakers, one gray, one black. "You look like something the cat dragged in. What were you up to last night?"

"Swearing, worrying, punching walls."

"We all were," Sally said, and sat back down next to Charlie.

He looked as wrecked as Lenny felt.

"Before we get started," Lenny said, "I just want to say that what we're involved in here is potentially quite dangerous, so if any of you have second thoughts, feel free to leave, and no one will think—"

"Get on with it," Charlie said. "You're making this sound like a bad caper movie."

Everyone muttered agreement.

Lenny shuffled through his pages of notes from the previous night. Too many, he thought, just like when he started a new course. "I've come up with some ideas, but I first want to hear yours."

Andy raised his hand, and for a moment Lenny felt himself back in front of a class. Andy was a short, smiley man with a rosy red face. "How come we don't just go to the police?"

"Good question. The thug who snatched Daniela keeps warning me not to. He said his boss has contacts all over the place. As you well know, Luther's brother is the police chief."

"Okay, then how about we grab someone ourselves?" Andy said. "We can't get up close to Luther on account of all the thugs protecting him, but we could maybe snatch the dean and make him tell us where they got Daniela hidden."

"We could if he were around," Sally said, "but he's in hiding until the reenactment."

Sally wore jeans and a baggy red flannel shirt of Charlie's. Her face was drawn, her hair a snarl.

"Then maybe we could lure him into a trap," Andy said brightly. "Tell him he's won the lottery, then grab him. I read how cops sometimes do that."

"The dean's not that stupid," Lenny said.

Andy looked at his hands.

"Sorry," Lenny said. "Sorry. I'm in a terrible mood."

Andy looked up. "Think we're not?"

Lenny took a sip of coffee, set the cup on the window sill and shuffled through his papers. The handwriting was a mess. Maybe the ideas too. "As you've already been told, they'll hand Daniela back as soon as Charlie signs the paper giving up the inheritance. That's when we—"

"Sorry!" Henri said, bursting through the door, briefcase in hand. He shook the rain off his Red Sox cap. "A bit late, *mon ami,* but the photocopier kept jamming."

Lenny introduced Henri to everyone.

He went from person to person, shaking hands and oozing charm. The Widow Bahr beamed and pulled a chair up next to her. He thanked her, sat down, opened his briefcase and handed Lenny some papers. "The latest reenactment schedule."

Lenny passed the copies around. It felt like the first day of class. Here's your syllabus, students. Study it carefully because this semester we're going to ignore linguistics and instead concentrate on saving an abductee. Warning: Some of us might get hurt or killed.

Lenny taped a drawing of the stadium to the wall. "As you can see, the building is shaped like a horseshoe, with the open end shown here to the right. Sally and Henri will be stationed in the British medical tent at the twenty-yard line near the open end. Andy will mingle with the Colonial forces at the other end of the stadium and keep in touch by phone with Sally. His job will be to find out if they really have Daniela with them, and—if so—who is guarding her."

"What do you want me to do?" The Widow Bahr asked.

"After the battle on the soccer field, the spectators and the reenactors will move to the stadium. The spectators will sit on the south side because the north half—that's at the top of the drawing— is closed for repairs. The British contingent—which will include Charlie and myself—will form up to the spectator's right, with the Colonial solders to the left, at the closed end of the stadium. After everyone's in place, Charlie and I will be summoned to the surrender table." Lenny turned to Henri. "Any idea who'll represent the Colonial forces?"

He shook his head. "The dean's keeping that a secret."

Lenny went back to the drawing. "Charlie will supposedly be signing the surrender paper but—as you well know—it'll in fact be a document giving up all rights to Harvey's will. Afterwards, Daniela gets handed over to us, and the dean will climb on his horse and lead his army around the inside of the stadium in a victory parade, followed by the marching band and floats. While everyone's attention is on the parade, it's my belief that some of Luther's goons, dressed as Colonial reenactors, will force Daniela, Charlie and myself at gunpoint into the back of a covered wagon and drive us away."

Andy raised his hand. "Where to?"

"Not someplace good."

No one spoke. Angel Warrior kicked the side of his stall, rain rattled on the roof, and gusts of wind shook the windows. Lenny's heart thumped.

What a goat rodeo, Lenny thought. A fake battle, a surrender ceremony that never took place, and a parade led by a scheming, preening academic on a big white horse. Add to that an anachronistic parade of floats.

'Anachronism' had for its origin the Greek word *anakhronismos*, from 'backward' plus 'time,' and…

And Lenny noticed that everyone was waiting for him to speak.

"The critical moment," Lenny said, tapping the drawing, "is after Daniela is handed over to us and before we're forced into the wagon at gunpoint. I'm going to insist that Daniela needs medical care—as some of you already know, I'm going to shout, swear, do whatever is necessary until I get the attention of the TV cameras. Then I'll scoop her up and rush her to the medical tent. Luther's goons won't dare stop us."

Approving nods all around.

Henri said, "Sounds good, *mon ami*, but then what?"

Lenny had been up until four in the morning asking himself the same question. "Uh… let's first hear your ideas."

Sally said, "Maybe after the parade starts, Daniela could just change into clothes we've brought for her and slip away."

"I've thought of that, but Luther will have men posted outside the medical tent and others guarding the stadium exit. Besides, Daniela's face is too well known."

Andy said, "What if we roll back the artificial turf, dig a hole, and bury Daniela with a breathing tube, then we can come back that night and dig her up."

"We won't have time to dig a hole," Lenny said, "and there'd be no place to put the dirt. Besides, I'm not sure Daniela would let us bury her alive."

Lenny thought of Daniela buried alive—or buried dead—and went cold. What had he gotten her into? If something happened to her, how could he go on living?

He started to drift toward the genesis of 'bury' but caught himself.

He turned to Andy, who was grinning.

"What?"

Andy shrugged.

"What?" Lenny said, only louder.

"I was just going to say something funny, you know, to lighten the mood. But I guess I won't."

"Go ahead," Lenny said with a sigh. "Let's hear it."

Andy looked around. "I was thinking about how we could stick Daniela into a cast like the one that guy wears who Luther hauls around on the back of his pickup. We could then just drive her right out of the stadium."

A few nervous chuckles.

The last time Lenny and Daniela lay naked atop his futon, he'd dreamily stroked her back, her slim hips, her long legs. He remembered telling her she was as tall and sleek as a dress store manikin.

Lenny said, "Andy, could you somehow get ahold of a manikin?"

"A what?"

"A clothing dummy, like the kind you see in shop windows. Female."

Andy looked around, then at his feet. "I'd feel kind of funny. The person I'd have to buy it from might think I wanted to use it for... uh... you know."

"Then steal one."

Andy looked up, relieved. "That I can do."

Lenny was confident that Andy could. If the man could swipe Oscar's body from a funeral home, then he'd have no trouble stealing a manikin from a Sears store.

CHAPTER 39

Ekomolurch

"Earthquake"

The meeting over, Lenny was halfway inside his car when his phone chimed. He stepped back out. "Yes?"

"It's going to be a scorcher today."

"Fuck you! Let me talk to Daniela."

"You're kidding, right? I called to tell you to be sure to hydrate. Oh, yeah, also to warn you again not to change your mind and go to the cops."

"You bastard. If you even—"

"Sports drinks are good, but just plain water's okay too."

The phone went dead.

Lenny stood staring at the phone, breathing hard, hearing his heart thump, fantasizing what he would do if he ever got his hands on the guy.

He drove to the stadium, parked and waited. He wanted to brainstorm with Charlie and take another look around inside.

Charlie thundered up on his noisy black Harley. He shut off the engine, lowered the kick stand and climbed off. "You look like *ool.*"

"I feel like *ool*."

They walked into the stadium, its artificial turf gleaming from the shower of the night before. Charlie pointed at a cluster of construction workers at the north side. "They should just knock the whole place down and start over. It's as ugly as a baboon's ass."

Lenny agreed. The place was an eyesore. The scoreboard at the western end read "Skammer's Stuffings," the one at the eastern end said "Skammer's Septic Services," and the bright red banner over the players' entrance urged football fans to procure their next vehicle at Skammer's Ford Ranchero.

Charlie pointed at the north side of the stadium. "Hey, look! It's your old buddy!"

Gerry Gerbil stood on a shelf directly below the glassy VIP lounge, staring into the distance, bewildered, bored, humiliated.

Lenny still puzzled over how blood had gotten onto Gerry's ear, and he was still pissed with the Sprocket brothers and their slip knots. What a useless pair, he thought, a total waste of the Earth's natural resources. They'd never done anyone any good and never would, either intentionally or just by accident.

A construction worker strolled by. Lenny said, "Excuse me, but could we take a moment of your time? I'm Lenny Thorson and this is Charlie Fox. We're members of the reenactment committee and are here to find out if the work will be finished before the event."

"I'm Peggy Carson," She said and shook their hands. She wore a yellow hard hat and possessed a powerful grip. "And to answer your question, there's not a chance in hell it'll be done. The northern half of the stadium is a disaster waiting to happen, and now cover your ears."

"What?" Lenny asked.

"Cover your ears."

Peggy did. So did Lenny, so did Charlie.

The noise hit Lenny like a whack to the side of the head, drilled into his brain, shook his whole body. He clamped his hands harder over his ears but could still hear someone singing "Sergeant Pepper's

Lonely Hearts Club Band" at the top of his voice and far off key.

The singing stopped and Lenny tentatively lowered his hands. His ears rang. "What in hell was that?"

"That's the tone-deaf techie who's installing the new sound system. The dean's having a monster unit put in. He plans to rent the place out for rock concerts."

Not surprising, Lenny thought. The dean would pocket kickbacks from the promoters just as he pocketed kickbacks from Luther for the stadium ads, the logos on the paper plates in the faculty cafeteria and the printing on the back of the marching band uniforms. "Is the stadium even safe?"

"The south side."

"What about the north half?"

Peggy rolled her eyes. "Luckily, this isn't an earthquake zone."

"That bad?"

"That bad."

Charlie pointed at the cannon a few rows below Gerry Gerbil. "What's that for?"

"It'll get fired after each touchdown," Peggy said. "Which in case of the Mighty Ghurkin Gerbils, won't be all that often. The dean also wants it for the reenactment. That's why that guy is working on it. Looks like he's getting ready to test it."

Charlie clamped his hands over his ears.

So did Lenny. "It shoots blanks, I hope?"

Peggy put her fingers in her ears. "You watch."

The cannon went off with a lusty *whoomph!* and puffed red, white and blue smoke.

Lenny lowered his arms. "Loud, but not painful."

Peggy took off her helmet and wiped the sweatband with a tissue. "Wait until it's miked up to the sound system. It'll knock your socks off."

"What a load of *Ool*," Charlie said.

"Of what?" Peggy asked.

"*Shit*," Charlie said. "It's Skalwegian."

Peggy nodded. "I gotta go now. The foreman's waving at me to get back to work. He's a real piece of... uh... *ool.*"

Lenny waited for her to leave, then said, "Now three of us know the word." He pointed toward the steps leading up the stadium. "Let's go up for a better look."

They climbed partway up, then stepped aside for three students in jogging shorts, thumping up the steps. One was the girl from Sri Lanka. Lenny didn't bother to say hello because she hadn't met his eye since the day Daniela went on TV and accused him of playing a part in Charlie's scheme.

But she stopped and jogged in place. "I got into Brown," she said, panting. "I start next semester. I wouldn't have made it without your help, Doctor Thorson. Thanks."

She smiled, held it for a moment, then turned and ran back down the steps.

'Doctor Thorson'—Lenny liked the sound of that.

"Miss the life?" Charlie asked.

"All the time."

"I even miss the army. My buddies, that is. Not the bullshit."

"Or people shooting at you," Lenny said.

"That especially. I'm hoping shootings are all in my past."

"I don't like the sound of that."

The girl from Sri Lanka waved from the bottom of the steps. Lenny waved back and watched her jog out the stadium.

Charlie said, "Andy called earlier and said he's rented the pickup for the day of the reenactment. It's the same model and color as the one that Luther's construction company owns. Andy wants to know if he should paint the company logo on the doors."

Lenny shook his head. "There's a chance the real pickup might show up at the same place. Besides, we'll have Daniela out the gate and on her way to somewhere safe so fast that no one will have time to notice."

At least that's what Lenny hoped. The thought that the caper might fail made his stomach seize. All he could keep down lately were toast and chamomile tea. He'd lost eight pounds on his new regimen.

Lenny recalled that 'regimen' descended from the Latin of the same spelling and is based on *regere*, which means…

Not now, Lenny told himself. He turned to Charlie. "The Widow Bahr keeps nagging me for a role, so I thought I'd ask her to drive the pickup with Daniela on the back."

"Sounds good. She's a tiger behind the wheel of her BMW."

"I still don't know how you and I will escape, though. Any ideas?"

"What if we call in a bomb threat and slip away in the confusion?"

"People might get hurt in the crush," Lenny said. "Besides, I doubt that Luther's guards would leave their posts even for a bomb threat."

Lenny and Charlie watched a tall man with a hammer and a tablet, walking along the row of seats below the VIP lounge. Every few steps, he would stop, whack the concrete with the hammer, shake his head, log the results, move on.

"We'll come up with something," Charlie said.

"We sure will," Lenny said with a lot more confidence than he felt.

They left the stadium and walked to the parking lot. Charlie put on his goggles, pulled on his helmet and threw his leg over the saddle. "Get yourself one of these babies, Lenny. When I'm out riding, I forget all my troubles."

"Too noisy, and I'm probably too big anyway."

Charlie slipped the key into the ignition. "Too big? This is a Harley, Lenny. It's made for big guys. I'm surprised they even let someone my size buy one. Both of us could ride on this thing, no trouble." Charlie scooched forward on the seat. "Hop on."

Lenny was tempted. He did want to forget his troubles, forget about how Daniela was tied up somewhere, and forget that he and Charlie had no idea of how they would escape from the stadium.

He threw one leg over the seat, then pulled back. "This thing is fast?"

"Like a rocket," Charlie said.

"How long would it take to carry you and me a couple hundred feet if you really pushed it?"

Charlie shrugged. "A few seconds. Why are you asking?"

"What if you drove the motorcycle into the stadium the night before the reenactment and hid it under a tarp at the spot where we're going to erect the medical tent? The next day, after we've gotten Daniela and everyone else out safely, you and I could climb on, head for the stadium exit and blow right past the guards. Think that would work?"

Charlie gunned the engine and grinned. "If not," he shouted, "at least we'll have a hell of a lot of fun trying."

CHAPTER 40

Reretrotu

"To walk backwards"

"Would it… uh… be out of order," Lenny mumbled into the phone the next morning, "to ask you to be so kind as to write a letter of recommendation for me?"

"Hang on Thorson, someone's just come into my office."

Lenny knew that the dean was stalling to give himself time to think. Lenny also knew that the dean wasn't anywhere near his office but in hiding until the reenactment.

It hurt to grovel, even if he was faking it.

Lenny shifted the phone to his right ear. From the rocker on Charlie's back porch, Lenny watched Andy Deezel slipping from one tree to the next inside the wood line at the far side of the pond. Deep into his role, he wore camouflage clothing, a black beret and combat boots, and he carried an M16. Andy had stolen the weapon from the Massachusetts National Guard but—to Lenny's relief— hadn't gotten his hands on any ammunition. Andy would soon complete the morning shift guarding the perimeter of Charlie's farm. Charlie's turn came next, then Lenny's. Because Lenny was having so much trouble sleeping, he'd volunteered for the dreaded midnight-to-eight slot. It had been Charlie's idea to bring him out to the farm for his safety and to post a guard around the clock. Charlie had also borrowed the neighbor's noisy Sheltie to warn of intruders.

During his dark and lonely patrols, Lenny worried himself sick about Daniela, and he beat himself up for his role in her abduction. He shuddered to think of how she was being treated—were they feeding her enough? Keeping her tied up around the clock? Molesting her? He felt as if he were living in a bad dream from which he couldn't shake himself awake.

But he also felt in charge of his life like never before. He was making plans, giving orders, making things happen, no longer accepting everything that came his way. His organizational skills and his imagination were being tested to the fullest, he knew, and that felt good. But he wasn't happy. How could he be happy with Daniela in danger?

Andy slipped farther into the woods, the neighbor's Sheltie found a squirrel to chase, and the dean came back on the phone. "All right, I'll write that letter, Thorson. But first you have to do something for me."

"Oh?"

"It's about your pal Henri. I want you to make sure he doesn't disrupt the reenactment."

The year before, Henri had shown up in the unauthorized role of Colonial-era pimp, driving a horse-drawn wagon with Joan and Jane as flashy camp followers. It had been a sensation with spectators, a trauma for the dean.

"I'll give him a stern lecture," Lenny said in his most assuring voice, "and make him promise to behave himself. This year we certainly don't want anything unexpected to happen."

"Then I'll write the letter, Thorson, but only after I've seen that you've kept Henri in line. I want everything to come off without a hitch."

"No hitches," Lenny said. "Not one hitch."

The dean grunted, and the line went dead.

Lenny pondered the origin of 'without a hitch.' Something horse-and-wagon related, he figured. He tried to picture the dean driving a team of horses or even atop a horse, maybe Angel Warrior in a rearward trot.

Lenny smiled for the first time in days, then called Henri. "I just phoned the dean with a phony request for a job recommendation."

"Why?"

"To give the impression that I didn't know he had a hand in Daniela's abduction."

"Clever. Did you learn anything new?"

"He wants you to behave yourself at this year's reenactment."

Henri hooted.

Lenny said, "Did you talk to the curator at the state historical museum?"

"Sure did, partner, and I charmed her into loaning us all their medical gear from the Revolutionary War era. I also charmed her into cooperating in other, even more exciting ways."

Lenny didn't pursue this. Women were always cooperating with Henri in exciting ways. "Have you picked up the tent?"

"A twenty-by-thirty. Also six cots, six chairs and three tables."

"Good. Keep me posted," Lenny said, and pocketed his phone.

Charlie pushed past with a wheelbarrow filled with horse manure. Since Daniela's abduction, he'd thrown himself into manual labor. He looked as exhausted and worried as Lenny felt. Charlie set the wheelbarrow down and wiped his forehead with the back of his sleeve. He asked, "Did The Widow Bahr agree to drive the pickup?"

"I'm just getting ready to call her."

"Good. Now I've got to get back to work and then relieve Andy. You wouldn't believe the amount of doo-doo Angel Warrior produces. Can't complain, though. I'm getting fifty bucks a bag." Charlie grabbed the wheelbarrow by the handles and trotted toward the barn.

Lenny phoned The Widow Bahr and explained how Daniela

would be smuggled out in a body cast.

"Great idea!" The Widow Bahr whooped.

"And I want you to drive the pickup."

The Widow Bahr whooped again.

"You'll stay outside the stadium until you get my call," Lenny said. "Then you'll drive inside and park next to the medical tent. We'll load Daniela on the back, and you'll hurry her to safety."

"Won't I be stopped?"

"The pickup's the same year, model and color as Luther's. The gate guards will assume it's his."

"Great," The Widow Bahr said. "Is that it?"

"Uh... just one more favor. As you're well aware, the dean will be leading the post-surrender parade, dressed up as George Washington. He's insisting on a white horse this year because George is often portrayed on one, which is why the dean has begged me to ask you for Angel Warrior."

Silence, then The Widow Bahr said, "Is the dean a good rider?"

"His office is filled with trophies."

Football trophies, but close enough, Lenny figured.

The Widow Bahr hesitated. "Does he know that Angel Warrior has a tendency to walk backwards?"

"Yes, and he says he loves a challenge."

Another silence, only longer. "Well, I guess that's all right if you're sure the man's up to it."

"Oh, he will be. He loves attention, and I'm sure he'll get lots."

Lenny pocketed his phone, leaned back in the rocker and smiled.

Andy phoned. "Come around front so I can show you what I got."

Lenny walked around to the other side of the house and found Andy standing at the back of his beat-up black Camaro. Andy popped the trunk and pointed inside. "I got that at two this morning from a strip mall near the college."

By 'that,' Andy meant a clothing dummy.

He added, "It's a lady, about five feet ten, just like you ordered."

"Perfect."

Andy tugged his earlobe. "You're sure you're not going to use her for something... uh..."

"Kinky?" Lenny said. "Nope."

"That's good," Andy said, and tapped the dummy's stomach. It produced a hollow sound. "Because she doesn't even have a—"

"I can see that," Lenny said.

Lenny carried the dress dummy inside, lay it face up on the kitchen table and poured himself a sixth cup of coffee.

Charlie came in, Andy's rifle over his shoulder, on break from guard duty. He grabbed a powdered donut and ate half in one bite. He looked exhausted and smelled of horse manure.

Lenny said, "You should get more sleep."

"Can't. I'm too wired. It's like waiting for a firefight."

"I wouldn't know," Lenny said.

"You might get your chance."

"Don't say that."

Lenny tore open the first of the boxes of cloth rolls he'd bought at a medical supply house, then read the instructions.

Charlie said, "Luther's okay with all this?"

"Yup. Henri asked him if he could borrow the man in the cast for display in the medical tent, supposedly to give the place authenticity. Initially Luther said no, but then asked the guy, and he said he wanted to play the part."

"What if Luther had said no?"

"I'd have gone ahead with the plan anyway. If Luther saw a second person in a full-body cast, he wouldn't know what to think at first. By the time he caught on, The Widow Bahr would have Daniela safely out of the stadium."

Lenny wrapped the dummy in thick strips of dry cloth, head to foot, leaving the fingers and toes uncovered. "By the way, the goon in the cast is called Bob Two."

"There's a Bob One?"

"Apparently," Lenny said.

The next four layers went on wet. "This will dry in six hours,"

Lenny said. "Then I'll saw the cast into two vertical sections, remove the dummy, and attach Velcro to the edges of the front and back halves."

Charlie watched Lenny work. "You're an unusual person, Lenny Thorson."

"You're not the first to point that out."

CHAPTER 41

Ukgillin

"To not recognize one's guilt"

The dean stepped into the Skammer's Construction Company trailer where it sat next to the stadium and settled into the chair behind the desk. Luther's three men were already there, dressed in reenactment uniforms. The dean had insisted on inspecting their outfits because the previous year, two numbskulls from Vermont had shown up in Civil War attire.

Against the wall to the dean's right sat the two killers imported from Chicago—tall, sleek and mean-looking—dressed in the blue officers' uniforms of the Colonial forces. Across from them slouched Goober Jones, a thin and narrow-eyed man just out of prison for stealing a freezer truck. He wore baggy brown pants and a suede jacket, his take on rough frontiersman's garb. He retained his prison pallor and sat hunched over as if still ducking under an upper bunk. The two thugs from Chicago called themselves Bob Three and Bob Four.

What a collection of dickbrains, the dean thought. Look at what a person has to put up with just to get ahead? Life's not fair.

Grace stepped inside and nodded brightly at the two men in officer's uniforms but ignored Goober. She wore tight black slacks, a gold blouse and bright-red lipstick. She sat on a folding chair and lit a cigarette.

The dean told her that there was no smoking in the trailer. She ignored him.

Luther waddled through the door, wheezed, and settled into a paisley armchair that squeaked in pain. From under half-closed eyelids, he swept his gaze across Goober and the two Bobs, then flicked a plump hand in the dean's direction. "You may proceed."

Dickhead, the dean thought. "Thank you." He stood up and tapped the drawing on the tripod. "We've got just two more days before the battle, and I want everything to go as planned, so listen up."

Someone snickered. A Chicago Bob, the dean guessed. Cretin. "The battle will take place on the soccer field to the east of the stadium. You three men who are with the Colonial forces will advance from the west, as I've indicated here on the left side of the drawing. I'll be there with you, commanding the unit from horseback. We'll engage the British army, who'll be approaching from the right. Luther won't be on the battlefield, of course, but in the stadium's luxury box."

The dean wanted it made clear that Luther wasn't a front-line soldier. The dean added, "He'll be watching us on television."

"Supervising," Luther said. "I'll be supervising."

Like hell, the dean thought, but said nothing.

Goober leaned forward and half raised his hand. "What if someone shoots us? I mean, from up close and like they can't miss. Aren't we supposed to fall down and play dead?"

The dean shook his head. "Don't get killed and don't get wounded, because then you'd be out of the action and not worth shit to me."

The dean didn't normally use 'shit' in conversations, but he knew that real soldiers did.

He continued. "We expect a couple thousand students and townspeople to attend. After the Colonial army defeats the British, the reenactors and spectators will shift from the battlefield to the stadium. The armies will assemble on the playing field, with the onlookers seated on the south side. The northern half of the stadium will still be under repairs and—as you can see from my drawing—that's the location of the luxury box where Luther and Grace will be seated."

"Supervising," Luther added and blew his nose.

Yeah, sure, the dean thought. "In the meantime, the armies will form up in opposite end zones, the Colonial forces to the left, the British to the right, just as they were on the battlefield. When called forward, a delegation from each side will proceed to the surrender table at the fifty-yard line. That's where the transfer will take place."

"Is that when we give the pretty lady back?" Goober asked.

"That's right," the dean said. "I'll be at the surrender table as will Bob Four and an artillery captain from the college faculty. Once Charlie Fox has signed the paper giving up his rights to Harvey's will, Bob Four will signal Bob Three to escort Daniela to the table."

Luther cleared his throat of a noisy wad of phlegm. "Who besides Charlie will represent the Brits?"

"Lenny Thorson. He'll be playing a captain in the British artillery. Bob Three will hand Daniela over to him."

Silence.

Goober let out a low whistle. "The Lobsterman! The guy who killed Bob One and Billy Butcher and messed up Bob Two so bad?"

The two Chicago Bobs exchanged glances.

"Which," the dean said, finger raised, "is the very reason we're making the transfer out in the open in front of television cameras and two thousand spectators. Thorson won't cause us any trouble there."

"You'd better hope he doesn't," Luther said. "Chicago will be pissed if we lose another Bob."

Again the two Bobs exchanged looks.

The dean said, "After the paper is signed, Luther has arranged with his bank to have $250,000 transferred by cellphone from his account to Charlie's and—"

"Are you fucking kidding?" Bob Four said. "You're actually paying the jerk?"

"No choice," Grace said. "We have to convince Charlie and Lenny that we're holding up our end of the deal. Or do you have a better idea?"

Bob Four shook his head.

"I thought so."

"After the signing ceremony," the dean said, "the Colonial army will celebrate by parading inside the stadium. I as George Washington will ride a white horse and lead the troops."

Someone snorted. The dean glared at the two Bobs but couldn't pick out the troublemaker. He added, "As a defeated army, the British won't of course be allowed to parade, but will remain in their ranks at the eastern end zone."

Goober leaned forward. "Can I shoot off the cannon?"

Imbecile, the dean thought. "I already have volunteers—two brothers from the football team. Now listen up: Right after the signing ceremony, Bob Three and Bob Four will force Daniela, Lenny and Charlie at gunpoint into the back of the covered wagon and drive them out the stadium." The dean glanced around the trailer. "Any questions?"

Bob Four said, "It'll look as suspicious as all hell that those three show up dead right after the reenactment."

"Not if we handle things right," the dean said. "Luther has already arranged with your boss back in Chicago to send us someone who specializes in fiery car crashes."

Goober raised his hand, "Do you really have to kill the nice lady?"

"Of course we do," the dean said, and to his surprise felt his throat tightening. What was this feeling? Guilt? Possibly.

Then again, the dean wasn't really sure what guilt felt like.

CHAPTER 42

Memeto nad ukmemeto

"Hope and despair"

The dean dropped by the next morning to see how Luther Skammer's lackeys were treating Daniela. He found her seated in a damp basement, gagged and blindfolded, her wrists tied together in front and her ankles laced to a wooden chair. Goober Jones was stretched out on his back on a folding cot, snoring, a Bart Simpson blanket pulled up to his chin. The dean woke Goober and sent him away.

An elk stood over Daniela's left shoulder, a zebra over her right, and directly behind her loomed a dusty grizzly bear with fist-sized patches of fur missing.

TV viewers would never recognize Daniela, the dean told himself. Greasy strands of hair clung to her forehead, mascara ran in streaks down her cheeks, drool leaked out the sides of her gag, and she smelled like a dumpster. But she was still a babe.

It had been fun showing her off that one time he'd talked her into going out with him. People smiled, called out her name, asked for selfies with her. But the fun stopped when they were alone in his car. Just a hand job would have been enough, but no, she'd slapped him away. Well, I'm in control now, lady, and you're tied up in the basement of Luther Skammer's taxidermy shop. I can do anything with you I want.

But he wouldn't, nor would he let her know who he was in case something went wrong during the reenactment and Lenny The Lobsterman came roaring after him. The dean didn't want a finger bitten off, or six months in a full body cast, or his head blown skyward. Daniela was safe. For now anyway.

She squirmed in her ropes and moaned through her gag.

What's she trying to say? She wants something to eat? She wants to piss? Water? It sounds like water.

The dean took a bottle from the table where a half-eaten meal lay in a Styrofoam take-out container. He bent closer. Snails, asparagus and chocolate mousse! You gotta be kidding!

He untied the gag.

Daniela turned her head to the side and spit a glob of gray mucus onto the floor. She grunted, then spit again. Drool ran down her chin and dripped onto her lap.

The dean held the bottle up to her mouth.

She drank in long gulps. Water ran down the sides of her mouth. She stopped drinking long enough to say, "You won't like it when my boyfriend gets his hands on you."

The dean shuddered, then hurried to tie the gag back on. Daniela was furious and stank like a dead possum, but she was still a babe. She has to die, though. What a waste of… uh… what's that word the Sprocket brothers keep using? 'Poontang.' Yeah, that's it. A waste of poontang.

*　　*　　*

Daniela heard the door close. Her blindfold had slipped, and she'd recognized Dean Sheepslappe. She might have known it was him anyway from his awful aftershave, the same stuff he'd worn that time on their date when he'd tried to run his hand up her skirt. The bastard.

She heard the door open and the guard return, the nice one. She could tell by his shuffle. Blindfolded for days, she'd learned to depend on hearing. Each of her three watchers had a different walk. This one dragged his feet.

Another guard had slipped once and called him 'Goober.' Was that his real name? Daniela guessed not. In any case, she was glad to have him back and to have the dean the hell gone.

The cot squeaked. Goober was sitting down.

"Need anything, miss?" he asked.

Do I need anything? I need my freedom, that's what. And a bath. And some privacy. And fresh underwear. But she shook her head.

"Make a sound if there's something you want."

Again the cot creaked. Goober was settling in for another nap. He'd be here for another few hours, then his replacement would arrive, a heavy-footed man who smelled of cigarettes, and after him the night guard, a limper who snored like a horse. All treated her decently, she had to admit. Several times she'd heard them talk in low voices about The Lobsterman, the strange nickname the killer had used on Juan. Odd, she thought, and why did she hear such fear in their voices?

After a few days, she'd stopped being afraid of the guards and actually felt comfortable with them, especially with Goober. When he was alone with her, he would untie her wrists and give her lotion to rub over the raw spots, then retie her hands, but loosely. When she had to use the bathroom, he'd walk her there and close the door, not like the other perverts who'd leave it open. And he'd bring her takeout from the best restaurant in town. It would arrive lukewarm but delicious. For lunch today she'd had snails, asparagus in butter, and a chocolate dessert. But because of recent bouts of nausea, she'd had to leave half her meal uneaten.

The ropes on her wrist and ankles chafed, the gag tasted like puke, her mask itched, and she smelled like a sewer. The place stank too, like moldy animal fur. She'd thought at first that she was locked in a cave with a family of dead bears, but soon decided that wasn't the case because the floor was flat and caves don't have bathrooms. She couldn't stop thinking about a book her mother had read to her long ago, about a naughty little girl who'd run away from home because she didn't like doing household chores and was adopted by a family of bears who forced her to cook, sweep out their cave and make their beds. A stupid story with a stupid moral, and one that had scared Daniela sleepless. Eventually, the girl's father came to rescue her—why not the mother?—and all lived happily ever after.

Daniela wanted to live happily ever after, and she wanted the dean dead and also two of her guards, but not Goober. Just a bit of prison time for him.

Except for occasional flareups, she'd gotten over her anger. She found this strange but guessed it was normal. Mostly she was achy, itchy, lonely and bored. She spent hours playing word games—Lenny would appreciate that if she ever got the chance to tell him—and she spent even more hours fantasizing what life would be like married to him.

She pictured their house—a white colonial with black shutters, roomy but not showy—with four bedrooms each painted a different bright color—she disliked white walls, detested wallpaper even more—with a spacious study whose three skylights faced south. She and Lenny would share the room, interrupt what they were doing from time to time to ask a question, or make a joke, or just tell the other how much they loved them—and there'd also be a glassy four-season room looking out over a wide backyard.

She'd have her charity up and running by then, and he'd be teaching at some Ivy League college. There'd be kids, of course—two, three, maybe four. Lenny would build an elaborate treehouse for them, run around the backyard with one or two on his back, teach them obscure word derivations.

Lenny.

She admitted that in real life the chances of his getting onto the faculty of an Ivy League school were minimal, as was the likelihood of his finding any teaching job whatsoever. Maybe he'd work at a salvage yard, something he knew how to do. She wouldn't love him any less.

Lenny.

She pictured him bursting into the room, knocking out her guards—with just a light tap to Goober—swooping her up in his arms and carrying her to safety like the father who'd saved his little girl from the bears.

Tears soaked her mask.

Daniela groaned, leaned back in the chair and banged its front legs against the floor. She had to talk to Lenny, had to tell him.

The cot squeaked. Footsteps. "You want something, ma'am?"

Daniela nodded.

She heard the cot squeak, then felt the gag come off. Warm saliva flowed out.

Goober wiped her chin with a napkin. "You have to go to the women's room?"

He always called it that, 'the women's room.'

"I want to call my boyfriend. I have something important to tell him."

"Uh… afraid not, ma'am."

"Please. Just a short call. I won't tell him where I am or anything."

"Sorry."

Daniela felt the tears flow, felt them seep under her eye mask and run down her cheeks. "I miss him so much."

"I'm really sorry, but I'd catch all sorts of heck if anyone found out."

"Only you and I will ever know. My boyfriend won't tell anyone. No one's more trustworthy than Lenny Thorson."

Silence.

"You mean… Lenny The Lobsterman? The killer?"

Goober's voice trembled.

"That can't be Lenny," Daniela said. "He's the nicest guy in the world."

Goober didn't respond.

Daniela listened to his breathing—short, hard bursts. He shifted from foot to foot.

The man's terrified of Lenny, she thought. How odd. "Please let me call."

A long pause, then, "Okay, but just one thing—when you talk to Lenny Thorson, you gotta tell him that Goober's been real good to you, okay?"

"Why?"

"Just in case."

Again, terror in the man's voice.

"Sure," Daniela said.

What had ever given Goober the idea that Lenny was a killer? And 'Lenny The Lobsterman'? What was that all about?

*   *   *

After two collapses, Lenny and Henri managed to get the medical tent to stay up. It sagged at the peak, and the center poles didn't stand quite straight, but both men thought they'd done a pretty good job for a couple of academics.

They lugged in six chairs, six cots and three tables. Charlie's motorcycle lay hidden under a blue tarp. The tent had gone up around it.

"*Merde*," Henri said and pressed both hands against the small of his back. "I hate working up to a sweat."

"It's just 'working up a sweat,'" Lenny said. "I actually like a good workout because it reminds me of the salvage yard. Physical labor relaxes me."

Except this time it didn't. Nothing relaxed Lenny. He couldn't stop worrying about Daniela. He'd lain awake most of the night, smelling her perfume on the pillows. He'd give anything just to hear her voice again.

Henri said, "I need a nap, partner," and stretched out on the operating table.

Lenny went outside, picked up a mallet and pounded the tent stakes deeper. He looked up to see two construction workers sauntering his direction. Luther's thugs, one tall, one short.

The tall one said, "Who's the guy sleeping inside?"

"A friend," Lenny said and hammered on a stake.

"Why did you pitch the tent so close to the exit?"

Lenny looked up. "Because that's where we were told to put it. Why are you asking?"

"What's under the tarp?"

"Folding chairs."

The two man stood around for a while, eying Lenny, then left.

Lenny watched them go. What was that all about?

He banged in the final stake and stood up just as a glockenspiel player approached. All morning he'd been walking back and forth nearby, all alone, tapping out tunes, the instrument hanging by hooks over his shoulders. Lenny thought it looked like an electronic keyboard with metal keys.

Glockenspiel was German, of course, and meant 'set of bells.'

The musician was a thin man with a thin black mustache, just how Lenny thought the player of this particular musical device should look. Lenny said, "Where's the rest of your band?"

"They hate the glockenspiel, *Greensleeves*, too." The man reached across his instrument and shook Lenny's hand. "I'm Jasper."

"Lenny."

Jasper looked the tent up and down. "Why did you pitch it so close to an exit?"

Again, that question. "It's where it's supposed to go."

"Can I look inside?"

"No. My friend's asleep."

"I'll be quiet," Jasper said, and pushed his way in.

Lenny said, "Hey!" then followed Jasper inside.

Henri lay snoring on the operating table.

Jasper picked a tool off a table. "This looks like a pair of long-nose pliers. What's it for?"

"Extracting bullets."

"Is it real?"

"Yes," Lenny said. "Now I have to get back to work, and you have to leave."

"Are you a doctor?"

"Of linguistics. I operate on words."

Jasper didn't smile. He pointed at the tarp. "What's that? More medical equipment?"

"Just folding chairs."

Part of the Harley's rear tire was showing. "Rolling folding chairs."

"That's funny," Jasper said, but didn't laugh. He went over, jerked the tarp back and whistled. "That's a beauty. I owned the exact same model ten years ago, only red. But after I got married, my wife made me sell it."

Lenny cringed. Why do people add 'exact' to 'same'? Does 'different same' make any sense? Of course not.

Also, Charlie had told Lenny that this model had been on the market for only three years.

Lenny pulled the tarp back over the motorcycle. "You have to get out. I have work to do." He stepped close to Jasper.

Jasper stepped back. "And I have to get practicing." He marched out of the tent, tapping *Greensleeves* as he went.

Lenny watched him leave. What was the guy up to?

His phone chimed.

"Lenny?"

"Daniela! *Daniela?* Oh, my God! Are you safe?"

"I can't talk for long."

Lenny's heart sped up. "Where are you?"

"I'm not allowed to say."

Lenny heard a man's voice in the background.

Daniela said, "Goober wants you to know he's treating me well."

"'Goober?' Uh... okay. But who's—"

"He's one of my... companions."

"Are you okay? Do you feel safe? Are you getting enough to eat?

"For lunch I had escargot, asparagus and chocolate mousse."

Lenny was quiet for a moment. "At least you haven't lost your sense of humor."

Daniela burst into tears.

"Don't cry, Daniela. Please don't cry. Things will work out. I'll make sure—"

"I've just been signaled to end the call. There's something I really wanted to tell you, but now I'm not sure I should. It complicates matters."

"Tell me."

Silence.

"Please, Daniela. Tell me."

"I'm late."

"Late? Late for what? Uh... oh... OH!"

CHAPTER 43

Lutketu ukeskumowa

"To fall down dead"

Lenny leaned against the wheel of the cannon, twin to the one facing him from across the soccer field. The eleventh reenactment of the Battle of Ghurkin Hill was to begin in fifteen minutes. Lenny felt as if he were taking part in a nightmare costume party. He hadn't slept more than a few hours the night before, ate nothing that morning and had a head full of horrible thoughts.

And one joyful one. Daniela was going to have his baby!

The dean's voice came over a loudspeaker. "Soldiers, take your place!"

Spectators lounged on blankets on each side of the soccer field, drank beer, ate chips and tossed Frisbees. Earlier, everyone had been free to roam the arboretum, where for the past three days dozens of bearded reenactors had camped in rows of white tents, cooked meals over open fires, cleaned weapons, rehearsed for battle, fed and watered the horses that The Widow Bahr had supplied, and attempted to talk like Revolutionary War soldiers.

Lenny wore the red coat, black hat and white pants of a British captain. He hated the outfit. It was too tight across the shoulders, too short at the sleeves, and the trousers bagged at the butt. In lieu of boots, Lenny wore black Converse High Tops.

Fellow reenactors, some of whom had traveled from as far as Ohio, at first scoffed at Lenny for his undeserved rank of captain and especially for his indifference to historical accuracy. Everything they carried or wore was authentic down to the slightest detail: every rifle, every powder pouch, every uniform button and even their underwear, which was hand-sewn by their wives.

Lenny's uniform had come with a long plastic sword that Lenny had worn on the wrong side until a surly corporal from Pennsylvania set him straight. The first morning of rehearsal, Lenny had felt miserable and useless and heard muttering from all directions.

The second day went better. Much better. Word got back to Lenny that the reenactors were whispering that he possessed a mob nickname, had killed a hitman with his bare hands, put another into a full-body cast and decapitated a third. Greatly puzzled, Lenny nevertheless saw no reason to deny the rumors. Starting on the morning of day two, reenactors stepped aside and snapped him salutes whenever he passed.

When the time came for the ragged Colonial army to charge the British lines, it would be Lenny's absurd and useless assignment to raise his plastic sword and point out targets for his cannoneers. Three frail Delaware brothers with blond flattops would then jerk the lanyard and produce a harmless cloud of white smoke. The boys griped among themselves that their weapon was of World War One vintage, but they never complained to Lenny. From day two they addressed him with a crisp 'Sir!'

Lenny peered through his binoculars and saw to his surprise that the Colonial cannoneers on the other side of the battle line were none other than the Sprocket brothers, commanded by Lenny's replacement in the language department, Bruce Something-or-Other.

Lenny scanned his own side of the field until he spotted Colonel

Charlie Fox. He'd asked to play a sergeant, but had been overruled because he had to sign the fake surrender papers, and a lowly enlisted men wouldn't be assigned to such an important task. Charlie was reviewing his troops now, barking orders, pointing here and there, back in the infantry.

Lenny lowered his binoculars. A kid ran past tugging a blue balloon with 'Skammer's Harley Heaven' printed on it. During the night, a crew had dyed 'Skammer's Lanes' in big red letters across the center of the soccer field. A booth distributed free Kool-Aid in blue cups reading 'Skammer's Wishy-Washy Laundry.'

Although Lenny felt like an idiot, he was nevertheless determined to save Daniela or die trying. For this he felt like a real soldier—a fool in his captain's outfit—but like a real soldier.

The oldest of the three Delaware brothers said in a trembling voice, "Sir, permission to load the cannon."

"Permission granted," Lenny said, then felt idiotic.

A white horse across the valley caught Lenny's attention. He raised his binoculars. And there he was, General George Washington— a.k.a. Dean Wesley Sheepslappe—posed atop The Widow Bahr's majestic and deranged white stallion. The dean had his sword raised and was shouting at anyone who strayed too close.

Lenny lowered his binoculars and turned to his gunner. "This wasn't a real battle but just a skirmish between a British patrol and a handful of local men who'd gotten drunk and went turkey hunting. Also, George Washington was a couple hundred miles away at the time."

"Yes, sir."

He doesn't believe me, Lenny thought.

His phone chimed. A major violation. His crew—busy loading the cannon—didn't look up or even change expression. Lenny guessed this must be how it felt to be a real captain.

It was The Widow Bahr, stationed on the Colonial side of the lines. "Good news, Lenny, They have indeed brought Daniela with them. The trade will go through."

"Great, great! How does she look?"

"Angry, hot, tired, but otherwise okay. She's being guarded by Goober Jones, a goofball ex-con who works for Skammer's construction company."

This had to be the Goober that Daniela had said was treating her well.

"But there are two other slimeballs hanging around," The Widow Bahr said, her voice stressed. "They're tough-looking customers, dressed up as officers but looking more like knee-cappers. The bulges under their jackets are no doubt guns. Wait, I have to go. I think the war is starting."

"Take care of yourself," Lenny said.

"It's only playacting."

"We hope."

The three Delaware boys were already standing at their assigned spots around the cannon, but Lenny nevertheless said, "Take your positions!" because it sounded good and it felt good to playact for a moment and forget his troubles. Maybe that's why his gunners had driven all the way from Delaware, to leave their own problems at home.

Three men guarded Daniela. Not good. But Lenny knew he shouldn't be surprised. He scanned the other side with his binoculars and spotted a man in a suede jacket, clutching Daniela by the upper arm. Goober Jones, Lenny guessed. Daniela wore a brown robe with the hood up and a look of fury.

Lenny was overwhelmed by fear and anger.

And joy.

A baby! His baby!

A voice broke through: "Sir, sir!"

It was the brother assigned to yank the lanyard. "Our troops are attacking, sir! The colonel wants you to give the order to fire!"

To Lenny's right, the commander of the artillery detachment—a local dentist with a dark reputation for pulling teeth rather than fixing them—waved his sword wildly as a signal for the cannon to fire. Lenny said, "Fire when ready!"

He knew that 'Fire' would have done the job and that 'Fire when not ready' made no sense, but 'Fire when ready' sounded good.

The cannon poofed a cloud of innocuous white smoke. Lenny said, "Keep firing until ordered to stop."

Another meaningless command.

Lenny heard the happy cheers of advancing soldiers, the pop of their blanks and the distant, soft 'whoomph' of the Sprocket Brothers' cannon. Overaged and under-exercised troops in colorful garb met at the center of the battlefield in clanking hand-to-hand combat, stagy and tentative. Officers on horseback trotted back and forth behind the lines, slapping their reins and raising their swords while they shouted their own meaningless orders. Across the slope, General George Sheepslappe Washington sat rigidly photogenic atop Angel Warrior, and spectators clapped and cheered.

Unlike the mounted officers who remained safely behind the British lines, Charlie led on foot from the front, giving frantic hand signals that his stumbling underlings either misunderstood or simply didn't feel like obeying.

Lenny counted four casualties so far. Although three dozen reenactors from each side had been designated by lot the night before to play the dead and wounded, most were ignoring their orders. A recent rain had muddied the field, and few men were willing to sacrifice their precious uniforms for the cause.

The whole thing looked stupid and artificial. Lenny had had enough.

"Sir, sir?" One of the boys said.

"Yes?"

"The colonel wants us to roll the cannon forward."

The dentist stood high in his saddle and frantically waved his sword. "Do what the hell you want," Lenny said. "I'm staying here."

The Delaware boys gave him a puzzled look, then rolled the cannon a hundred feet forward and recommenced firing.

Lenny tried again to locate Daniela through his field glasses, but she was hidden behind cannon smoke.

A feeble *pop!* then, "You're dead!"

Lenny turned and recognized the corporal who'd harassed him

about his phone the first day of rehearsals. He was a tall gaunt man with a black unibrow. Again he shouted, "You're dead!"

Lenny turned his attention back to the battlefield. The smoke had cleared somewhat, and he spotted Daniela and the three men guarding her.

"You gotta fall down dead!"

Screw the plan, Lenny thought. Why not just charge across the battlefield, shove the guards out of the way, grab Daniela and carry her off?

But The Widow Bahr said the two scary thugs were armed. Better to stick to the plan.

The Sprocket brothers fired their cannon, and again Daniela disappeared behind a cloud of smoke.

The reenactor stepped around in front of Lenny. "I killed you dead. You ain't following the rules."

Lenny was scared for Daniela, sick to his stomach, and fearful his plan wouldn't work. It certainly wouldn't if he had to play dead.

"There ain't no way I'm gonna get cheated out of my kill!" The corporal said. "Them's the rules!"

"Fuck the rules!"

The corporal took a swing.

Lenny blocked it with his left, then stepped back.

Reason with the man, Lenny told himself. After all, reason always wins out in the end. Anyone will listen to reason if it's presented in the correct fashion.

Lenny said, "Let's talk this over. I think..."

The corporal seized his rifle by the barrel and swung.

Lenny ducked, planted his legs, stiffened his back, and threw a hard uppercut.

Thunk!

His jacket ripped at the armpit.

The corporal stumbled backwards, then fell, arms outstretched. His rifle flew one direction, his hat in the other. He lay motionless.

Spectators clapped and cheered.

CHAPTER 44

Hoceketudo oolont oralopa!

"Get lost, shithead!"

The Colonies won, the crowd cheered, and a dozen dead or wounded soldiers lay on the battlefield, having carefully positioned themselves away from puddles. Spectators packed up blankets, diaper bags, picnic lunches and six packs and headed toward the stadium. Lenny joined the commingled spectators and warriors from both sides. The event now felt like a peculiar, warped pause in space-time during which soldiers rose from the dead, and the wounded—except for his unconscious and ungrammatical tormentor—stood up, brushed mud from their prized uniforms and exhibited neither amazement nor gratitude for their miraculous recoveries.

Spectators clambered up the concrete steps to claim seats in the stadium's south side. Yellow tape closed off the other half, where Lenny spotted Luther and Grace high up in the luxury booth. Signs read, "Construction Zone—Keep Out!"

My $197,000 at work, Lenny thought.

He found Henri inside the British medical tent on the twenty-yard line at the open end of the stadium. Henri wore a white apron streaked with ketchup. He gave Lenny a goofy, left-handed salute. "Maybe our side lost, but you fought a like a tiger, Lieutenant Thorson."

"Captain," Lenny said. "That's *Captain* Thorson."

Sally wore a nurse's white uniform and sat at a small table, a phone in each hand. Her job was to get updates from The Widow Bahr and Andy, both behind the Colonial lines.

Bob Two stood propped up against a center pole, a black, tri-cornered hat balanced on his head.

Lenny said, "It looks like we're as ready as we can be."

Henri nodded and wiped his hands on his apron. They trembled. The first time Lenny had seen him nervous.

Bob Two grunted. Sally got up, fed a lobster tail through the mouth hole in his cast, sat down again.

Lenny pointed at the two men stretched out on cots, one dressed as a British private and the other as a frontiersman. Both lay on their back and held tissues to their nose.

"Fistfight," Henri said. "They gave each other bloody noses. They mistook this for a real medical tent and wandered in. Sally stuffed cotton up their noses and sent them to bed."

"Get them out of here," Lenny said.

Henri saluted. *"Oui, mon capitaine."*

Lenny stepped outside, pointed his binoculars at the VIP booth and spotted Luther and Grace, him smoking a cigar, her dozing. Directly below them, Gerry Gerbil stared woefully into the distance. And below him, Tom and Titus Sprocket leaned on their cannon. Tom smoked, and Titus licked a blue ice cream cone.

A girl holding a similar cone walked past Lenny, followed by two adults chewing on lobster tails.

The two soldiers with the bloody noses stumbled out the tent and hurried away.

Henri stepped outside and put his hand on Lenny's shoulder. "Smile, *mon ami*, we're on television."

A shaggy-haired man pointed a shoulder-held camera at Lenny and Henri. Lenny looked up to see himself and Henri portrayed twenty feet tall on the screens over both end zones. Lenny took a step toward the cameraman. He lowered his camera and scurried away.

"There's Daniela!" Henri said, pointing to the other end of the stadium.

She stood beside Goober Jones in his suede jacket with the dangling fringes, her head down.

Lenny's heart pounded. He wanted to rush over, punch Goober and the other guards unconscious, grab Daniela up in his arms and run like hell.

The PA system squealed, the crowd groaned, and Bradley Noyze said, "Some kindly and anonymous individual has generously donated three hundred pounds of lobster tails to today's fine proceedings. You can locate the booth at the west end of stadium. One per person, please. Also, the same donor has supplied our fine local dairy, Skammer's Bovine Princess, with several hundred bags of frozen fruit for the delicious ice cream that many of you are already enjoying. The flavor is… uh… *poison berry*?"

A rustling of papers followed a brief off-mike discussion. "That can't be right," Bradley said. "This seems to be some kind of sick joke."

Lenny turned his binoculars toward the media booth high overhead. Bradley wore a Red Sox cap pulled down so far his ears stuck out. A couple weeks earlier, Daniela had told Lenny that the station's hair stylist had plans to spike Bradley's hair on the day of the reenactment, add pink streaks and walk off the job.

A trumpet blared from the PA system, followed by an advertisement for Skammer's Air Conditioning Services.

Bradley came back on the air. "I can't tell you how happy I am to find myself once again on a college campus. It brings back so many warm memories of my student years."

Daniela had told Lenny that Bradley had flunked out of three colleges, the final one a correspondence school based in Nigeria.

Bradley added, "Please join me in recognizing the good work of a fine gentleman from our community and the builder of this beautiful stadium. I am of course referring to none other than our own Mr.

Luther Skammer, who you can see sitting in the luxury booth on the far side of the playing field accompanied by his charming wife, Grace. It is he who supplied those colorful balloons that your children so happily tug about on strings, and it was he who donated over two hundred packets of Kool-Aid to the ladies manning the refreshment counter. Take note, lefty professors—not all capitalists are evil-doers! Far from it. So let's hear it for Mr. Luther Skammer!"

There was little to hear. At one time or another, every member of the community had lost quarters to broken driers at Skammer's Wishy-Washy Laundry, experienced shoddy car repairs at Skammer's Ford Ranchero, or had their rents doubled at Skammer's Happy Village Garden Apartments.

Undaunted, Bradley continued, "And let's give a big hand for our friend Gary... uh Gerry, watching over us from the other side of the stadium."

The crowd reacted more favorably to Gerry Gerbil. A frontiersman's hat sat atop his football helmet, and he looked miserable.

Charlie appeared at Lenny's elbow. "They're signaling us to move."

Finally, Lenny thought. His heart sped up. No more planning, practicing, worrying. The time had come—now or nothing. It didn't seem real.

He followed Charlie to the thirty-yard line, where the two waited for orders to proceed to the surrender table at midfield. The band finished a thumping Sousa march, followed by Bradley saying, "On this joyous day, when we've all come here to happily celebrate..."

Mumbling in the media booth. A sharp, off-mike argument. Then more from Bradley: "Of course men died in the actual battle, but still, you have to admit that the sun is shining and the sky is blue, and what I'm saying is that we should always look on the bright side of life."

The band launched into another Sousa march.

The dean stood at the opposite thirty yard line. A goon in an officer's uniform stood next to him. The third man as Lenny's replacement in the language department, Bruce Something-or-Other, playing the part of a French officer advising the Colonial army. He looked like a pale, puzzled boy dressed up as a captain of the artillery, proud of a uniform too loose at the neck, too long at the sleeves, an innocent taking part in a deadly prisoner exchange.

The band stopped playing and Bradley said, "Notice how high our brave Colonial soldiers hold their heads, and the stark contrast with the cowardly British. I for one have no respect whatsoever for soldiers who surrender."

"*Ool,*" Charlie said.

A WDRK cameraman pushed his lens close to Charlie's face.

Charlie said, "*Hoceketudo oolont oralopa!*" ('Get lost shithead!'), and the man stepped back.

Bradley said, "Representatives from both sides will now march to the surrender table, where the victorious and noble Colonial army will accept the signatures of the badly defeated British contingent."

That was the signal for Lenny and Charlie to walk to the fifty-yard line, where a folding table sat over the *Ford* in 'Skammer's Ford Ranchero.' The dean, Bruce Something-or-Other and a towering thug stepped forward at the same time.

Daniela stood fifty feet back, eyes down, her hood covering much of her face.

Lenny's heart leaped.

Bradley continued: "And now the three Colonial officers and the two representatives of the British will take their seats at each side of the table."

Lenny sat to Charlie's left and directly across from the man the dean had addressed as 'Bob Four.'

Bob Four studied Lenny for a moment, then leaned down to Bruce Something-or-Other and said in a low voice, "The Lobsterman."

Bruce Something-or-Other said, "Huh?"

The dean nodded at Lenny as if they were meeting in his office to discuss his next semester's course load.

Lenny wanted to pound the dean's face to pulp.

A television camera hovered in front of Lenny. He repeated

Charlie's earlier order: *"Hoceketudo oolont oralopa!"* and the cameraman stepped back.

The dean slid a manila envelope across the table toward Charlie. He pulled out a single sheet of paper, read it, then signed at the red Xs.

Bradley announced over the PA system that he'd tried to enlist in the Marines right after 9/11 but was turned down because of toe warts.

Charlie handed the paper to the dean, who glanced at it, nodded, took out his phone and held it up for Charlie. "That's your account number?"

Charlie reached into his pocket for a piece of paper, read it and nodded.

"And $250,000 is the amount agreed upon?"

Again Charlie nodded.

The dean tapped the phone a few more times and showed it to Charlie. "The funds have been transferred from Luther's account to yours."

Bruce Something-or-Other said, "Huh?"

Lenny stood up and leaned far across the table, his face inches from the dean's. "Turn Daniela over to me right this minute, or I'll rip your head off!"

The dean scrambled to his feet, knocked over his chair and stood behind Bob Four for protection. "Tell Bob Three to bring her here."

Bob Four signaled to Bob Three.

Bruce Something-or-Other looked even more confused.

Bradley said, "And with the signing of this treaty, the Revolutionary War comes to an end."

Mumblings in the media booth.

"I meant to say, this particular battle comes to an end."

Bob Three clutched Daniela by the upper arm and led her to the table.

Bradley said, "And now the lovely wife of the British captain, captured by the Colonial forces during the battle, is returned to her husband in a grand and noble gesture of friendship."

The crowd went "Oooh!"

Daniela held her arms out and rushed to Lenny. Her hood fell back.

Bradley said, "Uh... oops... uh... ladies and gentlemen, I'm... um... certain some of you might recognize Daniela, my junior assistant co-anchor."

The crowd whistled and clapped.

Lenny hugged Daniela, spun her around. She smelled of sweat and animal fur.

Bradley said, "Uh, let's take a break."

A commercial for Skammer's Lanes appeared on the television screens at each end of the stadium, but not before the crowd heard Bradley mutter, "What the fuck is that grand-standing cunt doing down there?"

Daniela hung heavily in Lenny's arms. He kissed her lips, her nose, her sweaty forehead, her lips again, then cradled her in his arms. She hugged him around the neck. Her hair hung free, her robe dangled and swayed.

Again the crowd went, "Oooh!"

The commercial ended, and a cameraman moved in for a closeup.

Lenny whispered, "Faint."

"What?"

"Faint."

Daniela said, "Why?"

"Just do as I say. And make it look good."

Daniela moaned, dropped her arms, let her head fall back and closed her eyes.

The camera slipped closer.

The crowd said, "Ohhhh!"

Lenny stared into the lens, "It's time to get this poor suffering woman to the medical tent!"

The crowd cheered.

"That's not part of the ceremony!" the dean hissed.

The crowd booed.

Lenny trotted off with Daniela draped limply in his arms.

The dean shouted at Bob Four, "Follow them!"

Bruce Something-or-Other said, "Huh?"

Lenny shouldered the tent flap aside and lay Daniela on her back on the operating table.

Bob Four stepped inside.

Lenny said, "Out!"

Bob Four hesitated.

"Out!" Lenny shouted and took a step toward Bob Four.

He backed out of the tent.

Lenny turned to Sally. "Step outside and keep an eye on that guy."

Sally nodded and hurried out.

Daniela raised herself on her elbows. "I'm free! I can't believe it! I'm free!"

"Not quite yet," Lenny said.

"What do you mean?"

Lenny brushed the hair from Daniela's eyes. "Are you claustrophobic?"

"I... I'm not sure. Why?"

"You'll soon find out."

CHAPTER 45

Nokmeltu

"To strike hard with the fist"

Lenny pulled Daniela's dress over her head and tossed it to Henri, who stuffed it into a bag marked 'Used Bandages.'

Daniela wore lacy black underwear.

Bob Two said, "Yum."

Lenny grabbed his cast by the feet, Charlie took him by the shoulders, and they laid him on the cot recently vacated by one of the soldiers with the bloody nose. Henri covered Bob Two head to foot with a gray blanket. He made muffled noises of protest.

Lenny reached under the cot, pulled out the body cast he'd created, unrolled it from a plastic tarp and laid it next to Daniela on the operating table. "A perfect fit."

"What *is* that thing?" she asked.

"Something I made especially for you."

"It looks like a cast."

"Exactly."

Daniela said, "You're not going to—"

"I'm afraid I am," Lenny said. "But you won't be in there for long."

He ripped apart the Velcroed halves, picked up Daniela and settled her into the back half. "Okay?"

"I suppose so."

"Then here goes," Lenny said. He kissed Daniela's forehead, pressed the front section in place, leaned close to her ear hole and whispered, "I know you're uncomfortable in there, but this is the best I could come up with. Soon you'll be far away from here and safe. And no matter what happens, remember this: I love you as much as any man has ever loved a woman, and I will do anything to make up for what I've put you through. I love you very, very much, and I always will."

"I have to pee."

Lenny straightened up. "Um… I… uh… guess I didn't make accommodations for that. The store dummy wasn't anatomically correct."

"I am."

"I know," Lenny said. "And you don't know how happy that makes me."

"Just how long do I have to stay in this thing?"

"A few minutes at most."

Outside, the band struck up *The Gang's All Here*.

From his cot, Bob Two hummed along.

Sally rushed inside. "The guy's coming!"

Lenny threw an army blanket over Daniela.

Bob Four stepped inside, phone in hand. "The boss wants you and Charlie Fox and the lady back on the field, so get your ass moving." Bob Four glanced around. "Where the hell is she?"

"She trotted off to the bathroom," Lenny said. "She ate four lobster tails and a boysenberry ice cream cone, and they didn't seem to agree with her."

Bradley's voice boomed over the PA system. "It's this man's opinion that the Revolutionary War would never have taken place if the two sides had spoken the same language. Communication between people is so important that we should make English the world standard."

Bob Four glanced around, "I don't see no bathroom."

"It's across from the ticket booth."

"Yeah? Well how come I didn't see her go past?" Bob Four stepped around Lenny, jerked the blanket off Daniela and thunked his knuckles on the cast. "When did Bob Two grow tits?"

Lenny said nothing.

Bob Four turned to Lenny. "What the fuck's going on here?"

Lenny glanced at Charlie, Sally, Henri. All were watching for him to come up with something to say. He had a reputation for making up stories on the fly.

But what could he say? That they'd replaced Bob Two's old cast with a new one? That it had warped in the heat? That Bob Two had in fact grown breasts?

Bob Four pulled his jacket back and reached for his pistol.

Lenny stepped forward and punched him under the jaw. Hard.

Thunk!

Bob Four rolled his eyes upward, dropped to his knees, then fell face down.

Lenny rubbed his throbbing knuckles.

Henri said, "*Magnifique!*"

Lenny and Charlie dragged Bob Four onto the empty cot, then gagged him and tied his hands and feet with extra tent rope. Sally covered him with a blanket.

Daniela said, "I still have to pee."

The band played *Greensleeves.*

Lenny shouted, "Sally, phone The Widow Bahr and tell her to bring the pickup around! Right now!"

"Got it!" Sally said and grabbed her phone.

Lenny turned to Daniela. "In ten minutes, you'll be safely out of here, and then we'll—"

"We've got a problem," Sally said, holding out the phone.

Lenny took it.

The Widow Bahr was breathing hard. She said, "The mayor's car is blocking the entrance, and I can't get past."

"It won't stay there long," Lenny said.

"Yes, it will. The goddamn thing's broken down, and a couple mechanics are fussing under the hood. I'll go find out what's wrong and call you back."

Lenny handed the phone to Sally. "A car's blocking the entrance." He grabbed a scalpel from the tool tray next to the operating table, cut an eye-level slit in the tent, snatched his binoculars and peered out.

The mayor was standing in the backseat of a red Mustang convertible, waving his arms and shouting at the mechanics. A banner read, "Scammer's Ford Ranchero, Dependability You Can Depend On!"

Lenny lowered his binoculars and turned to Daniela. "Can you stay in the body cast a bit longer than we'd planned?"

"If my bladder can."

"Good," Lenny said, then added, "Someday we'll laugh about this."

"No we won't."

CHAPTER 46

Ekplok aksomvulk

*"Although true lovers may part, they remain
forever together in spirit."*

Lenny pulled the tent flap a few inches aside, peered out and watched
the dean spur Angel Warrior unsteadily to the fifty-yard line. A weak
cheer went up.

Bradley announced, "You of course recognize the gentleman
portraying General George Washington atop that magnificent white
steed as none other than our own Dean Wesley Sheepslappe from
Ghurkin College. Soon he'll raise his sword to start the parade
and lead his brave and victorious soldiers around the inside of the
stadium, followed by the marching band and many colorful floats."

The crowd cheered.

The dean raised his sword, and the Colonial soldiers shuffled
forward, followed by the band, struggling with *When The Saints Go
Marching In.*

A cluster of men and women followed the band, desperately trying
to keep in step. Each wore a shiny purple bowling shirt with "Luther's
Lanes" printed on the back.

Miss New Skalvik came next. She sat enthroned on a float of red paper roses and wore a puffy-sleeved pink dress and a gold crown that kept slipping down over her eyes. Four ladies-in-waiting held baskets and tossed hard candy to the spectators, some of whom tossed it back.

A black flatbed truck drove close behind, four portable toilets on back. Three couples in Colonial clothing rode on the float, shuffled their feet and didn't make eye contact with the crowd. A big red banner read, "Skammer's Happy Shacks: A Revolution in Portable Hygiene."

The crowd booed. Luther Skammer's portable relief stations had a reputation for faulty hardware. At a construction site a month earlier, Luther himself had been trapped in one overnight. Daniela had reported this on air and was fined $250 by the station manager for giggling.

Lenny thought about Daniela's giggle, about her eyes, her smile. He thought about how she liked to tickle his chin to wake him in the morning.

The porta-potty truck bumped the float in front.

Miss New Skalvik swung around on her throne, lifted her crown from her eyes and gave the driver the finger.

Next came a John Deere tractor pulling the 4-H float, driven by a girl with bib overalls and parsley-colored hair. The wagon overflowed with bundled corn stalks, piles of pumpkins, baskets of tomatoes, and goats, chickens and one white rabbit that hopped down and bounded across the football field and out the exit. The crowd cheered.

Sally's phone rang. She listened, then held it out to Lenny. "It's the Widow Bahr again. They still don't have the car fixed."

Lenny took the phone. "Tell them to push the damn thing into the stadium and out of the way."

"I did," The Widow Bahr said, "but the mechanics are afraid that Luther will go ballistic if the crowd sees how one of his cars has broken down."

"Talk to the mayor. Maybe he can get them to change their mind."

"I tried, but he won't listen to me. Or anyone. He's red-faced and apoplectic, and his wife's swearing a blue streak. So what should I do?"

Lenny said, "Let me think," and lowered the phone.

Again the porta-potty truck bumped into the Miss Skalvik float.

Of course!

Lenny lifted the phone. "We can't wait any longer. Push the Mustang out of the way with the pickup."

The Widow Bahr whooped.

Lenny peered out the slit at the rear of the tent.

The Widow Bahr revved the engine, spun the tires and rammed into the Mustang.

The mechanics jumped back.

The hood banged down.

The mayor toppled onto his wife's lap. His three-cornered hat flew.

The Widow Bahr shoved the Mustang into the stadium, spun it around until it pointed in the opposite direction, then gunned the engine and roared toward the tent.

Lenny said, "Get ready, everyone!"

He and Charlie lay Daniela on a stretcher. Sally lifted the front, Henri the rear.

Seconds later, the truck slid to a halt outside.

"Get moving!" Lenny shouted.

Sally and Henri took off at a trot, the stretcher between them.

Lenny eased the tent flap back to watch.

Sally and Henri struggled Daniela onto the bed of the pickup, dragged her forward, propped her up against the rear window, then jumped down. Sally thumped the driver's side door. "Get rolling!"

The Widow Bahr gunned the engine and roared straight for the exit, leaving burn marks across the artificial turf. The guards jumped aside, and the pickup flew out the gate.

*   *   *

Sally hugged Charlie, Henri, Lenny.

"Okay, okay," Lenny said, pushing free. "Let's get moving." He turned to Henri. "Bring the medical wagon around front."

"I still think you and Charlie should come along."

Lenny shook his head. "They'll search the wagon."

Henri hesitated.

"Get going!" Lenny shouted.

Henri gave Lenny a quick salute and rushed out.

Bradley said, "The ice cream's gone, folks, but there's still plenty of lobster tails."

Lenny heard the snap of reins outside, the whinny of a horse, cursing in French.

Charlie said, "Time for you to get moving, Carrot Top."

Sally lingered, bit her lower lip. "I hate to leave you."

"Lenny and I can manage."

She hugged Charlie. "Take care of yourself, you old goat. I love you.

"I love you too. And no matter what happens, don't worry. There's an old saying that goes, '*Ekplok aksomvulk.*'"

Sally tilted her head back. "What does that mean?"

"'Although true lovers may part, they remain forever together in spirit.'"

"All that in two words?"

"Skalwegian is a rich language."

Charlie put his arm around Sally's shoulders and steered her to the front of the tent.

She kissed him on the cheek, stepped back, gave him a long look, then slipped outside.

Lenny and Charlie watched her climb onto the wagon beside Henri. He shook the reins and shouted in French. The two horses leaned into their collars, the wagon creaked, the wheels turned.

A minute later, Charlie said, "Do they have horses in France?"

"Lots of them," Lenny said.

"Apparently they never let Henri LeBeau get near one."

The wagon weaved, sped up, slowed down, jerked to a stop, jerked to a start, swerved, knocked over a taxidermized bear with a chest banner reading 'Skammer's Stuffings' and then rolled over it. The wagon ripped off a front paw, a rear leg, kept on going.

Sally grabbed the reins from Henri.

Two men in Colonial uniforms stepped in front of the wagon. One held the horses back, and the other climbed aboard and searched the wagon.

"I hope Sally can keep her cool," Charlie said. "She has a tendency to fly off the handle."

"I've noticed."

Bradley said, "Uh... um... it now appears that our brave Colonial soldiers are searching the medical wagon for cowardly British escapees."

"Or for a missing TV personality," Lenny said.

"*Bradley nak ool ank espaska,*" Charlie said.

Lenny agreed. Bradley did indeed have shit for brains.

Bob Two mumbled, "Tsshursty."

"He's hungry again," Charlie said.

"I think he said he was thirsty."

"He'll survive," Charlie said. "Look! They're letting them go!"

Sally snapped the reins, and the horses trotted to the exit. The gate guards stepped back, and the wagon rumbled through.

Lenny took a deep breath, let it out, took another, let it out. The weight of the world had lifted from his shoulders. Daniela was safe. Sally was safe. Henri was safe. The baby was safe.

Lenny turned to Charlie. "Now it's our turn."

CHAPTER 47

Klagmentok

"Diversion"

Charlie jerked the tarp off the motorcycle, stood it upright, grabbed the handlebars and swung his leg over the saddle.

Lenny snatched a scalpel from the tool tray, cut a six-foot vertical slit in the rear of the tent and peeked out.

A row of flutists marched past, then trombonists, then drummers. Charlie said, "Hop on."

Lenny held up his hand. "Wait for the band to clear out."

It was playing the Ghurkin College fight song to the tune of the *Notre Dame Victory March*. The crowd sang along.

> *Rally students of Ghurkin College:*
> *Sing her glory and sound her fame,*
> *Raise her Pink and Taupe,*
> *And cheer with voices true,*
> *Rah, rah, for Ghurkin College.*

"What a god-awful piece of music," Charlie said.

"At least it's not *Greensleeves*."

The band switched to *Greensleeves*.

"Okay, they're out of the way," Lenny said, and climbed onto the back of the motorcycle.

"Hang on!" Charlie shouted. "We're going to burn a big mother of a black streak right across the dean's goddamn artificial turf!"

Charlie turned the key, pressed the starter and the Harley turned over.

And over.

And over.

Charlie tried again. And again. And again.

"Maybe you flooded it," Lenny said.

"No, I didn't flood it, goddamn it! I'm not that stupid! Get off!"

Lenny did.

Charlie got down on his knees, squinted at the engine, then sat back on his heels. *"Ool!"*

"What?"

"Some shitweasel removed the spark plugs during the night."

"It might have been the glockenspiel player."

"Who?" Charlie asked.

"One of the bandsmen. Yesterday he got inside the tent and spotted the motorcycle."

Charlie got to his feet and kicked the rear tire.

Bradley said, "Let's everyone give a big hand for the marching orchestra!"

Few clapped.

Lenny said, "No choice now but to make a run for it."

"Nope."

Lenny and Charlie spun around.

A tall thug stepped inside the tent. "You ain't going nowhere."

A short thug followed. Both wore Colonial uniforms, both held revolvers.

Lenny recognized them as the men from Luther's construction crew, the ones who'd come around asking questions.

The tall thug waved his gun. "Where Bob Four? And where's the woman?"

Lenny glanced in the direction of Bob Four, tied to a cot and covered with a blanket. "Uh... he took her away. Luther called and said to bring her to him."

"Yeah? Then how come I didn't see them go past?"

"*Mmffth!*" Bob Two said.

"What in hell was that?" the short thug said.

"In a cashttt," Bob Two said. "Schee eshcaped in a cashttt!"

Lenny lifted a corner of the sheet, grabbed two lobster tails off a plate and stuffed them into Bob Two's mouth hole.

Bob Two said, "*Grmmpf!*"

The tall thug said, "Who's that?"

"A hungry reenactor," Lenny said.

The two gunman exchanged glances. The shorter one said, "He looks like that bandaged-up jerk that Luther hauls around on the back of his pickup, but it's not him because he got driven out of the stadium."

"You're quite right," Lenny said. "The gentleman I just fed lobster tails to is in fact an injured reenactor who was playing a British lieutenant until he fell off his horse. He's a pharmacist from Vermont. Or is it New Hampshire? I always get those two mixed up. In any case, he was leading his troops down that slope over there by the tennis courts, you know, the clay ones, and he'd raised his sword and was just turning to look back when he—"

"Shut the fuck up!" The taller man said and ground the barrel of his revolver into Lenny's stomach. "And raise your hands."

Lenny did.

"You, too," the shorter man said to Charlie.

The two thugs shoved Lenny and Charlie outside.

The taller man phoned Luther, explained that Daniela and Bob Four were missing, listened for a moment, then slipped his phone into his pocket. "The boss is going to have his guys check out everyone who leaves the stadium after this stupid parade ends. He'll also want to see you two."

Lenny glanced over at Charlie. He looked worried.

But whatever happened, Lenny told himself, Daniela was safe, and that's all that mattered. Would it be a boy? A girl? He hoped for a girl, a miniature of Daniela—dark hair, cute, thin, a bit sassy. What would Daniela tell the child about her father when she got old enough to understand? Your dad died saving us. He was big and funny, a linguist, a bit eccentric, often lost in the clouds, grew up in a junkyard.

"If you folks will look across the playing field," Bradley said, "you'll see that two of the college's finest football players, Tim and Titus Sprickels, are preparing the cannon for firing."

Lenny bent down to Charlie and whispered in his ear, "Wait for a diversion."

"Like a cannon going off?"

"Exactly."

CHAPTER 48

Dropplesteedetu

"To fall off a horse"

The two goons steered Lenny and Charlie to the west end of the stadium and away from the exit. "We're gotta wait here until the parade's over," the taller man said.

Lenny felt the revolver pressed into his back. His arms ached from holding them overhead, sweat streamed down his temples, adrenalin rushed through him, and his heart thumped. Just like before a fight, he thought, sitting on the stool in his corner, gloves laced up, mouth guard in. Nothing to do but wait for the bell. Or the cannon.

He watched a big red balloon float upward, trailing a banner that read 'Skammer's Ford Ranchero.' It caught the wind and drifted over the stadium and off to freedom.

Lenny ached to float away and be free. He wanted nothing more than to be back home eating a late breakfast with Daniela, sharing the Sunday paper, anticipating a stroll in the school's arboretum, then a tumble after lunch, a long nap, and a movie in the evening while snuggling in front of the TV. Bliss. Freedom.

'Freedom' has as its origin the old English word…

Lenny didn't pursue this. His thoughts drifted back to Daniela and the baby, a girl with big dark eyes.

At the other side of the stadium, Tom Sprocket fiddled with the cannon, and Titus licked a boysenberry ice cream cone. Bruce-Something-or-Other stood stiffly nearby, his arms hanging limp to his sides, the sleeves down to his fingertips, a lost expression on his pale, innocent face.

Lenny felt a sharp stab of doubt. The test of a few days earlier had been ear-shattering for him and Charlie. Did the techie dial the volume back? Remove the mike completely?

No deafening explosion meant no diversion, no escape.

Lenny wondered if he should just swing around and knock out the guy guarding him. But that would leave the other knee-breaker still standing, his gun pressed into Charlie's back.

Could he and Charlie just take off running? Would the two goons dare to shoot into a crowd?

Probably. These were Luther's men, after all.

Lenny half turned but kept his arms up. "Charlie's going to be filthy rich pretty soon. A multi-millionaire."

"Yeah, I heard."

"So I'm sure he'd be more than happy to share his wealth with you."

The goon grunted. "If we let you go."

"Exactly," Lenny said. "Think of what you could do with a million dollars."

The goon hesitated, then said, "I'm thinking of what Luther would do when he caught up with us. I don't want to die with a goddamn taco stuffed down my throat."

"But he'd never find you. You could get plastic surgery, move to Mexico and—"

"Shut the fuck up and turn around."

Lenny did.

Miss New Skalvik smiled wanly at the crowd. Behind her came the portable potty truck, the John Deere, the other floats—once, twice, three more times the possession circled past.

Sweat ran down the back of Lenny's collar, the gun dug into his spine, and his pulse pounded in his ears. He wanted the bell to ring, the fight to start.

After one more turn, and the reenactors and the band filed out the stadium, followed by all the floats but one. The potty truck had again rear-ended the Miss New Skalvik float and sent her and her attendants tumbling onto the AstroTurf.

The dean sat in the saddle, clutching his sword, taking his time, basking in glory. Angel Warrior shook his head and whinnied.

Bradley said, "In a moment, ladies and gentlemen, General George Washington will wave his sword as a signal for the firing of that cannon you see partway up the far side of the stadium. This will mark the dramatic climax to this exciting and edifying ceremony. It will interest you to know that it's an authentic Revolutionary War weapon, and it's…"

Whispering in the booth.

"Or Civil War, which was also a long time ago and pretty much the same thing. So watch carefully and…"

More whispering, then the mike went dead.

The dean spurred a reluctant Angel Warrior to the far side of the stadium and stopped directly below Gerry Gerbil and, higher up, Luther and Grace in the VIP booth. He had his feet up on a table and puffed on a cigar. Grace was slouched in an easy chair, a drink in one hand, a cigarette in the other and a magazine spread across her lap.

With great drama, the dean lifted himself high in the saddle, raised his sword, and Angel Warrior walked backwards.

The dean jerked the reins, dug in his heels.

The horse kept going.

Spectators laughed and clapped.

Bradley said, "That beautiful white steed, Angel Warbler, has been trained to operate in reverse. It's a beautiful sight, ladies and gentlemen, a first-class example of fine horsemanship."

Then the dean fell off.

The crowd hooted and whistled.

The dean jumped to his feet and limped forward, shouting and swearing. He raised his plastic sword and banged Angel Warrior on the rump.

"Uh… that, ladies and gentlemen," Bradley said, his voice filled with doubt, "appears to be the signal for the firing of the ceremonial cannon."

The short thug said, "It's about fucking time."

Bradley said, "For added realism, a microphone has been attached to the cannon's muzzle, which will channel the explosion through the stadium's remarkable new sound system."

Lenny and Charlie lowered their arms and clamped their hands over their ears.

The tall thug ground his gun into Lenny's back. "What the fuck do you think you're doing?"

"My friend and I are exchanging a sign of enduring friendship. It's an old and much-loved Skalwegian tradition."

"Get your hands back up, assholes!"

Lenny and Charlie raised their arms.

At the far side of the stadium, Titus Sprocket handed his cone to his brother, grabbed the lanyard, turned to Bruce-Something-or-Other, and said loud enough to be picked up by the mike, "Sir, Private Sprocket requests permission to fire!"

His voice echoed off both sides of the stadium.

The sound system squealed.

The crowd covered their ears.

Bruce-Something-or-Other said, "Are you sure? I didn't hear the dean give the order."

"He doesn't give an order. He just waves his sword," Titus said.

"He wasn't really waving it. He was hitting his horse. I'm not convinced we should—"

"Who gives a shit?" Titus said. "I'm firing this mother."

He jerked the lanyard.

CHAPTER 49

Vak rorum

"Not again"

Nothing happened.

Titus pulled the lanyard again.

Again nothing.

"Fuck!" Titus shouted.

He jerked the rope a third time.

Nothing.

"What a piece of crap!" Titus shouted.

He and Tom got down on their knees and tinkered with the cannon.

Lenny and Charlie exchanged looks.

The short goon said, "What a goat rodeo."

Titus stood up. "One more fucking try."

He pulled the lanyard.

KABOOM!!!

The ground shook, the air shook, Lenny's innards shook.

For a moment Lenny didn't know where he was, who he was.

The two goons yelped and covered their ears.

Lenny spun around, hit the tall guard under the jaw, punched him in the gut, hit him again.

He went down.

Charlie grappled with the other man. Both fell. Both jumped to their feet. The thug bent down for his gun.

Lenny dropped him with a single blow to the side of the jaw.

Lenny and Charlie pushed into the panicked crowd and headed toward the exit.

Charlie said, "Where did you learn to punch like that?"

"All linguists can. They won't give us a degree otherwise."

"I figured."

A refrigerator-sized chunk of concrete broke loose from the upper edge of the far side of the stadium, bounced down the empty steps and rolled to the forty-yard line.

Lenny and Charlie turned to watch.

The crowd slowed, murmured, rushed on, pushing and shouting, grappling with kids and drink coolers.

Tom and Titus Sprocket abandoned their cannon and ran toward the exit. Bruce-Something-or-Other followed.

Angel Warrior galloped behind, with the dean in pursuit.

A baby carriage tipped over and spilled its contents right in front of Lenny. The woman grabbed her child, still bundled-up, still asleep. Lenny picked up a bottle of milk and a stuffed blue bear, one ear chewed off, and handed them to the woman. She ran on.

He thought of Daniela's baby, his baby, of playpens and pacifiers, dirty diapers even. His heart raced.

Lenny pushed ahead, Charlie right behind.

Charlie pointed at the far side of the stadium. "Look!"

Lenny slowed down.

Gerry Gerbil shivered, shuddered, then leaned forward and slowly—very slowly—plunged head-first off his ledge.

He somersaulted once and crashed at the exact spot that the dean and Angel Warrior had occupied just before the horse decided to walk backwards.

The crowd slowed, murmured, sped up.

Lenny felt oddly sorry for Gerry Gerbil.

Then everyone slowed, stopped. A jam at the exit.

"Nothing to worry about," Bradley said, his voice booming brightly over the PA system. "The stadium is as sturdy as the ground itself. If we can't trust Luther Skammer to erect a building that's safe, then who can we trust?"

Then Bradley scrambled out the booth and bounced down the steps two at a time, shoving people out of his way.

Lenny pushed against the crowd. It moved a couple feet, stopped, moved a couple feet more, stopped again.

A loud *Crack!*

Everyone turned to look across to the other side of the stadium.

Someone shouted. "It's the VIP lounge!"

Luther jerked the inside door handle, kicked, pounded his fists.

"The door frame's warped," Lenny said.

"Like one of his defective portable privies." Charlie said.

Luther stepped back and rammed his shoulder against the door, bounced back, fell.

He jumped to his feet and beat his fists on the window looking down on the playing field, his mouth opening and closing, soundlessly calling for help.

Grace pounded on his back, her rubbery red mouth twisted in anger.

Another sharp *Crack!* filled the stadium.

The VIP booth shuddered, sagged, leaned forward.

Luther pounded harder on the window. Grace pounded harder on his back.

The booth wavered, paused, broke free, tumbled down and smashed onto the empty seats below.

Glass flew, chunks of concrete flew, chairs and television sets flew.

The crowd clapped and cheered.

Charlie said, "*Ool.*"

Lenny and Charlie pushed on, stopping, starting, shoving, apologizing.

They passed Miss New Skalvik, her crown missing, her high heels in one hand, the dirty hem of her pink gown in the other. She muttered, "Fuck! Fuck! Fuck!"

Lenny knocked down a trombone player, said "Sorry" and pulled him to his feet.

The north side of the stadium shivered, cracked, crumbled. Concrete dust rose in a swirling gray cloud.

Red Coats and Colonials ran side by side, united in their desperation to reach safety.

Lenny veered around two vendors taking swings at each other. Coke cups and bags of popcorn flew.

The crowd sped up. A lane cleared to the exit.

"We're going to make it!" Charlie shouted. "I knew we would. There's an old Skalwegian saying that goes…"

The first bullet hit him in the leg. The second in the chest. He stumbled and fell.

Spectators screamed, slowed, stared, rushed on.

The glockenspiel player swung his gun toward Lenny and fired. The first shot snapped the plastic sword at Lenny's side. The second missed and struck the covered wagon.

Lenny charged, rammed his shoulder into the shooter, dumped him onto his back, snatched up the glockenspiel and brought it down hard. Once, twice, three times. More.

Teeth broke, ribs cracked. Metal keys flew in all directions, end over end, tinkling in the air.

Lenny lifted the glockenspiel high overhead, ready to kill.

The man squirmed, moaned, spat teeth and blood.

Lenny saw the unconscious boxer lying at his feet, eyes vacant, blood running from his mouth, twelve hours to live.

Lenny lowered the glockenspiel.

"Not again," he said to the chubby man who'd stopped to watch, open-mouthed. "Not again."

Lenny dropped the glockenspiel, rushed over to Charlie and knelt beside him.

He lay on his back and stared at the sky, his expression blank, his jaw slack.

The crowd flowed around them.

Lenny shouted, "Is anyone a doctor?"

No reply.

"A nurse? An EMT?"

Everyone kept running.

Lenny lifted Charlie in his arms, carried him to the covered wagon, lay him in the back and scrambled onto the driver's bench. He shook the reins and shouted at the horses. The harnesses squeaked, the horses snorted, the wagon moved. "Coming through!" Lenny yelled. "Injured man on board!" The crowd parted.

Lenny drove out the gate, turned left onto the street and snapped the reins. The horses broke into a slow trot, their hooves clicking on the pavement. Lenny's pulse pounded in his ears.

He turned in his seat. Charlie lay on his back, motionless, his left leg twisted at an odd angle beneath him, his shirt front soaked with blood. "Hang on!" Lenny said. "The hospital's only three blocks away!"

Charlie said nothing, eyes wide open and staring at something far, far away.

CHAPTER 50

Seven Months Later...

Nakushkush

"Slush"

Lenny sat under the oak tree below which Oscar was buried and watched the neighbor's Sheltie splash in the pond. It was a warm Saturday afternoon in May, not a cloud in the sky, the breeze cool and fresh. Lenny wanted to relax but couldn't. A big day lay ahead.

"Ten," Henri said and got to his feet. "That's makes sixty push-ups today."

Henri had taken up with a cardiologist four years his senior. She made him exercise, cut back on red meat, drink less wine and get more sleep. Henri's suits hung loose, and he often smelled of sweat.

Four months earlier, Henri had proposed to Jane, then Joan, or maybe Joan, then Jane. Both turned him down. They now worked as high-paid systems analysts at a Boston computer company, where no one could tell them apart.

Lenny said, "I counted eight."

Henri dusted off his hands. "Eight, ten—does it matter, boss?"

Henri enjoyed calling Lenny 'boss' but never treated him as one. Henri still arrived late for his classes and unprepared.

One month after the reenactment, and one week after Lenny was cleared of all wrongdoing, Ghurkin College not only rehired him, but appointed him chairman of the language department. Lenny wasn't sure how long he'd remain, however. Based on his Skalwegian research, both Tufts and Boston University had expressed an interest in him.

Lenny arranged for the college to send his $200,000 grant back to the government.

He fired the incompetent sister and brother, hired qualified replacements, laid down strict rules against automatic A's for jocks, and kicked ass.

The campus had changed a lot over the past seven months. The dean was gone, as were Elspeth and even the Sprocket brothers.

Two weeks earlier, Lenny had received a surprise letter from Titus Sprocket. Fearing they'd be held responsible for destroying the stadium, the brothers had fled the country to play football in the European league, but they ended up in France working as elephant handlers for a traveling circus. Titus said he was writing because he'd met a bareback rider who said she'd once known him and wanted to say 'Hi.' Titus wished now he'd learned some French, and he was sorry the way Gerry Gerbil got all busted up.

Gerry's replacement as school mascot was a gnu ('Hugh Gnu').

Henri eased himself down beside Lenny and adjusted his tie. "You heard that the dean's getting twenty to thirty?"

Lenny nodded. "Kidnapping and kickbacks, with more charges on the way."

Various members of the Skammer organization as well as Bob Two, Bob Three and Bob Four had been arrested and were awaiting trial. Goober Jones was reportedly hiding in the mountains of Guatemala.

State inspectors had ordered the stadium leveled. During rubble removal, a decaying body was found with the forefinger missing from its right hand. An investigation was opened.

During a meeting of the entire college faculty, Lenny had stood up and proposed that the stadium not be replaced, but that the college instead lease a field from the high school. This was approved by voice vote. Lenny then declared that the dean had often told him that he regretted having built the stadium in the first place and that he would have much preferred a park with hedges, rose trellises, stone benches and gravel paths. Again the faculty concurred by voice vote, and work began immediately on the Juan Jorgenson Memorial Garden of Peace.

Angel Warrior became a YouTube celebrity. The Widow Bahr turned down dozens of offers for him, one a quarter of a million dollars.

Henri got up, removed his jacket, jogged in place for a minute, then sat down. "I got an email from Elspeth. She's as happy as a pig in clover."

"I'm glad to hear that. And it's 'a cow in clover.'"

With the dean gone, Elspeth had been promoted to his position but resigned after just eleven weeks. Three more of her poems had appeared in the *New Yorker*, and her tome, *Lament to Franco's Last Victim*—which featured her ode to Juan along with works previously published in small magazines—became a best-seller in the world of poetry readers. Elspeth moved to Washington, D.C. soon after her appointment as U.S. poet laureate following her predecessor's imprisonment for road rage.

"Nervous?" Henri asked.

"Yup."

"Still think you're making the right decision?"

"Absolutely."

"So do I, old buddy," Henri said, and reached over to pat Lenny on the back. "We've gone through a lot together, you and I."

Lenny nodded. Events seemed unreal now and far in the past: documenting a language that turned out to be bogus, the lost job, Daniela's abduction, and the caper that somehow succeeded. And of course Charlie's shooting.

Lenny lay in bed night after night and replayed the event over and over in slow-motion—Charlie twisting as the first bullet hit his leg, then the second to his chest, his tumble to the ground.

Henri said, "You did good."

"As good as I could."

Henri had started sprinkling his conversations with 'did good' and 'I'm good,' picked up from his students.

"Have you and Daniela found a bigger apartment?"

"We're still looking."

"You're a lucky man."

Lenny nodded. For the first time in his life, he in fact thought of himself as a lucky man.

Three nights after he'd vacated the Moon View Revolving Restaurant and moved in with Daniela, it started turning and never stopped. It spun faster and faster, clanked, shuddered and howled and finally wrenched itself free of its moorings, slid over the edge of the building and crashed and burned in the parking lot below. A video of its demise went viral. Arguments broke out online as to whether or not it had levitated.

Henri pointed down the slope. "They're coming."

Charlie still needed a cane, but was visibly improving. Sally clutched his arm. Charlie had on the blue suit he'd worn at Daniela's news show, now sagging at the shoulders from the weight he'd lost. Sally wore a lavender dress. Her curly hair had turned completely gray after the shooting.

Daniela wore a lacy white knee-length dress.

"*Magnifique!*" Henri said, clapping his hands. "*Une déesse.*"

Daniela did indeed look like a goddess, Lenny thought, and his heart melted. It humbled him to be marrying this creature who was so stunningly beautiful and so stunningly nice.

And so stunningly pregnant.

They'd held off the ceremony until Charlie was well enough to give his niece away. Daniela was getting along better with him now. So was Sally, although the two still argued all day long.

Lenny and Henri jumped to their feet and hurried down the slope. Lenny hugged Daniela.

She said, 'Oof' and stepped back, rubbing her baby bump.

Henri hugged everyone and kissed them on both cheeks, including Charlie, who grunted and wiped his face on his sleeve.

Daniela looked happy and relaxed since her time away from WDRK. She planned on returning in six months but would stay for just one year while she saved up enough to start her foundation. Because the new station owner feared an outcry from a sympathetic public if he didn't keep Daniela on, he promised her a raise and her own news shows when she returned. He'd already fired Bradley for his vulgarities during the reenactment, his misinformed observations, and for knocking down a cluster of cub scouts while fleeing the stadium. Bradley had eventually found work at an Idaho television station as part-time historical advisor.

Lenny put his arm around Daniela's waist as best he could and walked her slowly up the slope. The others followed. Once they reached the top, Sally and Henri helped Charlie ease down on the grass, then sat beside him. Daniela stayed on her feet for fear of grass stains. Lenny stood beside her.

Daniela said, "I hope Andy didn't get locked up again."

Charlie said. "He'll be here."

Andy was just out of the county jail for stealing traffic cones.

Daniela had objected to letting her uncle's army buddy and newly licensed justice of the peace conduct the ceremony, but gladly gave in after she found out the role he'd played in her rescue.

Lenny checked his watch for the one-hundredth time. "The others aren't here yet, but it's still early."

Henri got up, did some push-ups, then sat down. "Ten more."

Lenny looked down at Charlie. "So, everything's settled?"

He grinned. "Yup."

Luther's finances had been so vast, tangled and secretive that the authorities never discovered the $250,000 payment to Charlie, nor did they find the paper relinquishing his rights to Harvey's will.

Charlie used the money to clear his debts and pay off the mortgage on the farm. After inheriting Harvey's estate, Charlie deeded Skalvik Island to a charity to be administered by his lawyer. Harvey's castle was turned over to the town for use as a homeless shelter.

Sally gleefully quit her job and now spent much of her time teaching yoga and meditation on the farm's back porch. Henri was her most loyal student.

Charlie never told Sally that the Skalwegian language was bogus, fearing many long nights sleeping in the horse barn.

While Charlie was recuperating, he and Lenny finished documenting the language. Invitations poured in for Charlie to give lectures, all of which he declined. Lenny got praise from his peers and requests to publish in scholarly journals, which he declined. Although the language was phony, Lenny still felt proud to have done a little something for his Skalwegian ancestors. Also, it pleased him to take part in what seemed like the ultimate tall tale. His dad would have beamed with pride.

Lenny finally broke down and confessed to Daniela that he and Charlie had made up the language. He waited for an angry lecture, maybe things thrown. Instead, she threw her head back laughed until tears flowed. Recent events had mellowed her, just as they had Lenny.

The collapse of the stadium and the death of Luther and Grace made the national news. Daniela was portrayed as a spunky survivor, and Lenny was called a hero for saving Charlie.

"Here comes the rest of the party," Sally said.

Andy walked alongside Daniela's two bridesmaids, one the hairdresser from WDRK and the other a distant cousin of Daniela's. Behind them came Daniela's other friends from the station and Lenny's from the college.

The Widow Bahr had politely declined her invitation because she said she hated getting dressed up. In fact, at that moment she wasn't dressed up at all, but was riding Angel Warrior naked at the far side of the pasture.

Henri was the best man.

"Andy's cleaned up nicely," Daniela said.

Andy had a fresh haircut and wore a dark suit, white shirt and blue tie.

The bridesmaids and friends hovered around Daniela, hugged her, patted her tummy, told her she glowed.

The WDRK hairdresser started to sniffle, then the two bridesmaids, then Sally.

Lenny felt a lump growing in his throat and turned away before he joined in.

Henri grabbed an overhead branch, did two shaky pull-ups, paused and whispered, "Who's the babe in the blue dress?"

"A third cousin from Cincinnati," Lenny said. "Daniela's only met her once, but wanted a blood relative at the wedding in addition to her uncle."

Lenny and Charlie had agreed not to tell Daniela that, during the marriage ceremony, the earthly remains of her father would be lying in attendance directly underfoot for eternity in a crate that at one time held 150 pounds of Gallahad Canned Ham.

Daniela broke free of her cluster of friends, walked over and hugged Lenny around the waist. "We'd better get this thing moving because the baby's kicking like crazy. I don't want to give birth on a hillside." She looked around, grinned, then whispered, "You're still sure it won't come out blue?"

"Pretty sure."

They often joked about conceiving a child on a pile of chilly boysenberry slush.

"It's believed that 'slush,'" Lenny said, pulling Daniela closer and kissing her on the top of the head, "slid into the English language either from a Scandinavian source such as the obsolete Danish term *slus* or from…"

Lenny let his words trail off. He guessed that perhaps his wife-to-be wasn't all that interested in the derivation of 'slush.' To tell the truth, neither was he.

APPENDIX

The following truncated vocabulary and syntax will be fully expanded with the soon-to-be-published *Skalwegian: Syntax and Vocabulary,* as compiled by Charles Fox and Dr. Lenny Thorson (Moosemeal Publishing, Goytersip, Idaho).

Pronunciation:

Surprisingly, the pronunciation of the Skalwegian language closely parallels American English.

Major Parts of Speech:

Although exceptions exist, Skalwegian grammar and spelling are highly regular.

– Adjectives end in -*ont.*
– Infinitives end in -*tu.*
– Imperatives are constructed from the infinitive plus -*do.*
– Negations take the normal form of the word preceded by -*uk.*
– Plurals end in -*a.*
– Present participles end in -*ant.*
– The simple past (the only form in Skalwegian) generally ends in -*an.*

Vocabulary:

Ak (prep.) – from
Aksomvulk (v.) – stick together
Ank (prep.) – for
Bleefuma (n.). – crooks

Ceho (n.) – love

Chootora (n.) – lips

Cokeka (n.) – freaks

Custolo (n.) – guardian

Cutkoske (n.) - lobster

Di (v.) – is

Domalopa (n.) – head

Dropplesteedetu (v.) – to fall off a horse

Dunklont (adj.) – black

Ehotkekont (adj.) – dangerous

Ekaketu (v.) – leap

Ekomo (n.) – earth

Ekomolurch (n.) –earthquake

Ekplok (n.) – lover

Ena (n.) – butt

Entahetu (v.) – look

Eskunowo (n.) – life

Espaska (n.) – brains

Estome – what; that which

Fastoua (n.) – perverts

Feegtu (v.) – greet

Flekont (n.) – blue

Gillin (n.) – guilt

Grattu (v.) – grate

Gurblok (n.) – gerbil

Haceketudo (v.) – get lost

Hacha (n.) – fate

Hocak (v.) – lose

Hoceketudo (imp.) – get lost, leave

Hotulu (n.) – canary

Klagmentok (n.) – diversion

Klanktu (v.) – desecrate

Kopa (pron.) – I

Koretu (v.) – dispose of

Krakont (n.) – badger
Kuchin (n.) – pain
Kucua (n.) – truths
Kuk (prep.) – like
Kurvaka (n.) – female doll
Leefonta (n.) – rats
Lopica (n.) – angel
looigtu (v.) – to gouge; to plant corn
Lutketu (v.) – fall down
Mekut – this/that
Mem (poss.) – your
Memeto (v.) – hope
Memut (pron.) – his
Mumutan (v.) – moved
Muntudo (imp.) – expect
Nad (conj.) – and
Nak (v.) – have/has
Nakushkush (n.) – slush
Nan (prep.) – of
Nat (n.) – man
Nehatu (v.) – lie down
Neke (n.) – four
Nervu (adj.) – correct
Nikken (n.) – fate
Nokmeltu (v.) – punch
Omukoo (n.) – anger
Oofala (inter.) – exclamation of surprise for good fortune
Ool (n.) – feces (vulgar)
Opanut (n.) – fox
Oponayetu (v.) – fool
Oska (n.) – bag
Posat (n.) – cat
Rako (n.) – horse
Reretrotu (v.) – walk backwards

Rimenum (n.) – poetry
Rippahak (n.) – dilemma
Rorum (adv.) – again
Shakensit (n.) – fear
Skeenkont (adj.) – naked
Snorken (v.) – sleep
Soku (n.) – pig
Ta (v.) – am
Tokluk (n.) – hen
Torwu (n.) – side
Ugg (n.) – child
Ukeskumowa (adj.) – dead
Vak (adv.) – not
Verlaktu (v.) – to behave
Weegen (n.) – butthead (loose translation, impolite usage)
Yeksliss (n.) – drizzle
Yopok (n.) – slacker
Zaknak (n.) – fool
Zeebont (adj.) – cute

ABOUT THE AUTHOR

David Gardner grew up on a Wisconsin dairy farm, served in Army Special Forces and earned a Ph.D. in French from the University of Wisconsin. He has taught college and worked as a reporter and in high tech. He coauthored three programming books for Prentice Hall and wrote dozens of travel articles and many mind-numbing software manuals before happily turning to fiction. His novel *The Journalist: A Paranormal Thriller* appeared in February 2021 (Encircle Publications). He lives in Massachusetts with his wife, Nancy, also a writer. He hikes, bikes, messes with astrophotography and plays the keyboard with no discernible talent whatsoever.

If you enjoyed reading this book,
please consider writing your honest review
and sharing it with other readers.

Many of our Authors are happy to participate in
Book Club and Reader Group discussions.
For more information, contact us at info@encirclepub.com.

Thank you,
Encircle Publications

For news about more exciting new fiction, join us at:

Facebook: www.facebook.com/encirclepub

Twitter: twitter.com/encirclepub

Instagram: www.instagram.com/encirclepublications

Sign up for Encircle Publications newsletter and specials:
eepurl.com/cs8taP